The
Treasure Trove

LIZ DAVIES

CHAPTER 1

NELL

'You're doing what?' Nell was convinced she must have heard her boys incorrectly. Ethan, the youngest of the twins by twenty minutes, had mentioned something about going backpacking for a year. They must have been discussing one of their friends, she was sure of it.

'Backpacking, Mum.' Ethan was practically hopping up and down on the spot with excitement. Adam, the more laidback of the two, was lounging against the counter in the shop, almost as though he wasn't taking part in the conversation. But she wasn't fooled – he was taking a very keen interest indeed, and she could feel his tension from several feet away.

'Who is?' she asked, eying up a display of knick-knacks on an antique table and wondering if the grouping worked. In her line of business, it was all about the presentation. She picked up a little silver casket and began polishing it.

'We are.' Ethan pointed to himself, then to his brother.

'You're doing what?' Nell repeated, giving him her full attention, feeling the first scratch of worry's sharp claws scrabble at her heart.

'Mum, I know you're getting on a bit, but I didn't realise you needed hearing aids,' Ethan teased gently.

'I told you she wouldn't get it,' Adam said to his twin, along with a sad shake of his head.

'What wouldn't I get?' Nell had a horrible feeling she was getting it, but she didn't want to admit it.

'Adam and I are going to take a year out,' Ethan explained slowly, in the same tone of voice people used when they talked to the very elderly.

Nell didn't appreciate it and she gave him a warning glare. 'But you've only just finished your degrees. I thought both of you were looking for jobs?'

It was Adam's turn to take the baton. 'We have, Mum, just not in the UK.'

'I'm sorry, I think I might be a bit dim here, but I honestly don't follow,' Nell said. How did taking a year out equate with finding a job?

'You're one of the brightest people I know,' Adam, always the diplomat, said, 'So don't go putting yourself down. There aren't many people who can turn their lives around as you have.'

'You can stop the flattery,' Nell said, her voice sharp. 'I want to know exactly what's going on.' She replaced the casket and gave her sons her full attention. 'Are you applying for jobs, or are you going to disappear off around Europe for a year? Which is it?'

'It's both,' Ethan said. 'And not just Europe — we're going to work our way around the world.'

'You're serious, aren't you?' Nell felt the ground tilt a little. She'd been so looking forward to her boys coming home for a while, and now her world was being shoved off its axis.

Using the table for support, she inched her way to the nearest chair and sank onto it. This was not what she had planned for the immediate future. She'd been without her sons for the best part of three years (if she ignored the holidays) and now that they'd finished their degrees, they were telling her they weren't coming home after all.

'We've planned it all out, Mum,' Adam said. 'We know exactly where we're going, how long we're going to be there for, and what kind of work we can pick up along the way.'

'I don't like the idea of this,' Nell said. 'Have you spoken to your father?'

'Hardly.' Ethan snorted.

Nell didn't blame him. He'd taken their father's betrayal the hardest out of the two boys. Nell wasn't entirely sure Ethan would ever forgive him. Adam, on the other hand, acted as a mediator between Riley and his brother. Nell just did what she could to keep things ticking along, and tried to avoid any nasty scenes. If they hadn't spoken to their father, then at least Riley couldn't condone their plans. There was small comfort in that.

She had no doubt the boys *had* thoroughly thought their year out. Adam was a stickler for planning, although Ethan was more of a by-the-seat-of-his-pants type of boy. The term "boy" wasn't entirely correct; her sons were twenty-one. They were men, albeit young ones, and they had every right to be in charge of their destinies – in the same way as she had every right to be worried sick about what they planned on doing.

'Why didn't you tell me sooner?' she demanded, and Adam gave her a look. 'All right,' she waved her hands in the air. 'I know *why* you didn't tell me sooner, but I wish you had mentioned it before now so I could be a bit more prepared.'

'You would have spent the past year talking us out of it,' Adam said.

She was aghast. 'You've been planning this for a *year*? I don't believe it.'

Her sons gave each other a slightly shamefaced look, and she realised they were utterly serious.

'Er, Mum, we're… er… going next week.' Adam had the grace to look contrite. Ethan just looked excited.

Their diverse reactions highlighted the differences between the twins perfectly. Adam was more reserved, more considered and deliberate in his approach to life. He tended to think things through, and weigh up the pros and cons. Ethan, however, embraced things wholeheartedly, with little thought to the consequences or the pitfalls. They balanced each other perfectly.

Adam had clearly considered how the news would affect their mother. Ethan would merely assume she'd be as excited as he was about the mad-cap idea.

Nell held up a hand. 'Stop right there,' she said. 'I don't want to hear any more.'

There was silence for a second or two as the boys looked at each other, then looked back at her. Even Ethan could sense the conversation wasn't going as well as he'd expected. Adam, she guessed, would have anticipated her reaction. He was the one who had most likely persuaded Ethan not to say anything to her until it was a fait accompli. Adam, no doubt, had got all their ducks lined up in a row, and he'd shoot her objections down one by one.

'You might not want to hear it, Mum, but it's happening,' Adam insisted, and Ethan nodded vigorously.

'We're—' Ethan began, but Adam cut him off.

'We'll… um… give you a chance to think about it, yeah?' Adam pushed his brother towards the door leading to the stairs to the flat above the shop.

'I don't *want* to think about it.' Nell didn't know whether to be angry, terrified, or distraught. She thought she was probably all three. She leapt to her feet. 'I'm going out,' she announced. 'You two can close up for me.'

'But, Mum—'

'Let her go,' Adam said to his brother, as she marched towards the door. 'She'll come around when she's had a chance to think about it.'

Nell yanked the door open, strode through it and slammed it shut behind her, wincing as the windows rattled. She would not come round. There was no way she was going to condone this idiotic scheme of theirs. Didn't they realise how dangerous it was out there? How expensive it would be? How unprepared they were?

The boys had grown up fast over the previous three years, and she wasn't just talking about being on their own in university because they hadn't been on their own, they'd had each other, so they were in a slightly different position to most other students. They hadn't had to go it alone. They hadn't been in a situation where they knew no one, and had no one to rely on. She conceded that they had been on different courses, but that was hardly anything major, considering they'd taken different A-Levels in school.

Their growing up hadn't been a result of going to university, but due to their father buggering off with another woman. At least it hadn't been his secretary, or one of his clients. But it had been a woman he worked with, and Nell still beat herself up over it, because she hadn't seen it coming.

The twins hadn't forgiven him. What had angered them the most about their father's affair, aside from their mother's distress, was that they had been forced to leave the family home. Riley had been quite clever in that regard. Her shitty ex-husband had waited until the boys left for university before he'd made his announcement, therefore compounding her empty-nest depression. Although, when she thought back, no time would have been a good time. Prior to the boys starting university, there would have been A-Levels to worry about, and prior to that, GCSEs.

The twins might have grown up due to their previously very safe and secure world crashing down about their ears, but she believed they were still woefully unprepared to go backpacking around the world. She might have come to grips with it being Europe for a few months, but a whole year spent in far-flung places where goodness knows what could happen to them, made her head ache and her heart pound.

And where they were going to get the money from to fund such a venture, was beyond her. Then she recalled Adam saying something about looking for jobs. How was that going to work? They couldn't just turn up on somebody's doorstep and demand to be given a job, although she was aware some agricultural activities needed seasonal workers, but where were they going to stay? Had the boys already got their first job lined up? Had they got the first night's accommodation sorted? Oh God, she hoped they didn't intend to sleep on the side of the road, or underneath a railway bridge, or something equally horrid and dangerous.

She realised she was probably being rather childish in storming out and slamming the door behind her, but Adam was right, she did need time to process what they'd just told her. And by process, she meant time to come up with a reasonable counter-argument for them not going.

She also realised it wasn't just concern for their safety that was making her feel sick; it was the thought of them leaving. She knew neither of them had been offered proper jobs yet (picking grapes didn't count) so she'd assumed they would live in the flat and help her out in the Treasure Trove until they were taken on by perfectly respectable companies in the UK. If she was totally honest, she had assumed Adam, with his business degree, would gradually take over the reins of the business.

It was only when she heard the gurgle of water that Nell realised her feet had taken her to the little bridge over Ticklemore's river. At this time of year, the river was little more than a stream, especially since it had been such a dry spring, and she leant against the side of the bridge and peered over. The drop was probably about twenty feet to the surface of the water, less when there had been heavy rains. But no matter what time of year, it always ran clear enough to see the pebbly bottom, and underneath the shadow of the trees lining the banks, she was sure she spotted the dark outline of a fish. Every so often an insect would alight on the water and a ripple would radiate out from it.

Despite the river running through the heart of Ticklemore, it was still a serene place and today she was thankful for the quiet solitude.

Nell rested her arms on the top of the bridge, the stone warm and solid, and she gazed unseeingly upstream, her mind's eye turned inward as she pictured her boys on their own in the middle of God knows where, being unable to speak the language and desperately wanting their mum.

Then she gave herself a mental shake. Although she wanted to, she knew she couldn't wrap them in cotton wool. Those days were long gone, and she'd never been an overly protective parent. To a certain extent, she had allowed them to make their own decisions and their own choices. She'd also given them far more freedom than many parents gave their children, as they'd been allowed to play outside, building dens, dibbling in the river for fish, climbing trees, and doing anything else little boys loved to get up to. Within reason, of course.

She, therefore, only had herself to blame for this current turn of events. She'd taught them that anything and everything was possible, and now here they were, putting her words into practice and deciding to see the world for themselves before they were forced to settle down. Although Nell wondered if Ethan ever *would* settle down. He was a true free spirit, and she had visions of him disappearing around the world and never coming back. Adam, though, was certain to return.

My God, what was she going to do for the next year without her boys?

Just when she thought everything was finally on an

even keel, life had a way of rocking the boat. She just hoped her heart could weather this particular storm without shattering against the rocks of worry.

CHAPTER 2

SILAS

Silas Long always hated this time of year, and this date in particular. He was never entirely certain he'd be able to survive it.

Denise hadn't wanted a gravestone. She hadn't wanted their daughter to be buried at all. She'd wanted Molly to be cremated, her ashes scattered God knows where. Silas hadn't been able to face that; he'd wanted somewhere to visit, somewhere where he could feel close to his only child. The difference of opinion had been another nail in the coffin of their marriage. But he'd got his way, and it had possibly been the final nail.

It all seemed so long ago, but at this time of year and, especially on this day, to Silas it felt like his daughter's death happened only yesterday. He could cope perfectly fine for the other three-hundred and sixty-four days, even including the day of her burial. But he couldn't cope on the anniversary of Molly's death.

He hadn't opened the Gallery at all this morning. Instead, he'd spent the biggest part of the day sitting next to his daughter's grave, and feeling so much sadness he thought he might never recover from it. But every year he did recover, hauling himself to his feet, the earth beneath him damp from his tears, to carry on with his life.

Until the next time, when he felt as though he was being torn apart all over again.

Whisky wasn't the answer. He'd been there, done that, and got the vomit-stained T-shirt to prove it. But after he'd made the two-hour round trip to the graveyard and had returned home, his hand alighted on the bottle, and he licked his lips in anticipation. He could almost taste it, the burning smokiness as the golden liquid tracked its way from his mouth down into his stomach.

It would warm him from the inside out, but he knew the feeling would be short-lived. So would be the accompanying numbness. He also knew from bitter experience that the oblivion would be equally fleeting, and if he wanted it to continue he had to keep drinking, and drinking, and drinking.

He might have considered it an option if alcohol

didn't numb everything else, too. Because he didn't know what he'd do if he wasn't able to paint.

Painting was the only thing he lived for now. It was the only thing he'd lived for since Molly had passed away. His obsession with it had been a bone of contention between him and Denise long before Molly was born, and the bone had grown to be the size of a skeleton after Molly died.

The only thing which had been able to pull him away from his canvas and his brushes had been his daughter. Then when she had gone, a short three years after she was born, the only solace he could find was in his art.

'I'm sorry,' he muttered, but he wasn't quite sure who he was apologising to. Molly, definitely, for not being able to protect her from the disease that had ravaged and consumed her tiny young body. Denise too, for not being the husband she had needed him to be. To his parents, who had been just as grief-stricken at the loss of their little grandchild.

He gave the whisky a fond pat, then closed the cupboard door. The bottle had remained untouched and unopened for the past seven or so years, but it served as a reminder, which was why he kept it. He had no objection to drinking – he often enjoyed a pint in the pub and he sometimes treated himself to a glass of wine with his evening meal – but on the anniversary of Molly's death he didn't dare drink. He knew if he did, he might never stop again.

Desolate and unsettled, Silas decided to do what he always did whenever he felt this way – he'd go to the Gallery. He'd done his crying, and now he felt compelled to paint. It would help with the grief, although it never eliminated it completely.

The sight of a blank sheet of paper, the feel of a brush in his hand, and the way an image in his head came to life, kept it at bay. It also helped with his crushing loneliness, because when he was immersed in the act of creation he could forget about his loss. After all, with Molly gone, the only mark he'd have left on this world would be the paintings hanging in people's living rooms, or decorating the walls of pubs and restaurants.

His cottage was on the outskirts of the village, practically in the countryside, and he had chosen it precisely for its location. He had neighbours, but they weren't too close, and so he felt as though he was surrounded by nature. He'd lost count of the number of times he'd painted the scene from his bedroom window, or the fields beyond his back garden. But not today – today he'd paint something else.

The walk to the village would do him good, would help focus his mind on the task ahead and not allow him to wallow in the past. He also hoped the fresh air would clear away the cobwebs.

Silas nodded to a few people and said the occasional hello, but he didn't stop to talk to anyone. He wasn't in the mood for polite conversation and neither was he in the mood to hear anyone else's woes. He had enough of those of his own, without being asked to bear another person's burden.

Which was why he had his head down, his hands in his pockets, and his eyes on the ground when he almost bumped into someone leaning on the bridge and staring into the distance.

He recognised the woman immediately. It was Nell Chapman, who owned the Treasure Trove, a shop which sold antiques and unusual items. He knew her well enough, but right now he didn't want to stop for a chat and she didn't look as though she wanted to talk, either.

He was about to walk on by, when something about her gave him pause. He couldn't put his finger on why, but for some reason he had to stop. There was a bench a short distance away, over the other side of the river, so he made his way across the bridge towards it and dropped down onto its wooden slats.

Nell was so lost in her thoughts she hadn't noticed him, so he tried to pretend he was there solely to enjoy the late afternoon sun. He didn't want to be caught staring if she happened to look at him, but he couldn't seem to keep his eyes off her.

Despite him and Nell having been involved in a couple of community things, along with several other people in the village, looking at her now, her gaze unseeing and inward, she appeared to Silas to be a total stranger. She looked sad, melancholy, as if she had the weight of the world on her shoulders. Maybe she did...?

He didn't know a great deal about her, other than she was divorced, had a couple of twin lads in their late teens or early twenties, and she was intelligent and canny. He'd heard rumours she'd started the Treasure Trove with little more than items from her own house, and had built it up to be the successful business it was today.

He often lingered when he was passing her shop because of the lovely things in the window, even though he had no desire to purchase any of them for himself. He had what he needed in his cottage and anything more would simply be clutter, but he could certainly understand the appeal of the items she sold.

She had a good eye for what people liked and for what was aesthetically pleasing. Some of the items in her shop were nothing but curiosities, and they sold well for that very reason. Others were genuine antiques, with a story behind them. The Ticklemore Tattler had run a series of features about some of the items she sold, and he'd found it quite fascinating to think that a chair in the window, for example, had had a life long before it had arrived in the Treasure Trove. Yet some things, he surmised, would never have their stories told.

He wondered what Nell's story was. Why was she looking so unhappy? She was more or less in profile, although he could see more of her back than if he had been at a total right angle to her. His eyes ran up and down her trim figure, noticing the curly dark hair cascading down to her shoulders, the sun catching an occasional lighter strand which he suspected might be grey.

Despite her leaning against the side of the bridge, her back was straight, dipping into a curve above her hips before flaring out again. Her legs were long, one of them bent slightly, and she looked as though she might be there for a while. A slight breeze ruffled the ends of her hair, and Silas could have sworn he could smell a faint hint of her perfume in the air.

She remained in the same position for several minutes and when she lowered her chin onto her clasped hands, he was struck by a real desire to paint her.

It was so unusual and so unexpected, he inhaled sharply and sat up straighter.

Silas didn't paint portraits. He didn't paint people,

and he didn't paint animals much either, unless they featured naturally in the landscape. He painted vistas, with lots of sky, often dramatic ones, with the light slanting at different angles, hitting the ground and illuminating hillsides, meadows and trees. He didn't paint people. Ever.

So what was it about the set of Nell's features and the angle of her body that made him want to capture her on canvas? Was it the sadness radiating from her, or was it the loneliness he could sense?

He was reminded of the painting by Edward Hopper, showing a woman sitting on her own in a cafe. The woman appeared introspective, sad almost, and the painting was quite evocative and thought-provoking.

Nell's appearance was definitely provoking some of Silas's thoughts, as he wondered what she was thinking, and what had happened to cause her to look so lost.

On second thoughts, he didn't want to know. Knowing would strip the beauty of it for him. It was the not knowing, which was inspiring him.

Suddenly he got to his feet, full of nervous energy. He itched to sketch her out and he closed his eyes briefly trying to capture the sight of her in his innermost eye, until she was ingrained on his mind as if he'd taken a photo.

He nodded to himself once, then opened his eyes to find Nell staring right back at him, her gaze deep and unfathomable.

It made him want to paint her even more.

CHAPTER 3

NELL

Sleeping on things hadn't made the situation any better, Nell concluded the following morning. Thankfully, today was Sunday, and she didn't usually open the shop on Sundays; five and a half days a week were more than enough, thank you. She liked to try to get out and about on Sundays because she had the shop to restock, which wasn't easy to do from an armchair.

Even if it had been, she was far too full of unspent nervousness to look things up on the internet; she needed to see things for herself. Boot sales were her favourite hunting ground, and today she had planned on visiting one about an hour and a half drive away.

She'd got up early, not just because she had a long drive ahead of her but also because she hadn't been able to sleep much, and so was on her way by six-thirty. She hadn't bothered with breakfast, just grabbed a cup of coffee whilst she was getting dressed, and she was planning to buy a hotdog when she arrived.

For Nell, nothing was more pleasurable than rooting around in other people's unwanted items. Most of the fun was in not knowing what she might find, and she'd been known to come away from some boot sales with absolutely nothing, and other times she'd bought so much she'd had trouble getting it all in the van. She teamed her visits to boot sales with trips to auction houses, and she would sometimes attend two or three auction houses on a Wednesday afternoon, to see their catalogue listings for herself. There was nothing like seeing an item in the flesh so to speak, and then she would bid online or over the phone if she couldn't make it to the actual sale itself.

It wasn't easy running the Treasure Trove singlehandedly, and the more successful she was, the harder it was becoming – which was why she harboured a secret hope that Adam would join her in the business. He'd always been the one to help out in the shop, much more than Ethan. Ethan had no interest in antiques or curiosities whatsoever. Adam, on the other hand, had an eye for it. She had, if she was honest, expected him to spend some time in an auction house or something similar, to get his eye in and to gain some experience. But her ultimate goal, even though she hadn't shared it with her sons, had been to have one or both of them as partners in the Treasure Trove.

Aside from worrying about her children's safety on foreign soil, there was the added concern that Adam might find something he wanted to do more than help run his mother's business. And she wouldn't blame him. It was hardly riveting work, managing a small antique shop in a small village. It wasn't exciting, and neither was it cutting edge. But, damn it, she was good at it, and so was he. Besides that, it was her livelihood, the only one she had. Without it she had no income and no idea of what else she could do.

She picked up an art deco lamp and examined it, wondering if it was worth the thirty-pound ticket price. It was quite pretty, but the wiring would probably need to be replaced and that would cost money. She put it back and picked up a ship in a bottle. It always amazed her when she came across a good one, because of the amount of detail and skill which went into making the model in the first place. She remembered seeing one when she was small and wondering how on earth anyone managed to get such a large thing through such a tiny neck. When she learnt the truth, some of the magic disappeared, but she still found them fascinating.

Her attention was caught by an age-speckled mirror on another stall, and she wandered over to have a look at it. It was a free-standing one, probably designed to sit on a lady's dressing table. The frame was ornate, and she was sharply reminded of a similar one she'd sold when she'd first started making a living for herself.

When the children were small, she and Riley had agreed she needed to stay at home to look after them. He had a well-paid job, and they could easily afford for her not to go back to work, so that's what had happened. She'd become a housewife, although she had fully intended to return to work once the children were old enough. But therein lay the problem. At what point do you decide your children are old enough for you to return to work?

It was an individual decision, and she had struggled with hers. When the twins started school seemed to be a logical point, but finding a job to fit in with school hours and school holidays was incredibly hard.

Starting secondary school was another milestone that might have meant her return to paid employment. But more often than not, she found herself having to drive them to school and pick them up; then there were extra-curricular activities that both boys were heavily involved in. So once again school hours became a necessity when she was considering going back to work. By the time the boys were old enough to sort themselves out, she had been out of the marketplace for far too long. She guessed she'd probably have to retrain, and had been planning on doing exactly that as soon as the twins left for university; without having two thundering lads in the house demanding this and expecting that, she'd have more time on her hands, and more peace and quiet to be able to throw herself into gaining some kind of qualification.

She'd been actively looking into college courses when Riley had told her he wanted a divorce, which then made going back to work something of a necessity.

When he had insisted on selling the house, she didn't have much of a leg to stand on. What she did have though, was the contents of the house. Riley hadn't taken an awful lot of interest in home decor, and he certainly hadn't paid much attention to the gorgeous bits and pieces she'd bought over the years which made it a home and not just a house.

It had been her passion, digging out lots of lovely little things (some of them not so little) and finding the ideal place for them in the house. Most of what she'd bought hadn't been terrifically expensive, although a few pieces had been, but Riley hadn't had any idea what any of them were worth. Absolutely no idea at all.

Nell did, and she might have been out of line, but she was determined Riley and his bit on the side weren't going to get their hands on the things she'd so lovingly sourced. There was also an alternative reason for wanting to sell them – they were worth money, and money was what Nell was sadly short of.

That was how it had started; Nell had initially listed a few things for sale on various websites and some auction houses, and most of them had sold, many of them for a great deal more than she'd originally bought them for. And so the idea of the Treasure Trove had been born.

As soon as she'd received her share of the proceeds of the sale of the house, she had put down a deposit on a three-storey building in Ticklemore's high street, and had managed to persuade a bank to give her a mortgage for the rest. Then she'd moved herself, her boys and anything else she could get her hands on that came out of the house she'd once shared with Riley, into the new premises, and it became a home and a business all in one.

It was never going to make her wealthy, but she was making enough to keep her head above water and that's what mattered.

Her days were filled with manning the shop,

finding things to sell in it, and doing household chores, and it had been that way for the past two years, punctuated by the various university holidays when both her sons were home.

Nell knew it couldn't last, not unless the boys decided to become perpetual students, so she had been expecting and preparing for some aspects of her life to change. What she hadn't been preparing for, or anticipating, was Adam and Ethan disappearing out of her life for a whole year.

The thought of not seeing them for so long saddened her without measure, but she knew that, despite all her objections and all her fears, they were going to do it anyway. Because if they didn't do it now, they would probably lose the chance. She wished she had been brave enough to do such a thing when she was younger, but she hadn't, and now it was too late.

So, along with the fear and the impeding loneliness, she was also pricked with envy. Her sons had the world at their feet, and they were just about to embark on one of the most exciting chapters of their lives. How she wished she could join them. For a brief moment she was seriously tempted to suggest it, before common sense reared its head and she understood she would be neither welcome nor wanted.

Nell drove home in a desultory fashion, feeling rather flat despite all the lovely pieces she'd bought. For some reason the thought of cleaning them up, doing the research, pricing them, then putting them on the shop floor didn't fill her with the same enthusiasm as it would have done a week ago, or even two days ago. It was work, nothing more, nothing less. It was hardly an adventure; she was doing it to keep a roof over their heads and to put food on the table. But with the boys gone she might as well live in a caravan and live off toast and tea.

She hoped one of the boys would be home to help her unload, but as she drove around the back of the high street and pulled into the little parking space her premises had been allocated, there was no sign of life from the flat. With a sigh, she clambered out of the van and locked it carefully. She could do with a cup of tea and five minutes to catch her breath before she considered unloading it.

Automatically, as she did every time she arrived home, after switching the alarm off she took a quick peep into the shop to make sure everything was OK, and she saw someone had their hands cupped against the glass and was peering inside. It happened quite often, so Nell took little notice and was about to close the door which separated the shop from her private quarters, when she looked again.

There was something familiar about the figure on the other side of the window, something she couldn't quite put her finger on—

Riley!

It couldn't be, could it?

It *was*. The man standing outside her shop and peering in was no other than her ex-husband. She didn't know whether she was pleased or cross. She supposed it all depended on why he was here. If it was to support her in her reservations about the boys going backpacking, then she would almost be pleased to see him. If it was to back them up, then she would be furious.

Riley rapped on the glass and pointed to the door, and Nell tried not to pull a face as she went to open it.

He looked older than she remembered, his hair receding slightly, the lines around his eyes deeper. He'd developed a bit of a paunch, too. She supposed they all had to grow old, but she hoped she didn't look quite as worn as he did. There had been the temptation to comfort eat after he'd left, but she had been so busy and had done so much running around that she'd barely had time to eat at all once she'd got over the shock and anger of his betrayal.

She opened the door wider and beckoned him inside.

Riley sauntered in, his hands in his pockets, the gesture reminding her very much of Adam, and he gazed around, his head turning from side to side as he took everything in.

'Nice,' he drawled.

Nell ignored the comment – had he expected her shop to be a tip? Surely he knew her better than that? Or maybe he didn't, because when push came to shove she hadn't known *him* at all, had she?

'They've told you then?' she said.

For a moment Riley looked startled, then he said, 'Who's told me what?'

'The boys, about their year-long trip around the world.'

'What year-long trip? What are you talking about?' He hadn't looked at her at all; he was still gazing around the shop, his eyes coming to rest on a piece for a moment before moving on.

Something caught his eye and he walked over to it and picked it up. It was the figure of a woman made out of bronze, possibly art deco. It was expensive, and she saw him examining the price tag.

He whistled. 'Not cheap,' he said.

Nell marched over to him, snatched it out of his hand and plonked it back on the table. 'What do you want? If you haven't come about Adam and Ethan, then why are you here?'

Riley turned slowly and looked at her properly for the first time since he'd entered her shop. 'Where *are* the boys?' he asked.

'They're out. If you want to see them, you'll have to come back later. Why don't you give them a ring before you come next time, and then you can make sure they are in? Or better still, meet them somewhere else? I don't want you here.'

'I know what you did,' he said.

Nell blinked. 'What are you talking about?'

'How you got started.' He gestured, his arm encompassing the whole room.

Nell wasn't fazed. She didn't care whether he knew or not. She'd spent eighteen years raising their children, making a home for the family, cooking a meal every night, cleaning up vomit, washing filthy rugby kit, ignoring the occasional smell of a strange perfume on her husband's clothes. All she'd had to show for it had been a small allowance towards the boys' upkeep which had stopped when they hit the relevant age, and an amount from the sale of the house which had been barely enough to put down a deposit on this place. She'd felt entitled to take what she could. After all, her husband had taken exactly what *he'd* wanted. It wasn't her fault that all he'd been interested in had been the grand seven-bedroom, three-reception room house. The contents of it hadn't concerned him in the slightest.

So why was it concerning him now?

A shiver of fear wormed its way into her mind, but she pushed it to one side. The divorce was finalised, done and dusted. They'd gone their separate ways over two years ago; Riley had no claim on her and she had no claim on him. As soon as the boys hit twenty, all financial ties had been severed, and the emotional ties had been severed well before then.

'You sold all the stuff *I* bought,' he said, his eyes moving restlessly around the shop again.

'I think you'll find I bought it,' Nell pointed out.

'With *my* money.'

'I thought the money was ours,' she said. 'Not just yours.'

'Ah-ha!' he pounced. 'So you admit you used my money to buy all those things you sold.'

'*Our* money,' she corrected him, yet again.

'In that case, I believe I'm entitled to half.'

Nell was shocked. It took her a few seconds to stop spluttering. 'I don't think so.'

'You'll find I'm right.'

'The divorce is finalised. All the finances have been sorted. If you'd had any objections, or had wanted any of the contents of the house, you should have said so at the time.'

'I didn't know about it, did I?'

'Perhaps you should have made it your business to know about it. It's not my fault your floozy didn't want anything out of our house. Perhaps if she had, you would have discovered its value.'

Riley's eyes narrowed, and Nell could see the cogs whirring in his brain.

'Little knick-knacks, you called them,' Nell continued. 'You didn't think they were worth much, and you turned your nose up because I'd got a lot of them from boot sales and second-hand shops. If you had paid more attention to what I was telling you, if you had paid any attention at all, then you would have realised some of those things were quite valuable indeed.'

'Like the chest of drawers you sold to the Proctors?' he asked.

'Exactly.' The Proctors, a husband and husband team from Hereford had once been acquaintances of her and Riley's. It was Dougie Proctor who had given her the idea of flogging stuff from the house in the first place, when he'd phoned to offer his condolences on the death of her marriage. He'd asked her what they intended to do with the contents of the house and would she give him first refusal on the George III mahogany serpentine chest she'd kept in the hall, and she'd jumped at the chance for some much-needed cash.

'I want half,' Riley announced.

'No chance.' There was no way she was letting Riley bulldoze her or bully her into acquiescing. He'd taken what he'd wanted from the house, therefore anything left was fair game as far as she was concerned, to do with as she'd pleased. If she had used the contents to furnish a new house, Riley wouldn't be coming around here now sniffing after them. But because she'd sold some of them – most of them, actually – and had made a fairly decent profit he'd become rankled.

'I bet you thought I wouldn't find out,' he said, his gaze focusing on her.

Nell shrugged. 'I couldn't care less whether you found out or not.'

'Do you want to know how? I bumped into Dougie Proctor, who told me how much he loved the chest, and that at nearly two-and-a-half thousand pounds, he'd bagged himself a bargain. Two-and-a-half thousand pounds, I ask you! I bloody well hope you hadn't paid that much for it.'

Nell remembered exactly how much she'd paid, and it had been somewhere in the region of a hundred-and-twenty pounds. She wasn't going to tell Riley that, although he had probably guessed it was nowhere near the amount she'd sold it to the Proctors for, because if she had paid more he'd have noticed that amount of money going out of their bank account.

'Can't remember,' she said.

'Half,' he repeated, holding his hand out as though she had that kind of money in her jeans pocket. Actually, she'd had a substantial amount about her person earlier today, but she'd spent quite a bit of it in the boot sale; which reminded her, she still had the van to unload.

She stared at his outstretched palm, and the seconds turned into minutes before he finally dropped his hand.

'I bet you do remember,' he said. 'And what about the rest of the stuff from the house?' His eyes swept around the shop. 'Don't tell me you don't know what you bought any of it for – there are bound to be records. I'm entitled to half and I'm going to get it.'

There were records – meticulous ones – but Riley wasn't getting his hands on them. 'You should have asked for them when we got divorced,' she said. 'And please don't threaten me.'

'It's not a threat, it's a promise.'

'Whatever.' She borrowed the word from Ethan, and decided it was quite apt. She even said it in the same tone of voice as her son used, as though she was slightly bored of the conversation. Which she was. Riley was wasting his time if he thought he had any entitlement to any of the items she'd sold from their house.

Then he said something that made her blood run cold.

'As you wish, but I must inform you I have spoken to a solicitor. He believes you've built this business on the back of monies that are by law half mine. Therefore, he believes, and so do I, that I am entitled to half of the Treasure Trove.'

And with that, her scumbag of an ex-husband turned sharply on his heel and marched out of the door, letting it slam shut behind him, and leaving Nell shaking with temper and worry.

What the hell was she supposed to do now?

CHAPTER 4

SILAS

It was unbelievably early, but Silas seemed to have lost all concept of time. Having woken at 5 a.m. and unable to get back to sleep, he was once again in his studio above the Gallery, paintbrush in hand, and staring thoughtfully at the canvas in front of him.

It wasn't quite finished yet, but he was pleased with what he'd done so far. He'd drawn Nell's outline, and put some rough colour in the right places, then he'd left it to marinade whilst he'd worked on the background. Landscape was his speciality, so it hadn't taken him long to achieve the mood he was after. Although when he'd seen her on Saturday, leaning against the bridge with her chin on her folded arms, the afternoon sun had been quite bright and summer was in full swing, he'd debated whether to paint the background as was, allowing the contrast between her contemplative solitude and the sun to speak for itself. But then he'd decided that it might seem as though she was simply admiring the view. Without a clear look at her face it might be difficult to tell, therefore he painted a winter scene, one with a storm brewing, and in his gut he felt he'd achieved exactly the mood he was aiming for.

He was desperate to start painting Nell herself, but he couldn't quite remember the curve of her cheek, or the way her hair fell about her shoulders, although he could remember the colour exactly – burnished chestnut, with bronze highlights, and those lighter strands visible at the temple, which gave away her age.

She wasn't a particularly tall woman, about five-foot-four, and she was slim, her figure almost girl-like, despite having two grown-up sons.

He'd thought before how pretty she was, with her classical features and her aquiline nose. Her eyes were a dark brown flecked with amber, but they wouldn't be visible in his painting. Neither would most of her face be. But he still had difficulty recalling the precise curve of her cheek, so there was only one thing for it – he'd have to pop in and see her.

He didn't want to ask her to pose, or even tell her the reason why he was visiting her; he'd just have a browse around the shop and hope to catch her at the right angle. Of course, she'd probably be standing upright and definitely wouldn't be leaning over a parapet with her head on her arms, but it would have to do.

Silas meticulously cleaned his brushes, the tools of his trade, and washed up after himself, then he changed out of his paint-spattered jeans and T-shirt, and back into the clothes he'd worn when he'd got dressed this morning to come into the studio.

The air outside was relatively cool, although he knew from the forecast that the temperatures were set to rise, and there was the tantalising aroma of baking bread and coffee on the breeze, which grew stronger as he walked past Bookylicious, and his mouth watered. Although he'd been drinking copious amounts of coffee over the past day or so, he hadn't eaten a great deal. It was one of the hazards he faced when he got stuck into a painting – it tended to consume him to the exclusion of all else. And he felt the seductive obsessive pull even more keenly with this one.

Although he was tempted to step inside the café-cum-book shop, he resisted and carried on towards the Treasure Trove. He wanted to see Nell far more than he wanted a Danish pastry.

Darn it, there were no lights on in the shop and when he tried the door it wouldn't open. So he cupped his hands around his eyes, and peered inside.

There was no sign of life whatsoever, and when he stepped back he noticed a sign in the corner of the window which said that the opening time was ten a.m.

Silas checked his watch – it was five past nine. He may as well have a coffee and some breakfast in Bookylicious after all. Not only did he need the fuel, but it would kill the hour or so he had to wait for Nell to open up.

He took a seat near the window because he liked watching the world go by, and waited for someone to come and take his order.

'We don't see you in here very often,' Hattie commented.

Silas gave her a fond smile. For an eighty-year-old she looked surprisingly sprightly, and she had a glow about her that he could only put down to having found love with Alfred. It didn't exactly give him hope for the future because he had no truck with love or any of its trappings, but it did give him a warm feeling to see two elderly people so happy together, and to know he had played a very small part in helping make it happen. He'd watched the romance between the pair grow over the course of setting up the Ticklemore Christmas Toy Shop, and although he wasn't interested in finding love himself, it did make him feel good about life in general.

'I'm in desperate need of coffee and breakfast,' he

told her, and after she scribbled down his order on a little pad she patted him on the shoulder.

'You look tired and sad,' Hattie observed. 'Has something happened?'

Something had happened, but it was a long time ago and Silas didn't feel like sharing. No one in Ticklemore knew about Molly, and that was the way he liked it. Although, when he first set eyes on the beautiful toys Alfred had made, he'd let his guard down for long enough to purchase a little wooden rabbit to put on Molly's grave. Hattie hadn't asked any questions then, and she didn't ask any now; all she did was give him another pat and a squeeze, then she walked away. He'd been tempted to tell her, but he hadn't. He wanted to be known as Silas Long the artist, not Silas Long the bereaved father. He didn't want anyone's pity.

He gazed idly out of the window, watching the world go by, until his coffee and Danish pastries arrived, then he set to with gusto, not realising how hungry he was until he'd taken his first mouthful. After having rapidly demolished the lot in record time, he was on his second cup of coffee when he became aware of a man sitting at the next table who was speaking into his phone with a raised voice.

Silas tried to ignore him. However, it wasn't easy. The man was holding a heated conversation, in hushed tones that weren't hushed at all.

'I'll have it for you as soon as I can,' the man was saying. 'You'll just have to be patient.'

There was a silence while the person on the end must have spoken, then Silas heard, 'It's going to take time, I told you.' Then more silence followed by, 'Well, if you do, you won't get anything, will you? It's up to you. Either you take me to the cleaners now, or you wait a little longer. I've told her I've spoken to a solicitor and, believe me, she'll cave.'

Silas's curiosity was piqued, and he wondered what that was all about. Knowing he'd never find out, he checked his watch and ordered another cup of coffee, watching the stranger pay and leave. He just about had time to drink it before Nell opened up.

For some reason as he thought that, his heart clenched, and he stared at his cup accusingly. He'd better not have anymore, not if the caffeine was giving him palpitations. He'd drink this one, then switch to tea for the rest of the day.

CHAPTER 5

NELL

Nell flipped all the lights on in the Treasure Trove, unlocked the door ready to receive her first customers of the day, and stood there gazing around at her little empire. It wasn't much, but she was immensely proud of it. It was exactly the sort of place she liked to browse around and, luckily, so did many other people. Of course some of those customers who entered her shop did so purely to look and had no intention of buying, but around half of those who came through her door made a purchase, and she got the same thrill from a sale now as she had when she'd first started out.

Originally selling the contents of the house one by painful one, had been more a case of sticking two fingers up to Riley than for the love of it. But she had got a nice bit of money from it, and the more she sold the more she realised she was good at it. She'd bought wisely and sold well, and her little business had kept her and the boys afloat since they'd been forced to move out of the marital home.

The thought of her sons sent a little pang through her. They'd be gone in a few days, and she didn't know how she was going to cope. Even when they were in university, the flat had never felt lonely because she knew they'd be back for the holidays, and they frequently came back for weekends throughout the term. Admittedly, it was usually to have their washing done and have a few home-cooked meals, but nevertheless she enjoyed their company, even though when they were home they were frequently out with their friends doing their own thing.

She'd still felt their presence – unlike Juliette who owned the Ticklemore Tattler, who'd found it very hard when her daughter, Brooke, had left for university for the first time. Juliette, though, had found consolation in taking over the newspaper and finding love with a former colleague who she'd known years ago and who had been a journalist like her. It had given her new purpose and new energy, and Nell was delighted for her.

Nell had enough purpose and energy already without adding love into the mix, just by keeping the Treasure Trove afloat. Even though she would love to have a significant other to sit on the sofa with, drinking a glass of wine and discussing her day, she was often too tired after a full day in the shop, and then having to do all the behind-the-scenes stuff, to want to hold a conversation with anyone except her pillow.

Today though, she wasn't feeling as enthusiastic as usual. In fact, she was feeling downright flat. She should have a chat with Juliette, because they say a problem shared is a problem halved, but she couldn't bring herself to discuss it with anyone. Talking about it would make it real, and at the moment she was trying to pretend it wasn't going to happen, despite the frenetic activity of the twins as they finalised tickets, accommodation, and routes.

The shop door opened and Nell quickly glanced up to see Silas Long, who owned the Gallery a few doors up from hers on the high street, step inside.

She was genuinely pleased to see him. He might be a bit of a grumpy git and could sometimes be slightly on the moody side, but she didn't mind that. She had a feeling there was something in his past that he kept closed off from the present. She had no idea what it was and she had no intention of prying. But she sensed the sadness in him, emanating from him like heat from a radiator. It wasn't obvious, although it was definitely there, and today she felt more of an affinity with him than was usual.

'How are you, Silas?' she asked, as he sauntered around, his eyes scanning the walls. Of course, he'd be looking at the paintings on sale. The silver hairbrush set just to his left would hold no interest for him, and neither would the antique lamp to the side of it. She hoped he approved of what he saw, and that if he didn't, he wouldn't tell her. She didn't claim to know much about paintings, but she reasoned that if it caught her eye it would catch someone else's. She did try to do due diligence however, and if she could make out a signature she would look it up.

'I'm well, thanks,' he replied. 'How are you?'

'Good, thanks,' she responded, even though she felt as far from good as it was possible to get. The thoughts she was having about Riley were downright bad, evil almost. She'd had a moment last night when she'd imagined burying him under the patio. The problem was that she didn't have a patio. And if she had one, she wasn't sure whether she'd want his body underneath it. Knowing Riley, he would come back to haunt her.

Silas continued to gaze around at the various paintings, and Nell took a moment to look at him. He might have said he was well, but he looked tired; he also looked pale, and she wondered if he was coming down with something, or whether he was spending so much time in his studio that he'd managed not to notice the beautiful weather they were having. She'd heard that he could be driven, and that when he was in painting mode it was difficult to divert him, but she didn't know whether it was the truth or a rumour.

She didn't know an awful lot about Silas Long at all. He'd come to Ticklemore several years ago and had bought a cottage on the other side of the village. He sold his paintings in the Gallery, his studio was above the shop floor, and he appeared to be a one-man band, a bit like Nell herself was. But at least she had the twins to help now and again (not for much longer, an annoying voice in her head reminded her), but she'd not heard of Silas having any family, and if he did, they didn't live in Ticklemore.

He was a damned good artist, though. His paintings were landscapes, and she had to admire his use of light and shade. From what she could tell they were all watercolours and very well executed; there was a touch of something else that drew one's eyes back to them again and again, and Nell suspected he painted a little bit of his soul into every one.

She would have liked to have bought one or two for herself, but she couldn't afford his prices and neither did she have any room to hang them – her flat was already jam-packed with items which were eventually destined for the shop, because she had a tendency to buy things and live with them for a while in her own personal space before being able to let go of them and put them up for sale.

Nell came out of her reverie to find Silas gazing at her critically, and she wondered if she had a splodge of jam on her cheek. Surreptitiously she glanced at the mirror beyond his shoulder, but couldn't see anything wrong with her appearance.

'Sorry, I'm just browsing,' he said. 'You carry on doing whatever you're doing. I'll give you a shout if I need you.'

'That's fine,' she said, but she still felt the weight of his stare, and she wondered what it was about her that interested him so much.

He must have realised he was being rude, because he turned away and walked over to a dramatic painting of some Welsh hills and moorland, with a sheepdog in the forefront. She watched as he bent forwards slightly, his nose inches away from the bottom right-hand corner of the painting.

'Is this genuine?' he asked, pointing at the artist's signature.

'I doubt it,' she said. 'If it was then I bought it for a song.'

'You're selling it for a song, too,' Silas said.

'I'm making a decent enough profit,' she assured him.

'If it's a genuine Oakman, you could make much more.'

'I know, but I don't know enough about art to decide if it is or isn't.'

'I do,' Silas said, 'but I would like to get a second opinion. Would you mind awfully if I took it with me?'

Nell shrugged. 'If you think it would do any good…?'

'I think it might,' he said. 'I promise I'll take good care of it.'

Nell didn't doubt him. If there was one thing she was sure of when it came to Silas Long, it was his dependability.

'I'll get it back to you as quickly as I can,' he promised, and she told him to take his time.

'If what I suspect is true, would you be happy for me to display it in the Gallery on your behalf? You could get ten times the amount you're asking for it, but the likelihood of it being seen here by anyone who'd want to pay that much is quite slim.'

'Fine,' Nell waved an arm in the air. If it was worth that much, she was glad to get it out of the Treasure Trove before Riley saw it. She was under no illusion that the man would be back. Her ex-husband was tenacious once he got an idea in his head. And if he *had* been to see a solicitor and was getting the ball

49

rolling in his attempt to take half of her business from her, she'd prefer to give the painting away rather than let Riley have it.

Silas was gazing at her curiously, and she wished she could summon some enthusiasm. If he had come into her shop just a week ago and told her he thought her painting was genuine, she would have been overcome with excitement, but now she could hardly muster a smile.

Realising she was being rude, she said, 'Thank you, Silas, I appreciate it.' But she knew her voice lacked warmth. She sounded as though she was just going through the motions, because that was exactly what she was doing.

She wrapped the painting up for the short walk between her shop and Silas's Gallery, and when he had gone she dropped down onto the stool behind the counter and buried her face in her hands. She felt like weeping. For all the progress she'd made since Riley had left her, she felt as though it was all for nothing. She was back in the same situation she had been when he'd told her he was moving out.

Worse, because she'd put her heart and soul into the business and the accommodation upstairs, determined to make a home for her children. Now she was in danger of losing all three. If she lost the business she'd lose the flat and she had a feeling she'd already lost her sons. They were young men, embarking on their own lives, and although she knew she'd always have a place in their hearts, she was very much on the side-lines.

And with her boys gone, what else did she have to live for except her business? If she lost that too, she didn't know what she'd do.

CHAPTER 6

SILAS

Silas unwrapped Nell's Oakman painting and popped it on an easel. Although he was desperate to go back upstairs to carry on with his own work, he was acutely aware he needed to do some housekeeping on the shop floor. Some days it felt as though he was doing two full-time jobs, one running the Gallery and the other creating the paintings to be sold in it.

Not for the first time he wished he had an assistant, someone who could man the shop for him to let him get on with what he really wanted to do. Besides that, he wasn't very good at sales, and he was the first to admit it. In his opinion, either people liked a painting and wanted to buy it, or they didn't. He wasn't in the business of persuading them, but neither was he in the business of telling them what a painting was about, or what its meaning was. Some of the pretentious gits who came through his door wanted to know what the hidden message was, but he tended to be quite blunt, telling them if they couldn't see what they were looking at then they needed to open their eyes. A painting of rolling hills was exactly that – rolling hills – and there was no hidden meaning, no interpretation.

His thoughts drifted to his work in progress directly above his head. For the first time in many years he was using oils on canvas, rather than watercolours on paper, and not only that but his depiction of Nell went against the grain – he wasn't exactly painting what he'd seen, although he felt he was being true to her because he was convinced that what he had been looking at that day on the ridge was an incredibly sad woman indeed. He had changed the background to make it more in keeping with the emotion he'd seen in her, so, in this instance, the painting did have a meaning, but he wasn't entirely sure what it was. However, he was the first to acknowledge that he might have misread her completely and she might have been contemplating renovating her kitchen!

He knew Nell about as well as he knew some of the other residents of Ticklemore, but that didn't mean a great deal. Despite being an active, if somewhat reluctant member of the community, he wasn't bosom buddies with any of them. The closest he'd come to a meaningful conversation had been with Hattie and he hadn't wanted to pursue that, either. But for all his reluctance to get involved, he realised there was something seriously bothering Nell.

He'd have thought the woman would have been as excited as he was when she'd heard her painting might be genuine and not a reproduction or a copy. But she hadn't been; she'd been almost dismissive, as if it was irrelevant. And that wasn't the reaction of the Nell he thought he knew. Once again, he might have misread the situation. Perhaps she *was* excited, and this was her way of showing it? But somehow, he didn't think so. To him, it seemed as though a spark had dimmed inside her, which only served to reinforce his initial impression of her on the bridge.

Silas wondered what had happened to affect her so. If he knew, perhaps he could help. He was reluctant to get involved, but he couldn't stand by and not do something to help if it was in his power. However, the only thing he felt he could do at the moment was to make good his promise and check out her painting. So, with the door to the Gallery open in a vain hope that it might attract some customers, he set about researching the artwork in front of him.

Several hours, a few customers, and a lot of Internet searching later, he thought he might have the answer. He wanted to show the painting to someone first though, before he said anything to Nell, and even though he desperately wanted to pop down to the Treasure Trove and share his thoughts with her, he held back. He preferred to give her some concrete news, rather than his surmising.

As if thinking about her had conjured her up, Silas glanced out of the window to see her trudging past, her hands in the pocket of her lightweight jacket, her head bowed. He wondered where she was going, and glanced at the time, surprised to see how late in the afternoon it was. He had worked right through lunch (which usually consisted of a sandwich eaten at his desk), and he suddenly realised that not only was he starving, but it was time he shut the shop for the day.

He was dying to get back upstairs to resume work on the painting he was coming to think of as *Entitled Melancholy*, but first he had better see to his rumbling tummy. Without further ado he threw an old sheet over Nell's Treasure Trove painting, grabbed his keys and locked up. It was time to pay Bookylicious a second visit of the day.

He would normally quickly nip out for a sandwich from the bakers, but they would be closed by now, so the café would be his best bet. Even if Maddison had run out, he knew she'd happily pop out to the kitchen and make him a fresh roll of some description. And while he was there, he might pick Hattie's brains. Hattie knew lots of things about lots of people – some of them things she had no business knowing. But if he wanted to find out what was wrong with Nell, then she'd probably be his best bet.

He couldn't work out why he felt he needed to know. Was he simply being nosy? Did he just want to discover the meaning behind his painting of her? If so, he was as bad as some of those customers he encountered now and again who thought they were bloody art critics.

Hattie raised her eyebrows when she saw him. 'Back again? That's twice in one day.'

'I can't stay away from your scintillating company.' He smiled at her.

'Pah! If you think I'm falling for that, you must think I'm stupid.' She narrowed her eyes at him. 'You're in here because you want something, and I'm not talking about the Eccles cakes, either.'

'Ooh, have you any left?'

'I don't think so, but I'll check. We were just about to close.'

'I know, I'm sorry, but I was working so hard I forgot to eat lunch.'

The old lady's face softened as she took pity on him. 'What do you fancy?' She stepped to the side so he could have a good look at the counter.

'Can I have one of those, and one of those, and a coffee to go, please?' he asked, pointing to a slice of quiche and a neatly wrapped sandwich. He could have made himself a coffee back in the Gallery, but it wasn't half as nice as their coffee.

'Do you want a cake to go with that?' Hattie asked.

Silas hesitated. He really shouldn't because he was conscious of not putting on too much weight, but there was one solitary slice of red velvet cake left and his mouth watered. 'Go on, why not?' He'd probably be working long into the night, so hopefully he'd burn off the excess calories.

Hattie began making the coffee, her back to him as she fiddled with the knobs and levers, banging little pots down as she worked. As he listened to the hiss of steam and the gurgle of hot milk, he wondered how to broach the subject of the owner of the Treasure Trove without making it seem as though he was interested in Nell.

'Go on then, spit it out,' Hattie said, her back still to him.

Silas winced. 'Spit what out?'

'You want to ask me something,' she said.

'How do you know?' he asked, bemused.

'From eighty years of being on this planet,' was Hattie's swift reply. 'I make it my business to read people, and you've been standing there like a fish out of water, opening and closing your mouth.'

'I'm worried about Nell,' he blurted.

Hattie turned to look at him. 'Why?'

'She doesn't seem herself. She seems… sad.'

'Having kids can do that to you,' Hattie said, giving him a measured look.

Silas wondered how much the old woman knew or guessed about his own circumstances, but he didn't say anything about himself – he was more interested in Nell. His own story was an old one and he knew it off by heart. Nell's on the other hand…?

'Her boys seem like nice kids to me, but I was wondering if one or the other was in any kind of trouble?' he asked.

'Oh, they *are* good kids,' Hattie agreed. 'Ethan is a bit of a rascal, but Adam keeps him in line.'

'So what have they done to make her sad?'

'They're buggering off for a year, backpacking around the world, I heard. Nell is going out of her mind with worry.'

Silas could see how she would be, but in these days of mobile phones and the Internet, it would be easy for her and the boys to keep in touch.

He wondered if she was lonely.

He knew the feeling well, but at least he had his art to occupy him – he could lose hours and hours whilst he was working. What did Nell do after she'd closed her shop doors for the day? To his surprise, he found he genuinely wanted to know, and he was at a loss to understand this sudden interest in her.

It must be because of the painting he was doing, he concluded. There couldn't possibly be any other reason that made any kind of sense.

CHAPTER 7

NELL

'I heard about the boys,' was Juliette's opening statement as she walked into the Treasure Trove the following morning.

Nell stiffened as her friend's arms came around her, before melting into the well-meaning embrace.

'Why didn't you tell me? When are they off? Is there anything I can do to help?' Juliette fired off a series of questions as she kissed her on the cheek then released her.

'Because I didn't want to admit it to myself, the day after tomorrow, and only if you can hide their passports,' she replied to each question in turn with a small smile.

'Seriously, I can have a good go at hiding their passports, but do you honestly think that will stop them from going?'

Nell let out a sigh. 'It might slow them down for a month or two, but it wouldn't stop them. They've got their hearts set on it, and in all honesty I don't blame them. I just wish I'd had the gumption to do the same thing when I was their age.'

'Oh well, there's always retirement to look forward to,' Juliette said, chirpily. 'When you pack all this in,' she jerked her head to indicate the shop, 'you'll have plenty of time to go travelling.'

'Not on my pension, I won't,' Nell grumbled. 'I'm far too old to sleep in a hostel. I don't mind roughing it a bit, but a night or two will do me. I prefer a soft mattress and clean sheets, thank you, and preferably a private bathroom, and things like that cost money.'

Juliette laughed. 'I know what you mean, although I don't want to rough it for even one or two nights.' She shuddered. 'The thought of sleeping in a dormitory with a handful of strangers fills me with absolute dread.'

'Did you come in here to commiserate with me, or was there another reason?' Nell asked.

'There are two reasons; the first one is that I wondered if you had something interesting I could do a piece on, and the other is that Hattie is up to her old tricks again.'

Nell thought about the painting Silas had taken away to examine. Maybe Juliette could do a feature on that? However, it might be weeks yet before Silas had an answer and besides, she didn't want Riley to get an inkling of what it might be worth, so she glanced around the shop to see if there was anything else worth writing an article about.

Most of the stuff that she bought and sold she didn't know the background to, but occasionally someone would pop in with an item they wanted to sell, and she was sometimes able to discover the full background of a piece.

She admired Juliette for turning the Tattler around; not too long ago the newspaper was almost on its knees, with the threat of closure hanging over its printed head. Now, though, since Juliette had bought it, she and her author-and-journalist partner had produced some amazing stories and articles. One of the regular columns featured different businesses in Ticklemore and the surrounding areas, and Juliette had written stories that were as diverse as they were interesting. One of Nell's favourites had been the origins of a small wrought iron gate, following its journey from the manufacturing process right through to its sale to an elderly couple who wanted it for the garden to stop their terrier from getting out. All too often people bought things without any knowledge of how they were made or where they came from. Which was why Nell liked to try to discover the provenance of as many of the items she sold as she could. Antiques were ideal for that, and even if she only knew the basics, such as the century they were made, or whether they were English or French or Bavarian, at least she had some idea.

Juliette was watching her patiently. 'Well?'

'I do have one or two things; come out the back and let me show you.' Nell led Juliette to the stockroom and pointed out the items in question. One of them was an intricately carved piece of wood, about five feet in length. She picked it up feeling its weight, and handed it to Juliette.

'What is it?' Juliette asked.

'It's a taiaha – a Maori fighting staff,' she said to her friend, and preceded to relate the story that she had been told by the lady who'd brought it in.

Juliette turned it over in her hands. 'That's fascinating. I can certainly use this one.'

'I may have something else for you in a couple of weeks,' she said. 'Silas came in yesterday and saw a painting he thought might be the real deal. He's taken it with him to do some research, but if it is genuine there might be a story behind it.'

'Funny you should say that, but I'm just about to pop along to the Gallery after I'm done here. Hattie wants Silas to come along to the meeting, and asked me to invite him.'

'What meeting?'

'Haven't you heard? Hattie's got some bee in her bonnet about youngsters not getting a fair crack of the whip when it comes to employment. Alfred is thinking of taking on another apprentice because Zoe is doing so well, and Hattie believes the rest of us should be doing our bit in that regard.'

'Are you telling me Hattie wants us to take on apprentices?'

'That's exactly what I'm saying.' Juliette leant a little closer. 'I bet you could do with some help now and again?'

Nell pulled a face. She had been hoping some of that help would have come from one of her children, but clearly not. Not yet. A few years down the line maybe. But in the meantime she'd simply have to soldier on alone, the way she had been doing for the past couple of years.

'I admit I could do with the help, but I'm not sure how much help an apprentice would actually be,' she said.

'I think that's what we're about to find out. The meeting is in the Tavern this evening, at seven o'clock. Please say you'll come; I think I might need the support.'

'Is everyone going?' Nell wanted to know. 'I can see how you, me, and Silas might be candidates for this apprenticeship thing, but I don't see where Father Todd would fit in. Or Benny and Marge for that matter. They're both retired, so I'm not sure if they fit the criteria. And would Benny want any help with his vegetable plot, anyway?'

Juliette rolled her eyes. 'I don't know, but when Hattie is in this mood it's easier to give in and go along, rather than try to fight her. She's more tenacious than a meerkat digging for a scorpion.'

'Why do I get the feeling I'm likely to get gobbled up and my bones spat out?' Nell said. She didn't particularly want to go, as she didn't see the point. She was in no position to take on an apprentice, and even if she could financially afford it, her heart wouldn't be in it. She had too many other things to think about right now, the most important being the fact that in two days' time her sons would be on a ferry, and she might not see them again for a whole year.

'Come on,' Juliette elbowed her gently in the side. 'It'll get you out the house and stop you brooding.'

She had a point, Nell conceded. Adam and Ethan were off out this evening with their friends, having one last get together, so she'd only be sitting on her own brooding. If the meeting had been tomorrow night it would have been a whole different matter, because that was her last night with her boys and she intended to make use of it. She was planning on cooking a nice meal and the three of them spending the evening together.

'Okay, I'll come, but I'm not promising anything, and I'm certainly not promising to take on an apprentice just to keep Hattie happy. I've got enough with Adam and Ethan as it is, without adding a teenager into the mix.'

'I feel the same way,' Juliette said. 'Although I strongly suspect Brooke won't be content in helping to run a small publication like the Tattler. I know for a fact she's going to want to try to get a foot in the door with a much larger organisation.'

It was sad, but true; village life wasn't for everyone, and many of the youngsters wanted to move away and spread their wings. Very often though, they returned to Ticklemore once they had children, to raise their own families here, remembering their idyllic childhood and conveniently forgetting how bored they were most of the time.

Juliette left with Nell's promise to meet her in the Tavern later, but as Nell returned to the task of trying to make sense of her invoices, she regretted saying she'd go out, despite there being plenty of solitary evenings in the weeks and months ahead. To her dismay, she realised that even when Adam and Ethan returned to the UK, there was a distinct possibility they might want a place of their own, rather than move back in with their mum.

She didn't fancy the company this evening, and she didn't fancy the reason why the meeting was being held. Even if she wanted to entertain the idea of taking on an apprentice, there would be little point – not with Riley back on the scene and demanding half of the business. She'd rather see the Treasure Trove go under than give him a single penny and it simply wouldn't be fair to take anyone on and build their hopes, only for them to be dashed on the black and slimy rocks of her ex-husband's greed.

Therefore, Nell decided not to go. Besides, the mood she was in, she'd only sour the atmosphere – she'd be better off being miserable all by herself, and she knew the others would understand.

CHAPTER 8

SILAS

Meetings weren't Silas's thing. The only reason he was going to this one tonight was because he felt morally obliged. And he was scared of Hattie. That Nell would probably be there was an added bonus. Since he'd spotted her on the bridge that day, she'd constantly been in his thoughts and he jumped at any opportunity to gaze at her. It seemed that gazing at the painting of her (which he'd almost completed) wasn't enough. He had a hankering to look at the real thing.

'Order, order!' Hattie announced grandly, and the hubbub around the table died down to a mutter. 'Father Todd not here?'

Everyone looked around as though they expected him to be sitting there and no one had noticed.

'What about Nell?' the old lady asked.

'She said she was coming.' Juliette got out her phone. 'I'll call her, but I expect she's on her way.'

'Right, while you do that, I'll get this meeting started. We haven't got time to wait about for lollygaggers.'

Silas smiled – lollygaggers, indeed. Hattie was a delightful mix of old-fashioned and modern, and she was a dab-hand on a computer.

Juliette put her phone on the table. 'She's not answering. I wonder if I should go and—?'

'I'll go,' Silas volunteered quickly. 'Just in case she needs a hand with the alarm or something,' he added hastily when he caught Juliette's surprised expression.

Hattie simpered at him and he narrowed his eyes at her, daring her to make a comment.

'Be quick,' was all the old lady said. 'And if she's not coming, make sure you get straight back here because this concerns you, too. Zoe, over to you. Silas and the others can catch up when they get here.'

Silas thought Hattie would set them homework or make them write out fifty lines if they didn't.

'I won't be long,' he promised, getting to his feet, and as he hurried away he heard Hattie say, 'You'd better not be.'

He met Father Todd on his way out. 'You'd better get in there, quick – she's waiting for you.'

'Oh, dear.' The Father looked flustered. 'Where are

you going?'

Silas might be wrong, but he got the impression Father Todd wanted to add "you lucky sod" to the end of his sentence.

'To fetch Nell – she's supposed to be here, but she's not turned up yet.'

'Have you heard about Adam and Ethan?'

'I have, which is why I'm going to fetch her.'

'You don't think she might be upset and wants to be left alone?'

'Probably. But with the boys gone, it'll do her good to have an apprentice about the place.'

'Is that what this meeting is about? To persuade Nell to take on an apprentice like Alfred did?'

'And the rest – Hattie has got all of us in her sights.'

Father Todd removed his glasses and wiped them on the hem of his jumper. 'Oh dear, I don't see how I can help.'

'I don't see how Benny and Marge can help either, but she's rounded us all up anyway.'

'I'll have to have a word with the man upstairs and seek some guidance,' Father Todd said.

'From God?' Did praying result in the giving of such explicit answers, Silas wondered irreverently.

Father Todd gave him a curious look. 'I'm going to speak to the bishop.'

'Ah, I see. OK. Right then, I'd best be off.' And with that, Silas darted along the pavement and hot-footed it to Nell's shop, feeling a right idiot.

Nell had a separate entrance to her flat around the back of the high street, and that was where he headed, hoping she'd hear him knocking even if she was on the top floor of the building.

Seeing a buzzer, though, he pressed it, and shortly afterwards he heard her voice. It sent a tingle through him, but before he wondered what that was all about, the door made a noise and clicked open.

'Nell? It's me, Silas,' he called, poking his head inside.

'I know, I saw you on the camera.' She sounded close and not at all like she was talking through the buzzer.

'Ah, right. Where are you?'

'In here.'

"Here" turned out to be a small office to the back of the main shop floor. 'Are you coming to the meeting?' he asked. 'I've been sent to fetch you.' It was only a little fib.

Nell appeared to be doing paperwork, and she put her pen down and looked up at him. 'I told Juliette I would, but I've changed my mind – I'm not in a position to take on an apprentice.' She waved a hand at her paper-strewn desk, as if to indicate she'd been doing her accounts and it wasn't looking good.

She, however, was looking very good indeed. The sadness in her eyes was still there, but Silas, to his consternation, was more interested in their colour and the softness hiding in their depths. He also had trouble dragging his gaze away from her perfect features and the curve of her lips.

'Neither am I, but I'm there,' he said, after clearing his throat and hoping she hadn't noticed him staring. Even though he hadn't quite finished the painting he'd done of her, he felt an urge to begin another. This time he'd call it something like "Temptation".

'No, you're not; you're here and pleased you've managed to escape for five minutes,' Nell shot back, accurately.

'Hattie is a force of nature, isn't she? Please come with me, I need the moral support.' He craved her company, too, for no other reason than he wanted to continue looking at her. Maybe this was the start of him moving away from landscapes and into painting people? He wasn't sure what to make of that.

'You mean, you need someone else for her to pick on when she doesn't get anywhere with you?'

'That's not what I meant, at all. I was hoping if we stick together, she might shelve the idea.'

'This is Hattie Jenkins we're talking about. The woman shelves nothing. She ploughs ahead regardless.'

'She's got a heart of gold, though,' Silas pointed out. 'There's not a mean bone in her body, and she's always willing to help everyone.'

'Now look what you've done. You've guilt-tripped me into going. Wait here. I'll put some shoes on and grab my coat.'

When she stood up and emerged from behind her desk, he saw she was wearing slippers. The slippers had a face and ears.

'Don't judge me,' she warned. 'My son bought them for me for Christmas, and they happen to be rather comfy.'

'As I've got older, I've found that comfort is king. Leave them on, if you like.'

'I don't think so! I don't want to ruin them.'

'I could always carry you,' Silas said, then reddened. Where the hell had that comment come from?

'No thanks, I'll be sick if you do a fireman's lift on me,' she joked, sidling past him and leaving him standing in her office chock full of embarrassment and confusion. It was clear where the embarrassment had come from. What wasn't so clear was why he had an image in his head of cradling her to him, carrying her in his arms like a bridegroom carrying his new wife over the threshold – there wasn't a fireman's lift in sight.

Thankfully, by the time she'd reappeared, he'd regained control of himself; so much so, that he was able to teasingly inspect her shoes as she pointed first one foot and then the other at him.

'Trainers,' he said. 'Everyone's second favourite footwear of choice. Slippers come first, naturally.'

'I can't see you in slippers,' she said, ushering him outside before setting the alarm.

'I never wear them. When I'm in the house I'm a sock man, usually odd ones.' This was a strange conversation to be having. Surely he could think of something more riveting to talk about than footwear, or the lack of it?

'I know what you mean,' she said. 'No matter how hard you try to keep them together and pair them up, there are always odd ones.'

Silas didn't like to admit he never bothered matching up socks. He simply grabbed the first two he put his hands on and hoped for the best. Even that was a lie, though — he didn't hope, because he didn't care. He'd given up caring about things like that a long time ago, at around the same time he'd given up caring about anything other than his painting. Although, if he was honest, the matching, or otherwise, of socks had never been high on his list of priorities. That had been Denise's domain. He'd just worn the damned things.

They arrived at the Tavern and never had Silas been more pleased to see other people. He'd made a right burke of himself jabbering on about slippers and socks, and he was relieved to deposit Nell in a chair and sink into the background.

Juliette had saved the seat next to her for Nell, and she sent him a grateful smile. The chair on Juliette's other side was occupied by Oliver Pascoe, her partner in both life and business. A good bloke was Oliver, Silas thought. Got his wits about him and a decent head on his shoulders. Everyone around the table was decent people. Except for him. He wasn't decent – he just went through the motions and pretended to be. Ideally, he'd like nothing more than to be left alone, but Hattie wasn't the sort of person it was easy to say no to. Ever since she'd set her heart on rescuing Alfred and his toys, and setting up the Toy Shop, she seemed to be on a mission to rescue him, too. Silas didn't like to tell her he was a lost cause, because it would mean sharing his darkest secret with her.

Forcing himself to pay attention to the proceedings, he quickly gathered that the driving force behind this meeting was Zoe and not Hattie, although Hattie was having great fun organising it. Zoe was Alfred's apprentice, and she was a brilliant one from what Silas could gather. She was a quick learner and she had an affinity with wood. Alfred claimed she was a natural and he invited everyone to take a look in the Toy Shop to see the toys she'd made. He joked that he'd soon be able to retire.

His daughter, Sara, who ran the Toy Shop, snorted loudly. 'As if!' she exclaimed. 'Neither you nor Hattie know the meaning of retirement.'

'You can talk,' Hattie retorted, and Sara looked bashful when everyone chuckled. Sara, a former head teacher, should have been enjoying her own retirement, but she'd found it so boring that she'd been persuaded (by Hattie, naturally) to run the Toy Shop to allow Alfred to concentrate on doing what he loved, which was to make handmade wooden toys.

Silas listened intently to Juliette, who was quickly bringing Nell up to speed.

'Zoe is quite the advocate for apprenticeships,' she was saying. 'Not only is she a brilliant example, but she has eloquently put forward the argument that youngsters today aren't finding it easy to learn a trade because all anyone seems interested in are paper qualifications and not practical application or experience. She says there are a number of people in college who would dearly love some hands-on training that they'd also get a small wage for, and not just have work experience which is of dubious benefit and they don't get paid at all. She's got a point.'

'Are you going to take anyone on?' Nell asked Juliette in a low voice.

'Definitely, if I'm allowed. Apparently, there are strict criteria.'

'What about Brooke?'

'Meh.' Juliette waved a hand in the air. 'She's after fame and glory, and she thinks she'll find it working for the BBC. She'll be a journalist, not a publisher. I don't need someone with a journalism degree – we've got two between us.' She indicated herself and Oliver. 'I want someone who will have a go at anything and wants to learn from the bottom up. How about you?'

Nell shook her head. 'I don't think so. I'm not in the right frame of mind. What about you, Silas?'

'Yes, what about you?' Hattie asked.

Silas pulled a face. 'I haven't thought about it.'

'Don't you think you should? You've got a talent, my boy. It's your moral duty to pass it on.'

Alfred said, 'You can't pass talent on, Hattie. You've either got it or you haven't.'

'I know that, but I also know that techniques can be taught, and running the Gallery doesn't need talent.'

'So you're suggesting I have an apprentice in order to run the Gallery?' Silas asked.

'How about both?' Hattie grinned ingratiatingly at him. 'You could have one for painting and one for business. And you could teach both of them about art.'

'There are courses for that,' Silas pointed out.

'Pish! There's a course for everything these days. It's a wonder there's not a course to teach you how to wipe your nose. Courses can only do so much. Don't you agree?'

Silas didn't know whether he agreed or not. He hadn't studied art at school; he was purely self-taught.

'Think about it,' Hattie urged.

'I will,' he said, having absolutely no intention whatsoever of thinking about it. But then he caught Zoe's expression. It was as though she knew what was in his head, and heat stole into his cheeks for the second time in less than an hour. 'I promise,' he added, this time meaning it, and the girl nodded.

'If Alfred hadn't given me a chance, I don't know what I'd have done. But whatever it was, I wouldn't be enjoying it.' Zoe paused and glanced around the table. 'Think if it was your child who needed a chance to prove themselves, who needed someone to take an interest and believe in them?' Her gaze came to rest on Silas and he was unable to look away. 'How would you feel if it was your daughter? Or son?'

Silas closed his eyes slowly before opening them again, fighting hard to hold onto his equilibrium. His daughter would never go through the trials and tribulations of trying to work out what she wanted to do with her life, what she was good at, what she disliked. What she wanted to be.

His heart broke all over again. Would the pain ever diminish?

He would have loved nothing better than to have shown Molly how to hold a brush, what a palette knife was used for, how best to prepare a canvas, sketch a face…

No amount of apprentices in the world could make up for what he'd lost – for what Molly had lost.

If he wasn't able to teach his own child, then he didn't want to teach anyone else's.

CHAPTER 9

NELL

Wasn't there an old saying about people making plans and the gods laughing? They must be having a good old chuckle at her expense right now, Nell thought, because they'd totally scuppered her intention of having one last night with her boys.

Or rather, the twins had.

It might have been a good idea to have shared her intention with them, but because she hadn't, they'd gone and made a plan of their own – one which didn't involve her.

'I've made your favourite,' she announced, as first Ethan, then Adam, emerged from their bedrooms, hefting rucksacks (was that all they were taking?), and piling up passports, visas, and assorted currency on the coffee table.

'Great, I'm starving,' Ethan enthused.

Adam was more cautious. 'What are we having, and when will it be ready?'

Nell noticed Ethan was wearing what he obnoxiously referred to as his "babe magnet" T-shirt. It was black with a skull on it. He used to wear it when he went clubbing, before he started uni.

'Cottage pie with honeyed parsnips, and it'll be about half an hour,' she said.

The boys exchanged glances. 'Stick ours on a plate, Mum, we'll warm it up when we get home,' Ethan said. 'Save us buying a burger on the way back.'

'On the way back from where?' Nell was getting twitchy.

'Hereford.'

'When? Tonight?' The twitch was turning into palpitations, as her heart thumped and thudded an irregular rhythm.

'Er, yeah? That's OK, isn't it? I mean, you didn't have anything planned?' Adam's expression was sheepish as the penny dropped. Ethan, as usual, was oblivious.

'Of course not.' Her tone was airy, her voice too high-pitched.

Adam gave her an astute look. 'Are you sure?'

'I just thought we could have dinner together – it'll be a while before it happens again.' She firmly shoved the worry that it might never happen again if all the imagined fears which had invaded her mind ever since they'd told her their news came true.

'What, like a Chapman Last Supper, or something?' Ethan quipped. 'What I want to know is, who gets to play Judas?'

'That'll be Dad,' Adam said, his eyes still scouring her face.

Nell's mouth tightened at the mention of Riley's name. She didn't want to sully this final evening with her boys by having his name mentioned. Oh, wait – she wasn't going to be spending the boys' last night in the UK with them. They were clearly going to spend it in a nightclub with their friends.

'How are you getting there?' She'd happily drive if it meant being with them for a few more minutes.

'Cazz.' Ethan patted his pockets and triumphantly brought out a condom.

Nell winced. 'Don't get in the car with her if she's been drinking. Adam, don't let him.'

'We're not stupid, Mum, and anyway, Cazz doesn't drink and drive.' Ethan replaced the condom and brought out a foil strip of tablets.

'What are those?' she asked sharply, fear prodding her with unkind fingers.

'Duh, paracetamol?' Ethan smirked at her. 'I don't want a hangover, so I'll take two before bed.'

'Have you got everything you need?' She'd asked

this question at least twenty times over the course of the past few days.

'Yeah, Mum, don't fuss.'

'I'm your mother, it's my job to fuss. It's the law or something.'

'It's fine, Mum. We're all sorted.' Adam came to stand next to her and rubbed her shoulder.

'Have you got plasters?' she blurted. 'You might need them.'

'Mum, it's fine,' Adam repeated. Ethan had moved closer to the door and was practically bouncing in his impatience to be off.

'It's only half-past six,' she said. 'Isn't it a bit early to be going to a nightclub?'

'Pub first, then house party, then club,' Ethan said.

'I see.' Her reply was weak, and she felt drained even thinking about it. 'Be careful,' she warned; it was the only thing she could think of to say, even though what she really wanted to do was to cuddle them close, one either side of her, and fill their heads with every good piece of advice she could think of.

'Catch you later,' Ethan said. 'Don't wait up.'

'What time will you be home?'

'Two, three. Whenever.' Her youngest shrugged.

'What time do you have to leave in the morning?'

'Ten, if we want to catch the eleven-fifteen train to London.' Adam was the more precise of the two. He was the one who would have done all the organising. Ethan had the madcap ideas – his brother found a way to execute them.

'I'll drive you to the station,' she offered.

'It's OK—' Ethan began, but Adam butted in.

'That'll be great, Mum. Thanks.'

'Er, yeah, thanks. Cazz—' Ethan said.

'Cazz will be waiting,' Adam interjected once more, and she knew they'd made other plans for the morning, plans which didn't involve her.

She hoped it was because they wanted to spare her the emotion of saying goodbye at the station, and not because they wanted to spare themselves the embarrassment of seeing her cry as they left. No doubt, they'd expect to be dropped off outside like a couple of parcels and not want her to wait with them on the platform for the train to arrive.

She understood, she really did – this was an adventure, and maternal tears and stranglehold hugs might take a tiny bit of the shine off their exhilaration to finally be on their way. Keeping a lid on her sadness at them leaving and not knowing when she'd see them again was going to be hard, but for their sakes she'd do it. Adam, she knew, would worry about her if she seemed anything less than calm.

Telling herself she could do this, Nell gave them both a hug. 'Have fun,' she told them and tried not to think about the kind of fun they might shortly be having. It was hard to accept that her babies had grown and were just about to embark on their own lives. Of course, the journey had started long before the one they were about to undertake in the morning – it had begun, had she only realised it at the time, when they had pulled themselves up on the furniture on chubby, wobbly legs, batting her steadying hands away.

It had been so gradual, the slow sure creep towards independence and not needing her any more, that she hadn't noticed it, except for the milestones of their first day at school, their first time walking to school on their own, their first night away from home without her, first driving lesson, first visit to a university... the number of firsts had seemed endless and disjointed, but they had all come together like many separate beams of light to illuminate this one moment. They were grown. They had become men. She had done a good job of parenting them, even though she said so herself. They were fine boys and she was so very proud of them.

But faith or not, pride or not, worry came with the territory of being a mother and Nell had never before experienced the level of worry that she knew would be hers for the next year.

CHAPTER 10

SILAS

Was a painting ever finished, Silas mused, staring at the canvas critically. There was always something to be tweaked and dabbed at, another line to be added, another that he wished could be taken away.

He was a watercolour man through and through, but for some reason before he'd started work on Nell's portrait, he'd dug out his oils, surprised they hadn't gone off or solidified. The medium seemed more suited for the effect he was trying to achieve than watercolours, or acrylics (he had a rarely-touched supply of those, too).

There had to come a point, though, when it was time to stop fiddling with it, and he was close to that point now; he might have already reached it.

This painting had taken him considerably longer to complete than any other painting he'd done in recent years, and he was undecided whether it was due to using a less familiar medium, or the subject matter.

He still didn't do portraits and he had no wish to paint anyone else. But if he had the chance, he'd paint Nell again.

Suddenly a memory of Molly leapt into his mind, so vivid that it floored him. She was sitting on the living room rug, holding a doll in her hands. It had been her birthday, and he and Denise had just received the diagnosis that all parents dread. The reality of it had yet to sink in, and they were trying to be normal for Molly's sake. Silas remembered watching her play, and despairing that his daughter might never get to cradle a child of her own the way she was nursing the doll. He'd been right. She never would.

The memory was so clear he could see the dust motes drifting in the air above her head, illuminated by the shafts of the surprisingly strong early-spring sunshine.

That birthday had been Molly's third and last.

Why was he thinking of that now? Was the universe trying to torture him some more, because it decided he hadn't been tortured enough already?

Molly's head had been bowed over her doll and she'd been rocking it in her arms. The memory was especially poignant because there'd been no outward sign of the cancer that would shortly ravage her, nor of the effects of the treatment she was about to begin. Her obliviousness to what was about to happen stabbed his heart even now.

But there was something else along with the memory, a yearning to do something he'd never, ever contemplated doing – he wanted to capture it in paint.

They'd taken photos, him and Denise, lots of them, hundreds of them, desperate to capture any and all images of their daughter. They'd taken so many, and he'd hardly looked at them since.

He hadn't been able to.

It wasn't like he wanted to wipe Molly from his memory Absolutely not. Despite having had her for only a few tragically unfairly short years, he cherished every second with her. Even the bad ones. Even the horrific ones. Even the final one.

It was more a case of his soul having been so badly damaged by her loss that he couldn't bear to see her beautiful little face without being torn apart all over again.

Yet, now this urge to capture her in oils.

It was late, far too late at night to be thinking about starting a brand new painting. The light was wrong (artificial), he was tired (nothing new), he was too emotional, the subject matter too agonising—

Subject matter? Molly was no *subject matter*; she was his *daughter*, but he'd never been able to paint her until now.

Silas knew better than to argue. If something was telling him to paint her, then paint her he would. There was one thing about the urge (the need?) which terrified him, though... What if, once he'd started painting her, he couldn't stop?

Did that way madness lie, or was this the beginning of the healing process?

There was only one way to find out.

Silas reached for a blank canvas...

CHAPTER 11

SILAS

Silas had wrapped the Treasure Trove painting well and had placed it carefully in the back of his estate car.

When he'd got up this morning, the last thing he'd been expecting to do today was to drive to London, but Vaughan had been very insistent. And Silas was now all fired up, so he'd agreed.

In some ways Vaughan was the exact opposite of Silas. Vaughan didn't paint; Silas did. Vaughan was methodical and meticulous and had a great attention to detail when it came to his job; Silas tended to splash paint on paper and see where it led him. Vaughan was a well-respected curator of fine art in the Tate Gallery in London; Silas was a struggling artist displaying his own work in a non-descript little gallery in a village hardly anyone had heard of.

How the two of them had ever become friends was a mystery to Silas. But they had, and right now Silas was very glad about it, especially since he'd woken up this morning to a quietly excited and demanding email from the guy. Vaughan wanted to see the painting in person, which meant Silas was quietly excited, too. Vaughan hadn't dismissed out of hand Silas's suggestion that Nell's painting might possibly be a previous undiscovered painting by Peter Oakman. Therefore Silas had decided to forgo opening the Gallery for today, and head to London instead. If he was quick, he might make it back in time to open in the afternoon.

He'd woken early (5 a.m.) as was his habit, and he'd tumbled out of bed, sleepy-eyed and yawning, intending to do some painting before he opened the shop for the day. However, a perfunctory check of his emails had him dashing into the shower before preparing Nell's painting for its journey. He was on the road by six o'clock, and parking the car by nine-thirty.

When Vaughan took him through to his office, and offered him a coffee and a doughnut Silas almost bit his hand off. He'd been so eager to get to London, he hadn't thought about breakfast.

Afterwards, Vaughan took Silas and the painting into another room, one in which coffee and doughnuts were never allowed, and he watched Vaughan unpack it and stood by, becoming increasingly impatient as the man made a thorough initial assessment of the painting.

'Well?' Silas demanded, when Vaughan stepped back.

'It appears to be genuine,' Vaughan said. 'Of course, I'll have to run a whole load of tests, but in my opinion the signature is genuine, and the painting looks right.'

By "right", Silas knew the term was used when the type of paper or canvas, and the paint, the technique, the backing, and everything else which made a work of art attributable to any particular artist, was correct. He also knew Vaughan was duty-bound to X-ray it and to do goodness knows what else to it, to ensure it was a genuine painting.

'I did a bit of digging after you sent me the photos,' Vaughan said, 'and Oakman visited this part of Wales not long before he died. I only know of one other work of his which didn't feature a Scottish scene, but as you are probably aware there are rumours he painted at least one other. I strongly suspect this is it. Can you leave it with me for a few days?'

'No problem. If it is genuine, how much do you think it would be worth?'

'Probably somewhere in the region of half a million pounds.'

Silas gasped. He needed to sit down. '*How much?* Are you sure?'

'You'll have to have it valued of course, but I'm fairly sure. One of his sold about a year ago for just over £500,000.'

'Gosh.'

'Indeed,' was Vaughan's wry reply.

Silas couldn't wait to tell Nell. She'd be over the moon. Even if it didn't sell for that amount, it was still worth a substantial chunk of money.

'I'd better wait until you're certain before I share the good news with its owner,' Silas said. He'd explained in his email that the painting belonged to a friend of his.

'You can tell the owner now,' Vaughan said.

'You're that certain it's an Oakman?'

'I am. The rest is a formality. I've been studying his work long enough to know a genuine Oakman when I see one.'

Silas was so elated he could have kissed the man. But instead, he shook his hand. And when he came to think of it, the only person he wanted to kiss, *really* kiss and not peck on the cheek, was Nell.

The idea was quite disconcerting, yet very tempting at the same time.

CHAPTER 12

NELL

Grouchy didn't begin to describe the mood Nell was in today, and had been for the past few days. Phone calls and WhatsApp messages didn't do anything to alleviate her loneliness and, despite getting regular updates from her sons (they didn't have any choice, because she contacted them obsessively), the worry was eating her alive.

Were they eating properly? Where were they staying at night? Were they (God forbid!) hitchhiking? Did they have enough sun cream, and if so, were they remembering to reapply it frequently? How were they getting their washing done? She sincerely hoped they weren't wearing the same clothes day in, day out, without giving them a swill. Mind you, the far-too-small rucksacks they'd taken with them suggested that was precisely what they were doing.

If they had been girls, they would have Instagrammed every meal, every road, every hostel… everything. Or Snapchatted it. But they were boys – they didn't bother photographing their food; they forwarded her silly memes that they'd got from one of their friends, which failed to answer any of her questions, apart from one – that they were still alive and had access to their phones.

Occasionally Adam would send her a smiling selfie, or a picture of Ethan. In each one he was pulling a silly face and wearing a cap back to front. It was neon yellow and clashed with his slightly pink nose – hence the sun cream concern.

She was furiously wondering where they were and what they were doing right now (she found herself doing that a lot) when the shop door opened. The Treasure Trove had only been open an hour and trade was brisk already, so she made an effort to tear herself away from her worrying and turned to greet her customer.

Shit. It wasn't a customer. It was Riley.

Nell's stomach turned over and her heart dropped to her leather pumps. She hadn't heard from him since before the twins had left, and she'd begun to hope he'd buggered off.

No such luck.

'I've come for what's mine,' he told her without

preamble, and she hurried forward, grabbed him by the elbow and dragged him towards the back of the shop, out of earshot of the other customers. The middle-aged couple were frequent visitors and often bought a small item or two.

'The Treasure Trove is not yours,' she hissed.

'I'll think you'll find it is.' He gave her a smarmy smile. 'Look, I'm a reasonable man. I'll settle for half. I think that's fair, don't you?'

'No, I sodding well don't.'

'Have you had a letter from my solicitor yet?'

Nell felt the blood drain from what she suspected was her already pale face. This was the second time he'd mentioned a solicitor. He must be fairly sure he had a claim on the Treasure Trove. What with the twins leaving, she'd sort of pushed his threat to the back of her mind, but now it was in her face and in her shop once again.

'Excuse me, can you tell me anything about this?' the male half of the couple called to her. 'And it says £85 on the tag – is there any room for negotiation?'

'You'd better not come down from that,' Riley murmured. 'Half of that is mine.'

'Oh, piss off,' she mouthed, and went to see to her customer.

She hated leaving Riley unattended, but what else could she do? And, as she was chatting with the couple, she kept one eye on him as he sauntered around the shop, picking things up one by one to check the price, and she was convinced he was making a mental note as to the complete worth of the shop's contents.

Thankfully, there was nothing left in the Treasure Trove that had originally resided in the house they'd once shared, and she didn't think he'd recognise anything even if there had been, but she didn't want to take the risk.

Finally the couple made a purchase (she'd agreed to come down by £5) and they were just opening the door to leave, when Silas walked in.

He moved to the side to let them pass, and almost before he'd stepped inside he said, 'I've got some fantastic news! Your painting is genuine. It's worth a small—'

Nell waggled her eyebrows at him, and he stopped talking immediately, confusion flooding his face.

Too late – Riley appeared around the side of a particularly fine dresser like an evil genie let loose out of its bottle. He'd been tapping the wood and trying to seem knowledgeable.

'Pray tell,' he said with an ingratiating smile. 'We're all ears.'

Silas glanced at her for confirmation and Nell shook her head a fraction, hoping Silas would take the hint, and Riley hadn't noticed.

'You are…?' Silas asked.

Riley came forward, holding out a hand, his face all smiles and white teeth. They must be veneers, Nell thought blankly. He never used to look quite so shark-like. Or had he, and she hadn't noticed because she'd loved him.

'Riley Chapman. Nell's husband.'

Nell spluttered, '*Ex* husband.'

'That's what I meant. Now, about this painting.' He let his unshaken hand drop to his side without missing a beat.

Silas's face was expressionless. 'I don't think that's any of your business,' he said, and Nell could have kissed him.

'If it's to do with the Treasure Trove, it *is* my business. And who are you, anyway?'

'Riley, stop being so rude. Not that it's anything to do with you, but this is Silas Long and he owns the Gallery up the road. He was about to tell me about one of his paintings when you so rudely interrupted him.'

She prayed Silas heard the "one of his paintings" bit and understood what she was getting at.

'A friend of Nell's, are you?' Riley smirked, his inference clear. He thought they were sleeping together.

'That's right, a friend,' Silas said, and Nell could have sworn he'd grown a couple of inches as he squared up to her ex.

It was curious that she hadn't realised quite how tall Silas was until he and Riley were standing so close and she was able to compare the two of them.

Riley must have been able to see it too, because he stepped back slightly. Silas Long was a powerfully built man, she realised, with broad shoulders, muscular arms, and a deep chest. Riley was slighter, less substantial, and she didn't just mean physically. Silas was more solid, in every sense of the word, and she had the warm feeling that he had her back and wouldn't let her down.

'Can you tell me about the painting later?' Nell said, anxious to dispel the atmosphere of hackle-raised dogs which had suddenly pervaded her shop.

'Yes, run along,' Riley said, making a shooing motion with his hand. 'Nell and I have business to discuss.'

'We do not!' Nell refuted hotly.

'I think you'll find we do.' Riley's calm and assured manner was starting to get to her, and she had a horrible feeling he was right – that he *did* have a claim on the business. Maybe it was time she had a chat with a solicitor of her own, and she should have thought about it sooner, but she'd been so wrapped up in the twins' departure there hadn't been room in her head for anything else.

'Haven't I seen you somewhere before?' Silas asked abruptly.

Riley looked him up and down. 'I don't think so.'

'I'm sure I have… It'll come to me.'

'Don't bother letting me know when it does,' Riley said. 'If you were important, I would have remembered you.'

'Riley!' Nell was appalled. He never used to be so rude. 'Apologise.'

'Don't speak to me like I'm one of the boys,' he retorted. 'I had enough of that when you were my wife.'

'How *is* Vanessa?' Nell's tone was arch.

Riley's expression hardened. 'I'm not here to talk about Vanessa. I'm here to talk about my share of this business.'

Without warning, Nell felt all the fight go out of her. She'd had enough of this, enough of *him*. She needed to think about what he'd said and consider her options, but she couldn't think straight with him in her face and with the atmosphere rank with testosterone and greed.

Silas was responsible for some of that testosterone, but the greed was pure Riley.

'Go,' she said. 'Just get out.'

'But—'

Silas moved closer to Riley. It wasn't by much, but it was enough. 'You heard the lady. She'd like you to leave.'

Riley shrugged. 'If that's the way you want to play it, Nell, then so be it. I've tried to be nice, but... You'll be hearing from my solicitor.'

'I thought I was supposed to have heard already?' she countered, trying to muster up some fire, but feeling weak and drained instead.

'Yes, I need to get onto him about that,' Riley said. He sidled towards the door, his parting shot of, 'See you soon, Nell,' leaving a bad taste in her mouth.

Silas waited for the door to close and for Riley to walk down the street before he said, 'I know it's none of my business, but do you want to talk about it?'

She wasn't sure whether she was prepared to share the details of her divorce with him. He was a friend, and was possibly turning into a good one, but... Oh, what the hell! Ticklemore was a small place and everyone knew everyone else's business. If he wanted to discover anything about her, all he had to do was ask around. 'I'll make us a cup of tea, shall I, then I'll tell you what all that was about.'

'You don't have to, if you don't want to.'

Nell, to her bewilderment, found that she did. 'If I don't, someone else will,' she said, to cover her confusion. 'I'm surprised Hattie hasn't told you all about my sordid divorce.'

Silas smiled. 'I'm sure she would have done if I'd asked her.'

Nell gave him a small smile back. 'You've lived in Ticklemore for how long now?'

'Five years.' He followed her out to the little office. She was acutely aware of how he filled the space.

'Riley and I got divorced nearly three years ago. He'd been having an affair.'

'With someone called Vanessa?'

'Yes. She is younger than me, of course. At least she wasn't his secretary, but they did work in the same office, and it seems she wasn't able to resist his money – he's a financial consultant. He wasn't able to resist her either, apparently.' Nell wrinkled her nose. 'He's not got any claim on the Treasure Trove,' she said, handing him a mug, and gesturing to him that they should go back onto the shop floor. She didn't like leaving it unattended for too long, even though she could hear the door open from miles away. It had a distinctive little squeak which wasn't intrusive enough to get on her nerves, yet alerted her to it being opened.

'I'm glad to hear it,' Silas said. 'Although, he seemed quite adamant.'

'He did, didn't he?' She put her mug on the

counter and sighed. 'OK, he might have a claim,' she admitted. 'It's no secret that I sold off most of the contents of the house. He'd waited until the boys had gone to university before he told me he was leaving me, but the affair had been going on for a while before that. He insisted on the house being sold. It was that big one at the end of Chrysler Lane.'

Silas's eyes grew large. 'The really big one? The one that looks more like a mansion than a house?'

'That's the one. Seven bedrooms, I ask you! We didn't need seven bedrooms; three would have been enough, but Riley wanted it, so we bought it when the boys were about ten and I spent the next few years furnishing it.' Silas raised his eyebrows and she added, somewhat defensively, 'It gave me something to do.'

'I'm not judging you,' he said. 'I'm just surprised it took you so long. I furnished my cottage in about a day. Admittedly, it's only got two bedrooms,' he joked.

'I could have done it faster by going to a department store, but I like unusual things.' She glanced around the shop. 'And I like a bargain. I also found I enjoyed the hunt. Scrabbling around in boot sales and second-hand shops is my speciality, although I don't have as much time as I'd like to do that now.'

'You need an apprentice.' Silas grinned at her.

'I probably do need someone, but I don't think I'm in a position to take anyone on.'

'Riley?'

'Riley,' she confirmed. 'As I was saying, I furnished the house over the course of several years, and filled it with all sorts of lovely things. Riley didn't notice and didn't care what I bought, as long as I didn't spend too much money – and he didn't care what I did with my time, as long as I never questioned what he did with his. To be honest, I never thought to. I believed him when he told me he was working late, or when he said he was going golfing all weekend with "the lads". Ha! Some lad she turned out to be.'

'Then what happened?'

'I found out about him and Vanessa. He left, started divorce proceedings, and put the house on the market. I had no job, no real chance of getting one, and no money. So I sold my jewellery, my designer handbags and some of my clothes. Then I started on the contents of the house.' She smiled, her mind full of memories. 'I did rather well. Apart from when Riley came back to pick up his personal stuff, to my knowledge he never stepped foot in the house again, and he certainly never questioned what happened to the furniture or the ornaments. He probably thought I took most of it with me or left it for the new owners.'

'Until now?'

'Hmm. He's bound to have known I'd set up my own business, but why has it taken him this long to demand his share?'

'Do you honestly think he is entitled to anything?'

Nell looked at him, despair filling her. 'I don't know. Maybe. I suppose legally the contents of the house were as much his as mine and should have been split between us, like the house was.'

'You need to speak to a solicitor,' Silas said, and she knew he was right. Suddenly recalling the purpose of his visit, she said, 'You have some news about the painting?'

'Oh, yes!' He slapped a hand to his forehead. 'Good news, brilliant news – I think it's a genuine Oakman.'

'It is? That's…' Nell trailed off, the implication making her mute.

'It's worth a small fortune, that's what it is,' Silas finished for her. 'I had it checked over by a friend of mine who works for the Tate Gallery in London, and he confirmed it. I hope you don't mind, but I had to leave it with him because he wants to run a few tests on it to back up his assessment.' He looked worried.

'Of course I don't mind. I'm just grateful for your help. It's very kind of you.'

'I'll fetch it later this week,' he said, 'and then I

suggest you get it valued by an auction house that specialises in paintings.'

'It's worth that much?' Her mouth was dry and she didn't dare hope.

'Vaughan gave me a ballpark figure of around £500,000 but he couldn't be exact.'

'Gosh.' Nell reached blindly for the stool behind the counter and perched on it, suddenly feeling rather faint.

'Are you all right?' Silas peered at her, concern etched on his face.

'I think so,' she said. 'I'll let you know in a minute when it's had a chance to sink in. I think I'd better get it insured,' she joked feebly.

'I tell you what, how about you come with me to London to pick it up, and we'll make an appointment with Carlfort's Auction House for the same day – they're probably your best bet to give you a valuation, and if you're happy with the amount you can arrange to sell it through them.' He stopped and cocked his head to the side. 'Sorry, I'm assuming you *do* want to sell it?'

'Yes, and no…' She was conscious of Silas's scrutiny. 'I'm worried about Riley. Once he knows about it, he'll be all over it like a rash. Though why he's so insistent that he has half of the business is beyond me. He's not exactly short of a bob or two.'

Silas shook his head slowly and pursed his lips.

'What?' she asked. His behaviour was a little odd.

'I thought I'd seen him before,' he said. 'And I have – in Bookylicious.'

'Okaay?' Nell wasn't sure where Silas was going with this.

'He was having a heated conversation with someone on the phone. Loudly. I couldn't help overhearing.'

'What was he saying? Do you know who he was talking to?'

'No idea, but I heard him say, something like... "you can take me to the cleaners now but if you do you won't get anything". He mentioned something about needing more time and then he said, "I told her I'd spoken to a solicitor" so I'm assuming the 'her' he referred to is you?'

Nell was astonished. 'Did he say anything else?'

'Yeah, he did. He told the person on the other end that they'd have to be patient, and he'll have it for them soon. He also said, "She'll cave". Are you thinking what I'm thinking?'

'I'm not sure what to think.' Nell felt decidedly wobbly – this morning was becoming quite surreal.

'I suspect Riley is in financial trouble, which is why he's decided to try his luck with getting some money out of you.'

'But he's not stupid – he knows that solicitors work in their own sweet time, and all the legal wrangling will take months.'

'He's hoping if he frightens you enough, you'll give him money to make him go away.'

'If he thinks that, then he *is* stupid.'

'No, I get the impression he thinks you're naïve enough to do precisely that, just to get him off your back.'

Nell raised a shaking hand to her brow. 'I might have been that woman once,' she acknowledged. 'But not any more.' She forced out a wobbly smile. 'You don't know any solicitors who deal with business law, do you?'

Silas put a hand on her arm and gave it a little rub. His touch sent a shiver through her. 'As a matter of fact, I do.'

CHAPTER 13

SILAS

Getting involved in Nell Chapman's private affairs hadn't been Silas's intention. All he had wanted to do was to paint her.

It had escalated though, as things so often did. He'd spotted the Oakman painting and now he was caught up in her life and he wasn't sure he could extricate himself. What was more worrisome, was that he wasn't sure he wanted to. There was something about Nell which drew him to her, something that brought out the protector in him.

Not that she needed his protection; this wasn't the eighteenth century and Nell was no shrinking violet. She was strong and independent, and ran a successful business.

But he had a gut feeling there were sides to Nell that she didn't often show to the world, and he was desperate to capture the essence of her. He hoped he'd done that a little in the painting in his studio.

He lifted the sheet he'd draped over it and gazed at it at least twice a day, no longer looking at it with his critical artist's eye, but looking at it like a man who liked what he was seeing.

And he did like Nell. A lot.

Too much? Perhaps. Because he had no intention of doing anything about it. He wasn't in the market for a relationship of any kind. Not even a professional one with an employee – which was why he hadn't taken on an assistant, no matter how much he desperately needed another pair of hands. He suspected Nell felt the same way.

Damn, there he was thinking about Nell again.

She was invading his thoughts far too often, but he couldn't help feeling tied to her in a way, and it was all this bloody painting's fault. He dropped the sheet back over it, and studiously ignored the other sheet-covered painting in the room. That one didn't get looked at during the cold light of day. That one, he saved for the wee small hours when he couldn't sleep, and the siren call of his daughter whispered in his heart.

God, he missed her.

Shaking himself, he selected a recently framed landscape of the Black Mountains and took it down to the gallery to replace a similar one he'd sold yesterday, then answered a couple of emails asking if he had a print of one of his larger pictures which he had yet to sell. He only sold original works, no prints, but as he replied to the query he wondered if he should branch out. Selling prints of the original artwork might generate more income, which would mean he would have more time to paint because he needn't keep the shop open all hours.

Darn it – he really did need an assistant.

He checked the time, and realised he had to get a move on if he wasn't going to be late picking Nell up. The Treasure Trove closed half days on Wednesdays so Silas was driving her down to London to collect her painting, then they'd just have time to pop into Carlfort's Auction House to get the thing valued properly.

'Heard any more from your ex?' Silas asked, after they'd been on the road for a while.

'No, thank God,' Nell said. 'But I'm on tenterhooks every day waiting for the postman. Thanks for pointing me in the direction of your solicitor friend. I've made an appointment for next week. You certainly know some useful people.'

'I wouldn't call Francis a friend – he handled my divorce, but he also specialises in the more complex family law where businesses are involved.'

Silas was acutely conscious of the quick look she sent him. He was also well aware that no one in Applewell knew very much about him at all. Even if they Googled him, there wasn't a great deal to discover about his private life.

'Her name is Denise and it ended a while ago,' he added. He wasn't entirely comfortable sharing this, but she'd shared so much with him that it seemed churlish not to reciprocate.

'Ah, I didn't realise,' she said softly.

'There was no reason you should have done.' His reply was mild.

'Does she live near here?'

'No. Cheltenham.' Denise had stayed in the house where they had lived as a family. Silas had run away, unable to bear the unrelenting memories. It was another thing that had driven them apart.

He could sense Nell was dying to ask more, but to his relief she didn't. Instead, the conversation moved onto less fraught ground and they chatted about art and antiques for the remainder of the journey.

'Drat!' Silas exclaimed when the motorway traffic slowed, then came to an almost complete standstill. He rolled his eyes at Nell and she tutted sympathetically back at him. 'Roadworks,' he said, nodding to a flashing sign above their heads. 'They weren't here when I brought the painting down last week.'

They crawled for about twenty miles until, without warning, the traffic began to move again – only for it to grind to another halt less than fifteen minutes later.

Silas groaned. 'If this doesn't shift soon, we're not going to make our appointment at Carlfort's.'

He was right – they didn't. They only just made it to the Tate before it closed, and Silas rang ahead to let his friend know they were on their way. He also rang Carlfort's to tell them they'd have to rearrange.

They were met in the Tate's foyer, and were shown into an office where Nell's painting sat in the corner.

'Thanks for waiting for us, Vaughan,' Silas said. 'The traffic on the M4 was horrendous, then we hit rush hour…'

'No worries. Here's the letter of authentication. Of course, you'll need to get it properly appraised for its fair market value, but I'm guessing that for insurance purposes the replacement value is what I already told you,' Vaughan said, handing Silas an envelope. 'I must say, it's a particularly fine example.' He turned to Nell. 'Where did you get it?'

'From a house clearance shop in Brecon.'

'Silas tells me you paid a pittance for it.'

She nodded, and Silas saw a flush spread across her cheeks. 'I did. I feel awful about it now.'

'Don't even think about it,' Silas muttered. 'It's their fault for not doing due diligence on it.'

'I didn't check it properly, either. I wonder if the company could tell me whose house it came from?'

Silas realised she was serious, and something stirred deep inside him. 'Are you thinking of contacting the original owner and telling them?'

She worried at her bottom lip and frowned. 'I suppose I am. I've been thinking – it doesn't feel right keeping it, not now I know what it's worth. The real owner might be in dire need of the money.'

'You *are* the real owner.'

'I don't feel it.'

'It's your painting – you do with it what you like.'

'You don't approve, do you?' she asked, looking up at him from underneath her lashes.

'Actually, I do. Just be careful, eh? There are sharks out there.'

She smiled at him. 'I know.' Then she stood on tiptoe and kissed him on the cheek. 'I'm so glad you're not one of them.'

Silas felt himself redden, and he was conscious of Vaughan's gaze shooting between the two of them.

'Listen, Si, I'm glad you've found—' Vaughan began, and Silas hurried to cut him off.

'Thanks for your help, Vaughan,' he interrupted. 'We'd better be off, we've got a meeting at Carlfort's and we're late as it is.'

'But I thought you'd sent our apologies?' Nell said, once they'd said their goodbyes and were outside the building, the box containing the painting safely in the back of the car.

'If you let him, Vaughan will talk for Britain,' Silas said, by way of explanation, but he had a feeling Nell hadn't fallen for his little white lie.

Vaughan was an old friend. A very old friend. One who'd known Denise, and had known about Molly. One with whom Silas hadn't had a great deal of contact over the last few years. And one who'd been about to blurt out information which he didn't want to share. Besides, his relationship with Nell was purely platonic, firstly as a business acquaintance and more recently as a friend of sorts. Not a close friend, but someone he liked and admired. Not only was she attractive, but she was a nice person through and through.

He cast surreptitious glances at her out of the corner of his eye as he guided the car through the insane London traffic and back onto the motorway, admiring the slight upturn of her nose, the curve of her neck, her long lashes, the arch of her eyebrow.

The urge to paint her was still there, but not as demanding, and he wondered whether it was because he was able to gaze on the real thing and not an imperfect image. Because however hard he'd tried, he didn't feel his painting had done her justice. She was far more beautiful in real life.

Their eyes met briefly and he hastily glanced back at the road.

'Is everything all right?' she asked.

'Of course it is. Why do you ask?'

'No reason.' She paused, then appeared to reconsider and added, 'You seem a little preoccupied.'

'Just thinking about what to have for supper,' he lied.

'I've got some chicken breasts in the fridge – how about I make us some sticky chicken, rice and chargrilled vegetables?'

Silas was mortified. 'I'm sorry, I wasn't hinting or anything.'

Nell's amused chuckle made the hairs on his arms stand on end – my God, the sound was sexy.

'I didn't for one minute think you were,' she said. 'But I'm going to have to cook for myself, so why don't you let me cook for you, too? Anyway, it's the least I can do. I intend to thank you properly for all the trouble you've gone to with the Oakman, but this will have to do for now.'

'I don't need thanking,' he said, 'It was my pleasure.'

'I'm going to take you out to dinner, whether you

like it or not,' she said, with another of her sexy chuckles.

'And do what? Force feed me steak and chips?'

'If that's what it takes for me to feel I've said a proper thank you. Although I was thinking of something more upmarket than steak and chips.'

'I happen to like steak. It's my favourite. And let's not go anywhere fancy – the Tavern is perfectly good enough.'

'Are you sure?'

'Absolutely.'

Silas didn't want a fuss. He didn't feel it necessary for Nell to go out of her way – he'd not done a great deal, just shown the Oakman to a friend, that was all. It was sheer luck that the painting was genuine and worth a bit of money.

That Nell was planning on returning it to its previous owner had been a shock. Silas wasn't sure he would be so honourable or generous under the same circumstances. He knew she was a nice person from his dealings with her when getting the Toy Shop off the ground and, more recently, when helping Juliette to turn the Tattler around. This went beyond nice – this was the action of a thoroughly lovely person.

Despite him feeling he didn't deserve her thanks, he found he was looking forward to spending the next few hours in her company.

Oh dear, he should knock this on the head, shouldn't he, before he started feeling more for her than was wise.

CHAPTER 14

NELL

Nell had surprised herself when she'd offered to cook a meal for Silas this evening, but when she thought about it logically, it was the least she could do considering what he'd done for her. It was nearly nine p.m. by the time they arrived back in Ticklemore and she had a feeling that if she hadn't asked Silas to join her for supper, he probably wouldn't have bothered to eat more than a slice of toast.

Silas parked the car and picked up the painting whilst Nell unlocked the door, then she took it from him and made her way to her little office.

'I might as well leave it wrapped up,' she said. 'It's safer that way. Less chance of it getting damaged.'

Nell stowed the painting, then took Silas upstairs to the flat. The whole of the first floor was given over to a decent-sized kitchen and a large family room; the floor above had two bedrooms (Adam and Ethan shared the bigger one, which wasn't ideal) and a bathroom. When she thought about it logically, no wonder the boys had opted to go backpacking for a year, rather than return to their rather cramped living conditions. With a sinking heart, she knew it was time for them to move on, and not for the first time she blamed her ex-husband. She had the feeling that if they'd still been living in the house on Chrysler Lane, her sons might not be so eager to fly the nest.

Silas must have sensed her mood, because he said, 'It's late. Why don't I get off home – you don't want to be cooking at this time of night.'

Cooking would give her something to do, and having company would take her mind off her thoughts, because she'd had a sudden vision of selling the painting and using the money to buy a property with enough bedrooms to allow the twins to have one each. But she knew in her heart that although she was perfectly entitled to do that, it wasn't morally right. Then there was also the mean thought that if Riley knew about it, he'd take half anyway. Which made her not as nice a person as she hoped to be, if the main reason she wanted to give it back to its rightful owner was purely to thwart Riley.

'Don't be silly,' she said to Silas, who was hovering uncertainly by the stairs. 'I have to eat, and so do you.

Come in and shut the door. You can make yourself useful by pouring us a glass of wine. I've only got white – will that do you?'

Silas did as he was told and followed her into the kitchen. Nell took the wine out of the fridge and handed him the bottle whilst she set out preparing supper. He was right, it was a little late to cook, but she wanted to delay being on her own for as long as possible. The flat was terribly empty without her boys and she didn't want to spend yet another evening staring blankly at the TV.

'Is there any point in getting the painting valued properly?' Nell asked. 'I mean, the rightful owner can do that, once I track them down.'

'*If* you track them down,' Silas pointed out, pouring the wine into the glasses he'd spotted in one of the overhead cabinets. 'You might never find out who it belonged to.' He placed a glass on the countertop within easy reach, yet not so close she was in danger of knocking it over. 'And you *are* the rightful owner in the eyes of the law, so it might be a good idea to have it properly valued if only for insurance purposes whilst you still own it.'

'Oh, I never thought of that. I'm not sure my insurance covers an individual item of that value. I suppose I'll have to make another appointment with Carlfort's.'

Silas swirled the wine in his glass and breathed in the aroma before taking a sip. 'Not necessarily. They can give an appraisal by email, as long as you send them some decent photos, and the letter from Vaughan would come in handy, too. I only suggested going there today because we were in London and they're just around the corner from the Tate.'

'That's a relief,' she said, tossing the chicken into a frying pan, along with a chopped onion and some garlic. 'I didn't fancy driving down to London again.'

A short silence followed, Nell desperately trying to think of something to say, and wondering if Silas was doing the same. He looked out of place in her kitchen, and she realised he was the first man to step foot in her flat since the removal men had left on the day she'd moved in, and it was an odd feeling. Not unpleasant, just strange. Nell was acutely conscious of his masculinity, the sheer maleness of him. He took up more room than she would have thought possible, despite him being tall and broad-shouldered. He seemed to fill the available space, until all she could think about was his presence. She could smell his aftershave, even though the aroma of garlic and onions saturated the air.

'I enjoyed today,' he said. 'And if you do have to go to London again, I'll happily come with you.' He cleared his throat. 'If you want me to, that is. I don't want to impose.'

'I'm hoping I won't have to,' she said, then realised how that sounded and added, 'but if I do, I'd love for you to come with me. And you most definitely won't be imposing.' She glanced up at him, to find him studying her intently. He seemed to do that a lot. 'Thank you,' she said, quietly.

'It was nothing. Vaughan's an old friend—'

'That's not what I meant. You didn't have to say anything about the painting. You could have simply bought it, and I'd have been none the wiser.'

Silas stared at her for a moment, his expression unreadable, then he said, 'I'm not that kind of man.'

He most certainly wasn't, Nell thought. Riley would have taken great delight in buying it for a song when it was worth a small fortune – no matter if the person he was buying it from was a friend or not. He'd probably be filled with glee to think he'd got one over on the fellow. Riley wasn't an honourable man. It was a pity it had taken over twenty years of marriage and two children before she realised it.

'No, you're not,' she agreed softy, and for a split second she wondered how different her life would have been if she'd married a man like Silas.

'He hurt you badly, didn't he?' Silas said, and Nell's eyes flew to his in shock.

It was as though he'd read her mind. Not trusting

herself to speak, she simply nodded. Silas wasn't only devastatingly handsome and a nice guy, he was empathetic and astute to boot. A heady combination and one not even she was immune to. It was a wonder some lucky woman hadn't snapped him up already, and she was suddenly aware she knew next to nothing about him. There didn't appear to be a significant other on the scene, but what did she know? Nell had an idea Hattie might, though...

'Yes, he did,' she replied, her eyes returning to the dish she was preparing, her attention mostly on the man she'd soon be sharing it with. The image of the two of them sitting at the table was strangely intimate.

'I won't,' he said.

She didn't need to ask him what he wouldn't do; she knew what he meant and heat stole into her cheeks. Was he coming on to her? And if so, how did she feel about it? It was a very long time since a man had shown her any interest, and she wasn't sure how to deal with it. Or whether she even wanted it. She was flattered of course—

'I've got my reputation to think about,' he added. 'I don't want anyone to think I'd rip them off, and word would soon get out. Besides, Hattie would probably kill me if she thought I'd taken advantage of you.'

Chance would be a fine thing, Nell thought, then

froze as she realised the direction her thoughts had almost taken her. Clearly he hadn't meant what he'd said in the way she'd taken it. Thank God she hadn't said anything and made a fool of herself. He wasn't interested in her in the slightest, and it had been foolish of her to think he might be, even for a moment.

At least the previously somewhat awkward mood had been broken and the atmosphere had lightened.

'Talking about Hattie,' she said. 'Have you thought any more about the apprenticeship thing?'

'I've not considered it. It's a great idea and very worthwhile, but I don't see me mentoring a teenager. What about you?'

'I don't think I'm in any position to – not with Riley wanting half the business.' Oh, dear, she'd gone and done it again, allowing her worry to bring them both down. She tried to lighten the atmosphere once more. 'Anyway, I've only just got rid of a couple of youngsters – why would I want to saddle myself with another one?'

She could tell from the look he gave her that she hadn't fooled him for a second, and he confirmed it when he asked, 'Have you heard from your boys lately?'

'Oh, yes. I speak to them every day. I don't think they appreciate me constantly calling them, but I can't help it.'

'You must miss them terribly.'

Her smile was soft as she said, 'I do.' She gave the pan a stir and checked on the rice. Nearly done. 'How about you? Do you have any children?'

'Would you like a top up?' He indicated her almost empty glass, and she nodded. 'Those vegetables smell nice.'

'Damn, I forgot about them.' Nell opened the oven door and peered inside. They were starting to soften and there was a hint of chargrill on their edges. Just the way she liked it. 'If you grab some cutlery out of that drawer there,' she jerked her head, 'and lay the table, that would be a great help.'

She began dishing up, listening to Silas pottering around in the living room, and thought how pleasant this was. It was rare for her to cook for someone else these days (although she probably owned Juliette a meal or two) and it made a lovely change not to eat alone. She'd never admit it to the boys, but when she was on her own in the flat, she often didn't bother with a proper meal. Take this evening, for instance – she would probably have heated some soup, and would have shoved the chicken in the oven tomorrow, as is, without going to all the faff of cooking it in a sauce. She probably would have had a salad with it, or she might have cut a few slices off and stuffed it between two pieces of bread and called it a meal.

'Careful, the plates are hot,' she said to Silas as she carried them through to the living room. He was already seated at the table, looking expectant.

He sniffed appreciatively. 'Mmm, that smells divine,' he said, tucking in with so much gusto she wondered if he bothered to cook much either.

She wanted to find out more about his private life, and was just going to ask when she realised he hadn't replied to her question about children. In fact, he'd deftly changed the subject. Or had he? Had the question simply got lost in the vital business of topping up their wine, and she was reading more into the lack of answer than was there?

Somehow, she didn't think so, because on reflection she'd noticed his face close up and she was almost certain she'd spotted a flash of pain in his eyes. He'd said he was divorced and she tried to work out how long ago that was. He'd opened the Gallery about five years ago, and the reason she remembered was that there had been the most wonderfully atmospheric painting of the ruined castle at nearby Hay-on-Wye in the window, and she'd been seriously tempted to buy it but hadn't had anywhere suitable for it. It had sold shortly afterwards.

But even back then, there hadn't been a hint of a

woman on the scene. She recalled how the Ticklemore gossip drums had speculated about the good-looking man who'd bought a cottage on Ryeslip Lane and had opened an art gallery, but she hadn't paid it a great deal of attention, too wrapped up in the demands of her family. She wished she'd been a bit more curious – because she was certainly curious now, all right.

Nell considered asking him again whether he had any children, or whether he was in a relationship, but she decided against it. It would come over as though she wanted to know because she was interested in him. That she was starting to become interested was neither here nor there. She'd had enough of men to last her a lifetime, and she'd only just got over Riley – the last thing she wanted to do was to become embroiled with another one when she wasn't entirely sure her ex was out of her life yet. Of course, she never would be completely shot of him because he was the twins' father – but up until a couple of weeks ago, she thought she was as done with him as she could reasonably expect to be.

No such luck.

And now she was allowing him to sully a nice meal with a handsome man. Silas was, she granted, a very handsome man indeed. There was no harm in her enjoying his company, and as long as she didn't forget herself and start treating him as anything more than a friend, all would be well.

But it was with a smidgeon of disappointment that she said goodbye to him later, and when he leant forward to kiss her on the cheek a wave of longing for something much more swept over her, and she took herself off to bed more exasperated and vexed than she had any right to be.

CHAPTER 15

NELL

These days, whenever Nell saw the postman pop his head around the Treasure Trove door, she winced, expecting to find a letter from Riley's solicitor among the flyers and the junk mail. This time, though, she noticed a parcel sitting on top of the small pile of letters that he'd placed on the table closest to the door.

She had to wait a while before she went to investigate it, because three elderly ladies were on a day trip to Ticklemore and they wanted a memento to take back with them.

'If I don't buy something wherever I go, I forget I've been there,' one of them said. She was wearing a lovely string of pearls and a face-crinkling smile.

'Won't a tea towel or a keyring do?' This was said by a lady with a sour expression, and carrying an umbrella and a mackintosh, as though she was expecting rain despite the glorious day outside.

'Nah, tacky. I want something nice. Ooh, look, my mum had one of these when I was little.' The first lady picked up a perfume bottle which was part of a dressing table set. It was quite pretty, made of coloured glass with a silver stopper. 'How much is it?'

The three of them peered at the price tag, while Nell peered at the parcel from a distance and tried to work out who it might be from.

'Any chance of some movement on that?' the third lady asked, and Nell suppressed a sigh. She bet they wouldn't dream of going into Tesco and asking for a reduction of a microwave or a duvet set. Programmes such as *Antiques Road Trip* had a lot to answer for, especially since Nell's prices were already reasonable.

'I'm sorry, but I can't go any lower,' she said, and she received a glare in return.

'It's too much, if you ask me,' the grumpy woman stated, but the woman wearing the pearls shrugged.

'If I like it and can afford it, why haggle over a couple of pounds?'

'Shall I wrap it for you?' Nell asked.

'Go on, then.' The woman handed it over.

'I don't see the point myself,' the argumentative one said. 'It's only more rubbish for the kids to get rid of when you're gone.'

'Who rattled your cage? You've been a right misery since we got here.' The lady who was making the purchase slotted her bank card into the machine. 'Has that son of yours been on at you again?'

'Barry wants me to sell up and move into an old people's complex,' the grumpy one said. 'When I told him, "over my dead body", I could have sworn he was measuring me up for my coffin.'

Nell's heart went out to her. No wonder she was miserable, if that's the way her son treated her. 'Are you ladies ready for a coffee and a slice of cake?' she asked.

'Why? You're not going to try to flog us that as well, are you?' Grumpy-lady asked, and got an elbow in her ribs from the woman with the pearls.

Nell chuckled. 'No, but I can recommend the café down the road. It's called Bookylicious and if you show them the bag with the Treasure Trove name on it, there's a fifty per cent discount.'

The grumpy woman brightened up. 'I could murder a cuppa,' she said, making her way to the door. 'Hurry up, I haven't got all day. If Barry had his way, I won't have today either.'

Nell watched them leave, then picked up the phone.

'Hattie? It's Nell Chapman. If three ladies come in and they show you a Treasure Trove bag, could you give them a fifty per cent discount and let me know how much I owe you.'

'Why?' Hattie demanded.

'Because the grumpy one needs cheering up.'

'Why?' she demanded again.

'Her son wants her to sell her house and put her in a complex of some kind. I felt sorry for her.'

'Hmph. Some businesswoman you are.'

'Yeah, yeah. Will you do it, and not let on?'

'Only if you take an apprentice on.'

Nell shook her head in exasperation. 'I can't Hattie. I wish I could, but I can't.'

There was silence for a second. 'OK, I'll give them fifty per cent off. You're a good girl, Nell Chapman.'

The call ended abruptly and Nell smiled. Hattie's heart was definitely in the right place, despite her steamroller, no-nonsense attitude towards life.

Her good deed for the day done, Nell hurried across to the table and picked up her post. As she did so, she immediately recognised Adam's handwriting.

Curious, she took it to the counter and used scissors to carefully open it. Inside the brown paper was a box, and inside that, nestled amongst a protective layer of cotton wool was a silver pendant in the shape of a chest. Inscribed in the tiniest of letters were the words Treasure Trove, and when she opened up its hinged lid, a photo of her sons was folded inside. It was so exquisite and so thoughtful, tears pricked her eyes.

A note lay beneath it, and Nell took it out, holding it in her hand for a moment, imagining the last person to touch this was her eldest son. Ridiculously, it made her feel closer to him. And when she read it (it was written by Adam but signed by both her boys), she let out a sob. **_Saw this and thought of you_**, the note said.

'Actually, we saw it and had to get it engraved,' Ethan said later that evening during a WhatsApp video call.

'Thank you, I adore it,' Nell said fingering the silver chain she'd threaded through the loop, and the pendant was now hanging around her neck. She thought she might never take it off. 'Where did you get it?' Somehow, she couldn't see her boys hanging around outside a jewellers.

'A market stall in Imperia. Someone we met there makes them.'

'Where is Imperia?'

'The southern coast of France.'

'I thought you were in Paris? Surely you can't have done France in a couple of days?'

'Mum, this isn't a grand tour.' Adam said, shaking his head and smiling. Nell wanted to reach into the screen and give him a massive hug. Ethan, too, although he was currently turning away to watch the rear ends of a couple of skimpily clad young women.

'Ethan!' she said.

He turned back. 'What? I was just looking.'

'Hmm. How did you get from Paris to Imperia? I hope you didn't hitchhike. And where are you staying? Are you eating properly?'

'Chill, Mum.' Ethan gave her a big grin. 'We got a train, and we're staying on the beach.'

'Oh, that's nice – what's the hotel called? I'll Google it.'

'No, Mum, we're sleeping on the beach,' Ethan said.

'I told you not to tell her,' she heard Adam hiss.

Nell wished he hadn't. The less she knew about what they were getting up to the less she'd worry. Maybe. Or maybe not. Worry was part and parcel of being a parent.

Suddenly, she was consumed with the need to gather them to her and hold them close, like she used to when they were little and the most important thing in their world was her. Letting go was hard enough when your offspring was in the same country as you. But having them so far away, and not knowing where they'd be spending the night, or what they'd have to do to earn their next Euro made it doubly hard.

'At least we're eating properly,' Adam told her.

'Yeah, if you don't count getting the squits from that guy selling burgers,' Ethan laughed. 'You should have seen him, Mum – he was green. And the smell!' Ethan wafted a hand across his nose.

'Thank you, that's quite enough detail,' Nell said swiftly, sending a silent prayer up to whatever god might be listening to bring her babies back safe and sound.

'Mum, something strange happened earlier,' Adam began, and Nell's stomach turned over.

Trying not to show the sudden anxiety his words made her feel, she said, 'Oh?' as casually as she could. It must be serious for Adam to mention it, because out of the twins he was the one most considerate of her feelings. 'What was it?'

'Dad called.'

'Your dad?'

'Whose dad did you think I meant?'

'What did he want?'

'You should have told him to piss off,' Ethan said.

'Mind your language,' she said absently.

'Well, he should,' Ethan muttered. 'I would have.'

'That's probably why he phoned me and not you—'

'What did he want?' Nell repeated, her tone a little higher, the volume a little louder. It was a while since Riley had bothered with his children. She thought

Christmas was the last time they'd heard from him, and even then it had only been a card and a voucher for Amazon. Riley had always left Christmases and birthdays to her – most of the time he'd had little or no idea what gifts he and Nell had bought them.

'He asked about the Treasure Trove.'

'What about it?' Nell felt sick.

'He asked what we were up to, where we were, and that. Then he asked about the Treasure Trove. He wanted to know if it was doing OK and could I remember how it had started. He said something about using stuff from the house. I didn't tell him anything, Mum, honest.'

'There isn't anything to tell,' she said. 'It's OK for you to talk to your Dad, you know. If that's what you want. I've never stopped you and I never would.'

'You're too soft, Mum,' Ethan said. 'After the way he treated you…'

'He's still your father.'

'I never would have guessed.' Ethan's response was sharp. She didn't blame him – Riley hadn't wanted anything to do with the boys since he'd moved out.

'One thing he did say,' Adam began, a worry line appearing in the middle of his brow. 'He said that the shop must be doing really well for us to be able to take a year out travelling the world. I tried to tell him that we're funding this ourselves, but he didn't listen.'

'He was probably worried you might run out of funds,' Nell said. The last thing she wanted was for the twins to know what their father was up to. Adam would only worry and insist on coming back home, and Ethan would get angry and he'd insist on coming back home, but she suspected he'd be more interested in knocking his father's block off than plying her with tea and sympathy.

Ethan snorted. 'Yeah, right. Not even you can believe that, Mum.'

'Is there anything going on?' Adam asked.

'Not at all. Everything is fine.'

'You'd tell us if it wasn't?' The line was still dissecting Adam's forehead, but Ethan's attention was back on the passers-by, especially if they were his age and female.

'Of course I would,' she said, hoping he wasn't able to pick up the lie in her voice. As much as she was desperate to see them again, she knew this was an opportunity of a lifetime for them and, despite her intense worry and inability to sleep, she would hate for their trip to be cut short because of her.

Damn Riley, the selfish, two-timing ba—

'OK, speak tomorrow, Mum. Take care of yourself.' Adam was still worried, she could tell.

'I've been taking care of myself since before you

were born,' she retorted. 'Shouldn't I be saying that to you?'

'You do, all the time,' Ethan pointed out.

The last thing she heard before the call ended was her youngest telling Adam it was his turn to get the beers in.

Dear God, her children would be the death of her. No wonder she was going grey.

But for once her thoughts didn't linger on what her kids were getting up to – she was focusing firmly on Riley and what he was playing at. If he thought he could get to her through their sons, he had another think coming. This was her children's inheritance he was trying to get his hands on, and she knew damned well if Riley got his grubby mitts on the Treasure Trove, he'd take every penny out of it that he could, and wouldn't give a hoot about his sons.

Riley could sod right off!

CHAPTER 16

SILAS

When Silas's phone rang, he reached for it automatically. It was only at the last moment that he glanced at the number and froze.

He knew whose number it was, but there hadn't been any contact either from it, or to it, for years.

'Denise.' His voice was as neutral as he could make it, given the incredibly short amount of time in which he had to compose himself.

There was a pause, then his ex-wife said, 'Silas.'

Another pause, during which Silas wracked his brains trying to work out why she would call him. Why now, after all this time?

'I saw the toy rabbit,' she said. There was a slight catch in her voice. 'Molly would have loved it.'

'You visit her grave?' The knowledge surprised him. That he'd wanted their daughter buried and

Denise had wanted to have her cremated had driven yet another wedge between them.

They'd fought over it, bitter and stubborn in their shared and separate grief. He'd got his way. And then he'd moved away. It must have seemed so cruel to her.

But he couldn't bring himself to apologise, even now. Visiting Molly was the only thing that had helped with the crushing pain. That, and his art. The number of nights he'd spent on the road, driving to be with her, were countless. He could cope with the days. Just. The nights, however, had been brutal and endless. He knew it would have been the same for Denise.

'I saw you,' she said, 'on the anniversary of her...'

Denise had always had difficulty with the word *death*. Or passing. Or any word that meant their daughter was no longer with them. Whilst Silas, on the other hand, had tended to be blunt. A spade was a spade, wasn't it? Not saying the word didn't mean it hadn't happened, or so he'd argued. He'd faced it head on at first. And then, when he hadn't been able to cope any longer, he'd stopped speaking about Molly altogether. The loss of her had bitten so deeply, it hurt to even think her name. It had been all he could do to stop himself from joining her.

'Is there anything wrong? Your mother...?' he

asked, praying Denise wasn't calling to give him bad news but knowing she must, because there couldn't be any other reason for her wanting to speak to him.

'There's nothing wrong. I wanted to tell you in person...' Another pause. Whatever she was about to say, he gathered it wasn't easy for her. 'I didn't want you to hear it from anyone else. I'm getting married again,' she finished.

Silas's mother had mentioned that Denise had a gentleman friend once, a couple of years ago, but Silas hadn't wanted to know. At the time he hadn't cared that his ex-wife had moved on. Oddly, though, he cared now and he found he was pleased for her. Denise deserved to be happy – Molly had been as much her daughter as his. More, as Denise had carried her for nine months and had breastfed her for just as long, Silas only feeding his daughter on the odd occasion when Denise expressed milk. All Silas had been able to do had been to worship Molly and marvel they'd produced something so perfect.

'I'm pleased for you,' he said, gathering himself.

'Are you sure?'

'I'm sure.'

'Thank you. I was worried...'

'My feelings are neither here nor there, but I appreciate that you care,' he said.

'I'll always care, Silas. You were her father – how

could I not?'

Silas clenched his jaw. He didn't want to hear this. There was no need to go raking up past feelings. He'd loved Denise passionately once, and a part of him still did care for her, but their once-invincible love hadn't been able to survive the devastation of their daughter's death. He *was* pleased Denise had moved on though; he wasn't lying about it.

'I hope you'll be happy. I mean that, Denni.' His old nickname for her came easily to his lips, yet sounded alien and out of place. He'd lost the right to call her that when he'd walked out. That right now belonged to another man. Silas hoped her new fella would treat her better than he had.

'Happy? Maybe,' she said. 'Content might be a better way to describe it. It hasn't been easy, getting on with life. How about you, Silas? How are you?'

'Good.'

'Liar.'

He grimaced. She knew him too well; even after years of no contact, she still knew him.

'You have to start living again,' she said.

'Like you have, you mean?' His voice was sharp, the words bitter.

But instead of arguing, as she once would have done, or been so wounded that she would have hung up on him, all she said was, 'Yes. Like me.'

Silas swallowed, the statement hanging in the air. On the other end of the line his ex-wife waited. He knew she was still there because he could hear her ragged breathing.

'I don't think I can,' he said eventually, and he heard her sigh, a whisper on the wind.

'Try,' was all she said, 'for Molly.'

Then Denise was gone, and Silas was left with bitter regret for how it had ended between them, and sweet nostalgia for how it had once been.

She was right. It *was* time he tried. The problem was, he didn't know how.

His heart heavy, his thoughts a deadweight in his head, Silas did the only thing he could... paint.

But as he began to cover the crisp whiteness with bold strokes, an image came into his head and it didn't have anything to do with the image he was creating on the canvas.

Nell.

CHAPTER 17

NELL

Still nothing from Riley, but the chat with the twins yesterday had unsettled her, so to keep herself occupied, in between customers she popped into the office at the rear of the shop and began the search for the Oakman painting's rightful owner.

She'd have to be careful, because the house clearance company would want to know why she was so interested and she didn't want to give anyone an opportunity to claim the painting was theirs. Not that she was accusing anyone of anything, but if Vaughan's guestimate was right, such a large amount of money could make people do strange things. Take herself, for instance – she'd been quite happy selling it for a couple of hundred pounds and never thought about contacting any previous owners, but now she had an inkling of its worth here she was attempting to hunt them down. Go figure.

First, she checked her records and found the details of the company she'd bought the painting from. They had a shop (more of a warehouse) in Brecon and she set about thinking of a plausible reason for wanting to know the painting's provenance.

She came up with the idea of saying she'd taken the paper off the back and had found a letter hidden there, and as it was rather personal she thought the owner or their relatives might want it back. The person whose house had been cleared might well be still alive (she thought of the grumpy lady who'd been in her shop yesterday) and she was excited to think that she might soon have some very good news for them indeed.

Having fired off an email to the house clearance company, Nell gave Juliette a call. 'Are you free for lunch?' Although the sign on the door of the Treasure Trove informed customers that the shop was closed between 1 and 2 p.m., Nell often didn't bother to shut the shop. But today, she felt the need to have a chat with her friend.

Juliette was more than willing, so ten minutes past one found them sitting in Bookylicious with the wonderful aroma of freshly ground coffee floating in the air, and a Ploughman's each on the table in front of them with a portion of curly fries to share.

'What's the gossip?' Juliette asked, smearing thickly-cut bread with yellow butter.

Nell speared a slice of ham before replying. 'Riley is back on the scene.'

'*What?*' Juliette swiftly lowered her voice. 'You mean like you two are back together?'

'No! Don't be daft – after the way he treated me?'

'I was thinking that, but one never knows. Stranger things have happened.'

'Not that strange, and not with me.' Nell shuddered. 'He's back on the scene because he's claiming half of the Treasure Trove.'

'What! This time Juliette sounded even more incredulous. 'He can't do that? Can he?'

'I think he might,' Nell said. She put her fork down, her appetite deserting her. 'When we got divorced the house was sold and split between us. All he wanted out of it was his personal things, like his golf clubs, and I was left to deal with the contents.'

'I loved the way you *dealt* with them,' Juliette said. 'Bet he had no idea what some of the things you sold were worth.' Her eyes widened as the penny dropped. 'Oh.'

'Exactly!'

'It's not your fault he couldn't be bothered with it. I bet he and that Vanessa were chuckling when he thought he'd dumped it all on you.'

'He's not chuckling now. He's saying I used some of the contents of the house, which he owned half of, to kick-start the Treasure Trove.'

'He walked away!' Juliette was practically spitting feathers, and Nell loved her for the instant and unwavering support.

'I'm worried he has a point,' she confessed.

'Like hell he does. The nasty little—'

'Now then, Juliette, who are you calling nasty, and what's wrong with your Ploughman?' Hattie asked, appearing at their table.

'Nothing, I'm sure it's delicious,' Juliette said. Apart from buttering a slice of bread, she'd not touched it.

'You'll fade away if you're not careful,' Harriet said. 'I don't believe in all this dieting fad.'

'I'm not dieting,' Juliette protested.

'Could have fooled me. If you two aren't going to eat anything, you should just have had a coffee. There are people in the world who'd be grateful for a meal like this. Talking of people being grateful, I've got a lovely young lady lined up for you to meet.' This last was said to Nell, who blinked at her owlishly.

'Why would I want to meet—?'

'Your apprentice. Her name is Tanesha, and she's a poppet. If you ignore the tongue-piercing.' Hattie stuck her tongue out and shuddered. 'I try not to look at it, but I can't help it. Anyway, she seems sensible enough for a seventeen-year-old and she can speak in proper sentences.'

Nell pressed her lips together, trying not to smile. Hattie was so straight you could use her as a spirit level. 'I told you I don't think I'm ready to take anyone on.'

'It won't cost you much, if that's what's worrying you,' Hattie said, pulling out a chair and plonking herself down on it.

'It's not the money,' Nell protested.

'What is it, then? Don't tell me you don't need some help in the shop, because you do. Working all hours isn't good for you, and I bet you're sitting here worrying about losing trade and that's why you haven't eaten your lunch.'

Actually, Nell wasn't. She wasn't worried about losing a sale – she was sitting there worrying about losing her whole business. Because if Riley was able to claim half, she might as well cease trading right now. Even if he didn't strip it of all its assets, she'd never be able to have him as a partner. She'd burn the place down before she'd let that happen.

'Honestly, I don't know why you bothered to order any food in the first place. Now, if you had an assistant…?' Hattie smiled beguilingly at her, all

149

scrunched-up eyes and wrinkles.

'You're not going to let this go, are you?' Nell asked. The old lady might well drop the subject if she knew the reason for Nell's reluctance, but Nell wasn't prepared to share.

'No, I'm not. Juliette is taking one on.'

Nell turned to her friend. 'You are?'

Juliette nodded. 'It makes sense – the more admin someone else can do, the more I can focus on growing the newspaper.'

'Now look here, young lady.' Hattie puffed herself up like a cross robin, her cheeks almost as red. 'I'm not letting you have an apprentice so you can dump the boring stuff on them. They are there to learn, not to make the tea.'

Juliette leant towards Nell. 'Anyone would think she was setting all this up herself. It's done via the college in Hereford, and Zoe's tutor is arranging it all.'

'I heard that, I'm not deaf yet.'

Nell smiled as Juliette rolled her eyes.

'It was my idea,' Hattie said. 'You'd never have thought of it. So I feel responsible.'

'Do you honestly think I'd use my apprentice as cheap labour?' Juliette looked hurt. 'I thought you knew me better than that.'

Hattie got down off her high horse and her

shoulders relaxed. 'I do, and I know you won't. But as I said, I feel partly responsible. Now,' she turned her attention back to Nell, who suppressed a groan, having thought she'd dodged the bullet. 'About Tanesha. I can set up a meeting with the pair of you for early next week. What do you say?'

'All right – but I'm not promising anything.'

Hattie rubbed her hands together in satisfaction. 'Now, all I've got to do is try to persuade Silas that he needs some help. He's like you – stubborn.' Creakily she rose from her seat, but not before patting the edge of Nell's plate. 'I want to see most of this eaten. The pair of you will waste away, and let's be honest, there's not a great deal of meat on either of you.'

'She can talk,' Juliette said. 'She's like a nail, straight up and down. Now, what were you saying about Riley before we were so rudely interrupted?'

'I'm seeing a solicitor on Wednesday and hopefully he can put my mind at rest. I do have some other news, though.' Nell picked up her knife and fork again and began eating, if only because she still had to pay for the meal whether she ate it or not, so she might as well finish it.

'Go on, I'm on pins here.'

Nell glanced over her shoulder to make sure Hattie wasn't in earshot, and that no one else was taking any interest in them. 'I've got a painting worth about half a million pounds,' she whispered, then sat back to enjoy the astounded expression on her friend's face.

'I could have sworn you just said—'

'I did. Silas spotted it when he came in one day.' Nell frowned. 'I have no idea why he came in – he doesn't strike me as the antique vase type – but I'm glad he did. I had it hanging in the shop with a price tag of a couple of hundred pounds, and he took one look and said he thought it was painted by Peter Oakman. He took it to London, to the Tate Gallery no less, and a friend of his confirmed its authenticity.'

'You lucky so-and-so. I assume you're going to sell it – what are you going to do with the money? Retire?'

'Hardly! I'm far too young to retire; what would I do with myself all day? Anyway, I'm not keeping it.'

Juliette, who had started making steady inroads into her lunch, dropped her fork, and it landed on her plate with a clatter. Eyes wide, she picked it up, never once taking her gaze off Nell. 'You're not serious? Are you going to donate it to a museum, or something?'

'I'm going to give it back.'

'To whom?'

'It's rightful owner.'

Juliette frowned and tilted her head to the side. 'I thought you said it was yours?'

'It is, technically. I bought it from a house

clearance place in Brecon, but neither the company nor I was aware of its value. And whoever owned it couldn't have been, either. I wouldn't feel right, keeping it.'

'I must say, you're far more noble than I would be.'

'That's what Silas says.'

'Are you sure about this? What with Riley, and all? Assuming he did have a claim on the Treasure Trove, this could pay him off and more, probably.'

'Please don't say anything – if he was to get wind of it…'

'Of course I won't say anything. But once everything with Riley is sorted, you must let me write a feature about it.'

'I will,' Nell promised. 'It mightn't come to anything anyway, if I can't track the owner down.'

'Thank God Silas realised what it was,' Juliette said. 'Imagine if you'd sold it, and then found out how much it was worth? Come to think of it, thank God Silas is honest. He could have bought it himself, sold it on, and you'd never have known.'

'He's a sweetheart,' Nell said absently, her mind on their trip to London yesterday, and the meal she'd cooked for him last night.

'Oh, yes?' Juliette was giving her a knowing look, and to her chagrin, Nell blushed. 'You like him, don't you?'

'Who wouldn't like a man who'd just given you a small fortune,' Nell quipped.

'You don't fool me, Nell Chapman. I've known you far too long. You have to admit, he's rather good-looking in a brooding sort of way. Has he asked you if you want to see his etchings yet?'

'Juliette! No, he hasn't. He's not like that.'

'Bet you wish he was.'

'I do not. Anyway, he's not interested in me like that.'

'Why not? You're gorgeous, and kind, and very solvent.'

'I don't know, there's something going on with him. He's lived in Ticklemore for over five years, yet there's never been a hint of a woman in his life.'

'Perhaps he's gay?'

Nell didn't think so. 'He's divorced and her name is Denise, so he probably isn't gay.' She thought of how she'd caught him staring at her when he didn't think she'd notice, and she knew he'd been appraising her, the way a man sometimes looks at a woman. Yet, he'd not made a pass at her, and neither had there been any other indication he thought of her in that way.

She said, 'There's a sadness in Silas Long. If you spend enough time with him, you can sense it. Half an hour in the pub, with lots of people around, and you won't notice. But get him on his own…'

'How much time *have* you spent with him? And when have you been on your own with him?' Juliette demanded.

'He took me to London yesterday to pick up the painting, then he came back to mine for supper.'

Juliette gave an unusually unladylike snort. 'And you say he doesn't like you? Pull the other one. Are you seeing him again?'

'Yes, but it's not what you think. I'm taking him out for a meal to thank him.'

Lips quirked in a smile, Juliette said, 'Believe me, if he didn't like you, he wouldn't have agreed to go out for a meal with you.'

'But we're just friends. It's a meal between two friends.'

'I'm still not buying it. You protest too much. Go on, admit it; you fancy him. And I'd bet my last column inch that he fancies you too. You've just not realised it yet.'

For the rest of the afternoon and evening, and for all of the following day, Nell couldn't help think that Juliette was right. Nell did fancy Silas. But she also thought Juliette was wrong, too – Silas wasn't the least bit interested in her. If it wasn't for her Oakman painting…

Anyway, it didn't matter whether she fancied him or not. He didn't fancy her, which was just as well because she had enough on her plate at the moment without adding a romance into the equation.

CHAPTER 18

NELL

What does one wear for a non-date, Nell asked herself, surveying the contents of her wardrobe with concern. She had business clothes, casual clothes, and dressy stuff from her days as Riley's wife. What she didn't have was anything she deemed suitable for a meal in the Tavern with a man she was seriously attracted to but didn't intend for that attraction to go any further. You don't find a section in Debenhams with that label, she mused.

'Stop being so silly,' she muttered, and instead asked herself what she'd wear if she was popping into the pub for a meal with Juliette.

Nell picked out a pair of slim jeans (not skinny, not at her age and not with her knees) and a floaty blouse in a soft aqua shade. She slipped her feet into some navy ballet flats and decided it would have to do. She was making an effort without wanting to look as though she was making an effort, so she kept her make-up minimal almost to the point of non-existence.

Then, cross with herself for caring so much, she grabbed her everyday work bag and headed out of the door.

The Tavern was fairly quiet, although a few locals were in, and she nodded to David, whose wife Sara managed the Ticklemore Toy Shop, and Benny who chaired the local AA (Allotment Association, he always added, after chuckling at his little joke).

Nell glanced around and saw that Silas had arrived before her, and had already claimed a table in the corner by the window. Feeling an unaccustomed flutter of nerves in her tummy as she walked towards him, she lifted her chin and told herself for the second time that evening not to be so silly.

He was staring out of the window, but Nell had a feeling his attention was turned inwards. If pushed, she'd be forced to describe him as melancholy, sad, even. He looked as though he had the weight of the world on his shoulders.

He didn't spot her until she was nearly at the table, but when he did, he half-rose from his seat and pulled a chair out for her. As she sat down, he leant across and kissed her cheek, making her blush furiously at the unexpected contact.

Her skin was tingling where his lips had touched, the heady scent of him wafting over her and filling her senses. Crikey, that was some aftershave he was wearing, she thought wildly; it was making her head swim and the sensation was rather pleasant.

'I got you a drink. I hope you don't mind. Logan told me what your favourite tipple is.'

Nell picked up the glass of Pinot Grigio and took a hefty swig. 'Not at all,' she said, feeling the alcohol's welcome hit on her empty stomach. 'This is lovely.' She licked her lips, wondering what to say next.

'Thanks for inviting me.' His smile was warm and his eyes crinkled at the corners.

'I'm the one who should be thanking you, for all your help with the painting.'

'It was nothing.'

Gosh, this was awkward. 'Do you come here often?' she asked, then let out a nervous giggle. 'That didn't come out right. I meant to say, are you a regular?'

'Not really. I pop in now and again.'

'Me, too. Now and again. Usually with Juliette.' Nell gave another odd giggle. 'Always with Juliette. And Oliver sometimes. He's Juliette's partner,' she added, in case Silas had forgotten. 'Not on my own with him, of course. Juliette is always with us.'

Silas was gazing at her with a quizzical expression, and Nell knew she was babbling.

'I hadn't forgotten,' he said.

'Of course you haven't. Silly me.' Nell caught her bottom lip between her teeth.

'Are you OK?'

'Yes, why do you ask?' She knew why he was asking; it was because she was spouting nonsense and coming across as a right idiot. And if her cheeks grew any redder, she could double as a tomato.

'You seem a little out of sorts.'

'I think the shock of finding out about the painting is finally getting to me.'

'Are you still planning on tracing its original owner?'

She nodded. 'I've sent an email to the house clearance company, so hopefully I'll hear back soon. It all depends on whether they keep detailed records, I suppose. But even if they don't, one of the employees might remember where it came from.'

Nell was starting to calm down. She felt more at ease discussing business, and although it hardly made for scintillating conversation, it was better than her nonsensical wittering.

'How about you?' she asked. 'Are you all right?'

'I'm fine.' He said it quickly, like an automatic reflex, but Nell had the impression Silas wasn't fine at all. The sadness she'd thought she'd seen in him previously was definitely there. She'd noticed it the first time she'd met him, but it hadn't registered properly until recently.

'Any more news on the Riley front?' he asked, putting the focus back on her.

'I've not had a letter from his solicitor, if that's what you mean, but he has kind of been in touch. Not with me, with the boys. He's been asking them questions about the Treasure Trove.'

'That's not good, is it?'

'No, it isn't. He's hardly bothered with them at all since he walked out, just cards at birthdays and Christmases, and the occasional text when he remembers, but today he actually phoned them.'

'Does he know they're out of the country?'

'Yes, he does.'

'Perhaps he's concerned about them?'

'Hardly. He wasn't all that concerned when we were living under the same roof.'

'I was trying to be charitable,' Silas said.

Nell took another sip of her wine. 'I know you were,' she said. 'But he doesn't need anyone trying to think the best of him. Least of all you, when you're so much better a man than he is.'

Silas looked uncomfortable. 'I'm not that much better,' he said. 'Unlike you, I would have kept the painting.'

'That doesn't make you a bad person,' Nell pointed out. If you'd bought it instead of me, you would be the rightful owner. It would be up to you what you did with it.'

'But that's what you are, and look at what you're planning to do with it.'

'To be honest, I think it's because of the way Riley treated me, the way he's continuing to treat me. I don't want to become like him, whose only focus is money.'

Silas chuckled, and his sexy laugh sent a tremor through her. She'd always known he was attractive, any fool could see that, but she hadn't realised quite how sexy he was. And that laugh …

'You're nothing like Riley,' Silas said. 'He sounds a right cad, and I'd say you are the polar opposite. I don't think you could be like him even if you tried.'

'I've had my moments,' she admitted. 'I should never have sold everything of value in the house.'

'What else were you going to do with it?'

Nell shrugged. 'I don't know.'

'Well, then, there you go. Did your ex not help? '

'Not at all. He took what he wanted then walked away.'

'I say again, what else were you going to do with it? Would you have been able to keep all of it?'

Nell laughed. 'Definitely not. My share of the house wouldn't have enabled me to buy anything large enough to fit all that furniture in. It was just enough to put a down payment on the shop and flat.'

'Do I have to say it again?' Silas grinned at her.

'No, you don't. I know I would have had to get rid of at least half of it. The problem is, I started selling things before the divorce was finalised, and the money I got for each item was sometimes considerably more than I paid for it.'

'It could be an issue,' Silas conceded, 'but let's wait to hear what the solicitor says. I take it you have made an appointment to see Ron?'

'Yes, I have, and that's something else I need to thank you for. I could have used the solicitor who handled my divorce, but it seemed so straight forward at the time I didn't think I needed anyone who specialised in anything. Now there's a business involved...'

'Not just a business, *your* business. The Treasure Trove is yours, I'm certain of it.'

'But I used items from the house to start it up.'

'So? You've already said Riley didn't want them.' Another sexy chuckle issued from his lips. 'I'm not gonna say it again, but...'

'What else was I going to do with it?' Nell and Silas chorused together.

Nell suddenly remembered where they were and why, and she got to her feet and walked over to the bar. 'Could I have a couple of menus, please?' she said to Logan, who handed them over.

'There's no meeting tonight is there?' he asked, 'because if there is, I haven't been invited. Don't get me wrong, I don't want to be, because there's no way I could take on an apprentice. But I was just wondering.'

Nell followed the direction of his gaze and her heart sank. Hattie and Alfred had just walked in. Typical. She knew she should have insisted on taking Silas somewhere else.

She grabbed the menus, and went back to the table, trying to avoid Hattie's gaze. However, she could feel it in the back of her head, and she guessed Hattie would be putting two and two together and coming up with half a dozen. Even if Hattie didn't get that far, Nell knew the old lady would be asking her some questions the next time she saw her, and that's assuming she wasn't going to walk over to their table and ask them right now.

Nell gave one of the menus to Silas, and proceeded to bury her nose in it pretending to study its rarely changing list of dishes. Once they had made their choices, Nell checked to ensure Hattie wasn't anywhere near the bar, before she gave their order to

Logan.

'No meeting,' Logan said. 'I asked.'

Nell had to grin at his obvious relief, but she was also conscious of the way he looked at her and Silas. That was the problem with Ticklemore, you couldn't keep anything quiet for long. Not that she had anything to hide (she did, but even that would come out soon enough) but she didn't appreciate being the talk of the village just because she was having a meal with a friend. If she had been with Juliette, no one would have batted an eyelid, but because it was a man and a woman enjoying an evening together, and because that man was notoriously reserved, tongues would be sure to wag.

She had the brief thought that it was a pity there wasn't anything to wag about, before Silas asked her a question about how trade was going and they started talking about their respective businesses, and the thought was forgotten. For now.

'How do you manage?' she asked, when there was a lull in the conversation. 'I'm surprised you don't have someone to run the Gallery for you, so you can concentrate on painting?'

Silas shrugged. 'I just like doing everything myself, I suppose. I usually paint when the Gallery is shut, although I have been known to nip up to the studio when things are quiet. There's a little buzzer that sounds upstairs when someone comes into the shop, so it's no bother to down my paintbrush and go downstairs. There's a camera in the Gallery too, so I can see who comes in. It's not like your place where there are lots of small items that somebody could easily pocket. Most of my paintings can't be hidden under a jacket.'

'Doesn't it interrupt your concentration though?'

'Sometimes, but that's just the way of it. When Mo—' He stopped talking abruptly and his face clouded over.

What on earth had he been about to say, Nell wondered, and then, as he glanced up and over her shoulder, she realised it was because Logan's mum was coming towards them with their meals.

Marie placed the hot plates carefully down on the table mat, and took the napkin-wrapped cutlery out of the pocket of her apron.

Nell smiled. 'Thanks, Marie. How are you?'

'Not too bad, and yourself?' She looked from Nell to Silas and back again, and Nell guessed what she was thinking. It was the same as everyone else was probably thinking.

'Good, thanks,' Nell said. 'Looks like Logan is keeping you busy?'

'It's Scarlet's evening off, so I said I'd step in. If I don't, Logan runs himself ragged.'

'It can't be easy managing a pub,' Nell said sympathetically. She knew how difficult it was running a business on her own without any help (the thought of Tanesha popped into her mind and she pushed it away) and she only ever had one or two customers in the shop at any one time. Logan had help in the form of a couple of barmaids and a chef, but she'd rarely entered the Tavern and for him not to be behind the bar.

At least she had Wednesday afternoons, Sundays and the evenings to herself, although she had been contemplating opening on Sundays as well, but the twins had scuppered that idea when they'd informed her they wouldn't be around for the next year. She couldn't rely on them anyway, knowing they had their own lives to lead, but she still harboured the hope that Adam, at least, would fly back into the nest and help her run the business.

Marie said, 'It doesn't do my bunions any good being on my feet for hours on end, but needs must.'

Hattie had clearly been listening, because she called out, 'No sign of your Logan settling down with a nice girl, then? What he needs is a wife to help him run the place.'

Marie's expression hardened, and she drew her lips into a thin line. 'He's got enough to do as it is, without chasing after girls. And my health isn't the

167

best, either.'

Nell was pretty sure she'd never seen Logan chasing after anyone, although she was the first to admit he worked very hard, so he probably didn't have the time or the opportunity to date much. She had a feeling he wasn't the type of man to hit on any of the punters, so it couldn't be easy for him to meet prospective girlfriends. Nell also didn't have any idea why the state of Marie's health should have any bearing on Logan settling down. Logan's mother sounded as though it were a barrier, when in fact, if Logan did find himself in a relationship, it would probably free up more of Marie's time so that she wouldn't need to help out in the Tavern. As far as Nell could see, it was a win-win situation.

When Marie walked back to the bar, Nell and Silas tucked into their meals, and conversation halted for a moment whilst they concentrated on eating.

After several mouthfuls, Silas said, 'This is the second decent meal I've had this week. I feel quite spoilt.'

'You don't cook for yourself much, do you?' Nell asked.

Silas looked sheepish. 'Not much. I can't be bothered. I do sometimes pop into Bookylicious and have one of their daily specials. Maddison does a mean lentil curry, and the Chinese takeaway down the road knows my number off by heart. I always tend to have the same thing, too.'

'I can see how you mightn't be bothered,' Nell said after chewing and swallowing one of her chips. 'I sometimes get a bit lax at feeding myself when the boys aren't home, but I do try to eat healthily if I can.' She pointed to her chips. 'Not that I'm doing that right now, of course.'

'There's nothing wrong with a chip or two if you fancy it,' he told her. 'It's clearly not doing you any harm.'

'That's because I try not to eat them too often,' she laughed. 'They go straight to my bum!'

Nell realised what she'd said, just as Silas replied with, 'You've got a lovely... er... *oops.*'

'I wasn't fishing for a compliment,' Nell hastened to tell him, her cheeks pinking up yet again.

'And I didn't mean to comment on your behind. Although it is lovely.' Silas was just as red as she was, and Nell bit her lip to keep the laughter in.

'Thank you. I think. It *was* a compliment, wasn't it?'

'Most definitely.' Silas couldn't look her in the eye and Nell's lips twitched.

She pressed them together, but it was hopeless, and a giggle escaped.

'Oh dear,' she chortled. 'I'm sorry I backed you

into a corner and you felt you had to say something about my...' She pointed to her backside, tears of mirth gathering in the corners of her eyes.

Silas was laughing, too. 'I wouldn't have said it, if I hadn't meant it.'

Gradually they both sobered and the mood calmed a little. Nell was still red with embarrassment, and so was Silas, but it had been good to laugh and let off some steam. She didn't think she'd found anything as funny in a long time.

Suddenly Nell was gazing at Silas and he was gazing back, his expression unreadable. Nell cleared her throat. 'Dessert?'

'What about your bum?'

Nell spluttered, and almost fell off her chair in mirth. 'For dessert?' she sniggered, and laughed even harder at Silas's face when he realised what he'd said and how she'd twisted it.

'Oh, God...' he moaned and buried his head in his hands. His muffled, 'I've done it again, haven't I?' had her gasping.

'I'm sorry,' she said when she could eventually speak. 'I don't normally behave like this.'

'I don't normally have women collapsing in hysterics,' he replied.

'How do you normally have them?' Nell quipped without thinking. 'Oh, damn, now it's my turn.'

'Shall we start again?'

'Let's. Would you like some dessert?'

'Yes, please, if you are having some. I fancy the tart—'

That was it – Nell howled, tears in her eyes, and her sides began to hurt. 'You slay me,' she managed to get out, holding onto her stomach and hoping she wasn't going to be sick.

It took a while to bring herself under control, and when she finally got enough of a grip to sit in her chair properly and not make wheezing noises, she realised most of the Tavern's clientele were grinning at her.

She took a deep breath. 'I'm going to behave now,' she told Silas.

'I'm not. I haven't had so much fun in ages.'

Nell was enjoying herself immensely too, but then she had to spoil it. 'I've got some cheesecake back at the flat, if you want to join me,' she said.

'Are you asking me back to your place for a coffee?'

Nell gaped at him. That wasn't what she'd meant at all. She'd been thinking about getting away from all those gawping eyes, but it sounded as though she was inviting him back for more than coffee. Abashed that Silas had interpreted her innocent offer as her coming on to him, she was about to put the record straight when Silas's barriers came down.

It was like looking through a window into the room beyond and suddenly having the curtains pulled across. 'I... um... I'll pass, if you don't mind. Maybe another time,' he said.

To Nell's chagrin, she knew there wouldn't be another time. He'd made his feelings perfectly clear and although it was plain he enjoyed her company he evidently didn't want to be more than friends.

That was OK because neither did she, but if she said so now it would seem like she was protesting too much.

Mortified, she smiled awkwardly at him as she finished her wine.

'Thanks for a lovely evening,' he said, as soon as she put her empty glass on the table.

'You're welcome. I'll go and pay. You can get off home, if you like, there's no point in you hanging around.' The bar was busy and there were a couple of customers waiting to be served. 'Thanks again for helping me with the painting and everything.'

'You're welcome. I enjoyed it.'

She watched him leave and as soon as he'd stepped through the door, Nell closed her eyes briefly. That was her well and truly told. And it had been the start of such a lovely friendship, too. Oh, well...

Nell hadn't been expecting to see Silas outside, but he was hovering near the Tavern's door.

Their eyes met and locked for a moment. Nell was the first to look away. 'I thought you'd gone home,' she said.

'I was going to—'

'You don't owe me any explanation,' she interjected.

'I believe I do. Nell, you're a beautiful, funny, intelligent woman, but—'

'Please don't say it's not you, it's me,' she said, aiming for as light a tone as she could manage. 'Silas,' she added rapidly before he had a chance to say anything more. 'It was only going to be coffee. Nothing else.'

'Oh.' He hung his head and shuffled his feet for a few seconds, before looking at her. 'You'll let me know how you get on with finding the Oakman's previous owner?'

Nell nodded. 'Of course I will. We're friends, aren't we?'

'We certainly are.' He seemed a little happier. 'And keep me up-to-date about how you get on at the solicitor's?'

She nodded again. 'Bye, Silas.'

'Bye.'

Turning around, she walked down the street,

determined not to look back. But he was watching her – she could feel his gaze, as light as gossamer, and all she could think of was how much she was going to miss him, even after this short amount of time. He'd made his position clear. He wasn't interested in her.

The problem was, after this evening, she realised she was most definitely interested in *him*.

CHAPTER 19

NELL

Nell eyed the plain white envelope with concern. Her name and address had been typed, not hand-written, and a first-class stamp was affixed to the front.

Gingerly, she turned it over to see whether the sender's address was on the back. but there was nothing there. She had an awful feeling she knew what was inside, and a part of her briefly considered throwing it in a drawer and pretending it didn't exist. However, she had an appointment with Francis Slade, who Silas had put her in touch with, in two days' time, and he'd want to know what it said. If, indeed, it did contain a letter from Riley's solicitor.

Still holding a faint hope it contained something else entirely, something innocuous, she slid the expensive-looking cream paper out of the envelope. Seeing the name Price and Waters, Solicitors, at the top, Nell quickly scanned it and groaned. It was as bad as she'd feared.

She read it again, but it didn't get any better with a second perusal. If anything, it was worse. Everything she'd worked so hard for since Riley had walked out of her and her sons' lives and into the arms and bed of another woman, was in danger of collapsing around her ears. God, she prayed Francis was as good as she hoped he was. Riley shouldn't be allowed to get away with this. It had taken her a long time to rebuild her life, to provide a home for her admittedly grown-up children, and arrive at the point where her newly-established business gave her enough of an income to support her and the boys. Riley hadn't given Adam and Ethan a penny, and she'd been forced to support them through university all by herself. She'd never told them that. It was bad enough that their father could only be bothered with them on their birthday and at Christmas. They didn't need to know he'd ditched his responsibility to them completely.

How she'd managed it, she didn't know. But she had. And now here was Riley, wanting to take half of the business which would eventually belong to the twins. What an absolute bastard. Nell thought she might explode if she didn't speak to someone soon and Juliette was the obvious choice to let off steam to. Juliette was the kind of friend who, if you told her you had a body to get rid of, would offer to bring a shovel and ask questions later. Nell was tempted to ask Juliette to bring a shovel right now, because if Riley had been within striking distance, Nell might just have clobbered him.

Unfortunately, after several rings, the call went to Juliette's answerphone.

Just my luck, Nell thought, as she paced around the shop. She was in such a state, she almost toppled a rather expensive lamp over, and she was sorely tempted to close up for the day. She might well have done if a young couple hadn't entered at that very moment.

She still had a desperate urge to share her bad news, and Silas had said he wanted to know how the meeting with the solicitor went, so...

'Silas? It's Nell. Can you spare a few minutes for a chat? This isn't a bad time, is it?'

'Hi, Nell, no, it's fine, I can talk. There's no one in the Gallery at the moment.'

Nell lowered her voice so her customers couldn't hear her private business. 'I've just had a letter from Riley's solicitor.'

'What does it say? Never mind, don't tell me over the phone. I'm coming over. Get the kettle on.'

Before she could assure him it wasn't necessary for him to pop round, he'd hung up and she was left holding a dead phone. With no other option, she did as he'd asked and dashed into the office to flick the switch on the kettle.

She was keeping an eye on her browsing customers and listening out for the water to come to the boil, when Silas strode into the Treasure Trove and gathered her to him.

Shocked at the unexpected intimacy, Nell sank into his embrace, feeling his strong arms holding her, hearing the solid steady beat of his heart as the side of her head pressed against his chest. The contact was brief, and over far too soon.

He released her and moved away a step or two, but it had been wonderful to be held by a man again – she'd forgotten just how wonderful. To be honest, for the majority of her marriage to Riley, being embraced by him had never felt this good. Apart from sex, contact between them had been perfunctory, rarely heartfelt, but Nell was certain Silas's concern was genuine, and that he'd realised she was upset on the phone without her having to say anything. Riley wouldn't have noticed if she'd had a complete meltdown, and even if he had he wouldn't have cared.

'Can I see it?' Silas asked and Nell was brought back to the present with a bump.

'Here.' She handed it to him and watched his face as he scanned it. Then he turned it over, to briefly look at the back, Grimacing, he read it again.

'You were right. He does seem to think he has a claim on the Treasure Trove, and so does Price and Waters. I bet this is a fishing expedition, though – he's shaking the tree to see if anything falls out.'

'He's not shaking anything from *my* tree,' Nell declared adamantly. 'I'm not going down without a fight.'

'That's my girl!'

Nell winced. She most certainly was not Silas's girl; he'd made that very clear. But at least he was in her corner and cheering her on.

'About the other night,' Silas said, into the sudden silence.

'Let's not talk about it.' He was here, that's all that mattered. For a while she'd thought their friendship was over – thank God Juliette hadn't answered her phone, and thank God Silas had. He could easily have ignored her call.

But he hadn't and, more than that, he'd come straight over.

'Tea!' she blurted, remembering. 'I boiled the kettle once. Keep an eye on the shop for me?'

By the time she emerged from the office carrying two mugs and a packet of shortbread fingers, Silas was busy wrapping up three purchases. He'd taken the tags off the items and had left them next to the till for her to ring up. Pleasantly surprised that he hadn't just shouted for her, Nell completed the sale, and once the customers left she thanked him.

'That's all I seem to be doing lately, saying thank you,' she joked. 'But seriously, thank you for listening. You're turning into my knight in shining armour.'

Silas shrugged and she knew she'd embarrassed him, but she didn't care. He was quite cute when he was all discombobulated.

'I'll come with you, if you like,' he said suddenly.

'I'm sorry...?'

'To your meeting with Ron. I'll come with you. If you want me to.'

'Would you? That would be wonderful. I don't mind going on my own, but some moral support would be more than welcome.'

They sipped their tea and munched on the shortbread biscuits in companionable silence for a while, Nell thinking how pleasant it was to have someone else in the shop who she didn't feel obliged to sell something to.

'I'm supposed to be meeting one of Hattie's apprentices,' Nell said. 'Has she persuaded you yet?'

'No, and she's not giving to. See? I told you that you're a nicer person than me.'

'Stop being silly,' she said sharply. 'You're incredibly nice, so don't put yourself down.'

He concentrated on the half-eaten biscuit he was holding, and she knew she'd embarrassed him yet again. She'd better stop doing that, or he really would ignore her call the next time he saw her number on his screen.

'I'm just teasing,' she said gently.

He peered up at her from underneath lowered brows. 'Ah, so you don't actually think I am a nice person?'

She shook her head at him. 'Now you're the one fishing for complements.'

'I thought you said you weren't,' he countered cheekily, and she gave him a nudge with her elbow.

'I wasn't,' she protested. It was her turn to be embarrassed as she remembered how complimentary he'd been about her bum. When he chuckled, she realised he'd achieved his goal to get his own back.

He stayed for a short time, but all too soon he told her he had to get back to the Gallery. As soon as he'd gone the shop felt incredibly empty without him in it.

The question was, was it having someone to chat to that she missed, or did she miss Silas himself?

Nell was pretty certain it was the latter.

CHAPTER 20

SILAS

A knight in shining armour, that's what Nell had called him, but Silas wasn't sure he either deserved the accolade or wanted it. He enjoyed Nell's company and he liked helping her, but he didn't want her to read more into his actions than he intended.

Feeling restless, he grabbed a small sketchpad and his box of pencils, locked the Gallery and walked back to the cottage to fetch his car. He'd been cooped up for too long and it was about time he ventured out for inspiration, and the urge to paint wouldn't be denied.

Llanthony Priory was where he was headed this evening. It would only take him half an hour to get there and it wouldn't be dark for ages yet so he'd have plenty of time. Maybe he could capture the sun setting over the ruins? Or better still, through the bare bones of the old stonework, with the soft glow of the sun hopefully providing a colourful contrast to the dark outline of the abandoned priory's tumbling walls.

He'd painted the priory before; there was something about crumbling buildings set in the natural world that got his creative juices going, and as far as romantic ruins went, the old priory was up there with the best.

But by the time he arrived, the glorious sunset had been transformed into gathering clouds of purple and grey and the air smelt of rain and copper. Thunder rumbled overhead as he got out of the car and began to walk towards the priory, and although he hadn't seen the preceding flash, he sensed it.

Silas hoped the storm would hold off long enough to allow him to capture the essence of the scene without getting a soaking. Unsurprisingly, there was no one else in sight, and he quickly found a suitable spot in which to sit and sketch.

As his pencil flew over the paper, he felt the first fat drop of rain land on his head. A flash lit the sky, and for a brief wonderful second, lightning zig-zagged across it, emblazoned on his retina, and the cannon-fire thunder made him jump. Crikey, that was loud, and he guessed the storm was more or less directly overhead.

Another heavy raindrop landed on his sketchpad

with an audible plop, and he knew he had only scant minutes left to complete his rough drawing before he got drenched.

Hastily, he scrabbled for his phone, knowing even as he aimed it at the lowering scene before him that no photograph would ever do it justice, but trying nevertheless to capture the amazing colours of Nature's wrath. He only just made it back to the car before the heavens opened and torrential rain cascaded from the sky like God's very own power-shower.

As he sat there, Silas, for the first time in years, wished he had someone to share it with. And it didn't come as any shock to realise the only person he'd want by his side was Nell.

So much for him not wanting her to read anything more into his actions than was there – because it was apparent there was a great deal indeed that she could read into them. He had been kidding himself, thinking he had been helping her out of the goodness of his heart. Silas wasn't Good Samaritan material. He was selfish and self-absorbed, and the reason he was going out of his way for her wasn't because he wanted to paint her for art's sake. It was because he was more attracted to her than he could ever remember being attracted to a woman before. Not even his ex-wife.

Sorry, Denise…

Ah, *Denise*.

He wasn't sure how he felt about the news that she was marrying again.

He was happy for her, but it unsettled him to think she was moving on. The two of them had been in an emotional limbo for so long, it was hard to even consider that love and life carried on.

After his daughter had been so cruelly taken, life for Silas had meant existing, getting through each day with grim determination and the least amount of heartache he could manage. It had been the same for Denise. Yet, she'd been able to move on, to move past her crushing grief. He was under no illusion that she would ever truly recover from Molly's death. He'd witnessed first-hand how devastated she'd been, but now she was trying to find happiness and he had to admire her for that.

As for himself, Silas wasn't sure he wanted to try. It would almost be like saying that he was over it. Over Molly. Pain and grief had defined him for so long, he didn't know how he'd cope if he ever let go of it. Who would he be then?

Silas was too scared to find out. He hadn't liked himself much at all over recent years. What if he liked himself even less? What would he do then?

It was best for everyone if he carried on the way he was. There was no need to inflict his misery on anyone else, least of all Nell. She didn't deserve it. She had enough to contend with as it was, without dealing with a man who was barely holding the broken pieces of himself together. And, if he was honest, he was terrified of opening himself up to love once more. If it didn't work out, he might shatter into a million pieces and never be able to put himself back together. Humpty Dumpty would have nothing on him.

He'd carry on with their friendship for now. Anyway, hadn't she said he'd taken it the wrong way when she'd invited him back to hers for coffee? So maybe he was the one reading too much into their relationship, and friendship was all she was offering?

It would have to be enough.

Despite the growing niggle that he liked her more than was good for either of them, not being friends with her, not seeing her again, was worse than cutting her out of his life altogether.

CHAPTER 21

NELL

Fancy popping into the Tavern for a quick drink later? Got news. Nell pressed send, and the text winged its way through the ether to Silas's phone.

His reply was immediate. *Sure. What time?*

Six? Too early to be called a date, she reasoned. One quick drink as she brought him up to date with what she'd discovered about the painting's previous owner, then they could go their separate ways.

Arrangements made, Nell left her office and went to the shop floor, taking her phone with her. She'd always had a tendency to carry it at all times in case the school rang, or the twins needed picking up; but with them God knows where and doing God knows what (maybe it was better for her sanity if she didn't know!) she was terrified she'd miss a vital call, even though she only ever spoke to them outside of the shop's opening times.

You'd think once they were adults, you'd stop worrying about your kids, she mused as she wrote out a price ticket for a piece of Moorcroft pottery and carefully tied it around the vase's neck.

'Oh, for Pete's sake —' she muttered when her phone rang and she recognised the number.

'Did you get my letter?' Riley asked, without preamble.

'If you mean, did I get the letter from your solicitor, then yes, I did.'

'Well?'

'Well, what?'

'Are we going to come to an arrangement, or are we going to do this the hard way? You do realise if this goes to court the legal fees alone would cost a fortune.'

'You must want the Treasure Trove really bad.' She hoped her confrontational reply concealed just how close to tears she suddenly was.

'Not as badly as you want it,' was his quick reply.

Riley was right. To him, this was just a game of one-upmanship. To her, it was her livelihood.

'Got money to throw away, have you?' she taunted, desperately trying not to let him see how much he was getting to her. She debated whether to let him know she had an appointment with a solicitor of her own, but she decided to wait until she'd spoken to Francis and had some more information and a better grasp of where she should go from here.

'More than you,' he said, sniggering.

'If that's the case, why are you so interested in the Treasure Trove?' she demanded.

'I want what's mine, and as you've used our possessions to fund the business I think it's only fair I should get my share. You can pay me what you owe in instalments if you like. I can come over right now for the first one. Shall we say £25,000?'

Nell spluttered. 'Shall we say not? I don't know what you think the business is worth, but I don't have that kind of money lying around.'

'Surely you must have some working capital to buy all those antiques?'

'Not that much.'

'Pity. I'd hate to have this drag on and on. You mightn't have a business worth worrying about once all the legal fees are paid.'

Nell wanted to cry. She had spent enough on the divorce – how much more was this going to cost? Solicitors weren't cheap. It might be better all round if she bit the bullet now and gave him what he wanted. She wasn't stupid, though – she'd have to get the business valued and even then he'd only receive fifty per cent of the profits. Considering she'd ploughed most of those back into The Treasure Trove in terms of stock, he'd get a lot less hard cash than he thought he was going to get. She'd paid herself a salary, of course; perhaps she'd have to do the same for Riley?

Crumbs, this was going to be so complicated that she couldn't see a way of *not* involving a solicitor. However, determined to wait until she'd at least spoken to Francis tomorrow, she had no intention of rushing into anything, no matter how hard Riley pushed. Surely waiting a few more days—

'Are you still there, Nell? Did you hear what I said?'

'I heard.'

'Let's talk about it. I'm sure we can work something out between us. Look, I'm in the area tomorrow, how about if I pop round for a chat?'

He wasn't going to give up, was he, not until he'd got his way.

'OK, you win,' she began, but before she could say anything further, he jumped in. 'I prefer cash, but a cheque will suffice, if necessary.'

'Excuse me?'

'I said—'

'I heard you the first time, but I thought you were joking. A chat, that's all that's on offer. at this stage. The Treasure Trove will have to be valued and—'

'Let's not bother with all that nonsense. I trust you. All we need to do is to draw up a partnership agreement. I can get my solicitor to do that for us, if you like. Anyway, we can discuss it properly when I call in. What are you doing this evening?'

'I'm busy,' she retorted.

'Tomorrow, then?'

'Make it the day after.' She still intended to keep her appointment with Francis. She wasn't going to build her hopes up, but there might be a way of extricating herself from this impossible situation.

'Hmm, you don't want to leave it too long. Price and Waters will want to start the ball rolling.'

'You're paying them. You tell them what you want done and when.'

'Keep your hair on, Nells. I just want the best for both of us.'

Rubbish, she thought. All Riley ever wanted was what was best for him. And it seriously got her back up to hear him call her Nells, as though the past few years had never happened. Then there was all this "we" and "us" rubbish he was spouting. A partnership with her ex-husband was the last thing she wanted – she'd prefer to sell the business and walk away before she'd let that happen. Of course, she'd still have to give him half...

Riley wasn't happy she was forcing him to leave

their meeting until the day after next, but he didn't have any choice. He was railroading her too much as it was, and she stood her ground, not quite hanging up on him but very close to it.

Nell was still seething and simmering when she shut the shop for the day, changed into something more casual and headed off to the Tavern.

'You look cross,' Silas said as soon as he saw her, indicating to Logan that drinks were needed. He'd only just arrived himself, she saw, for he didn't yet have a pint in front of him.

Nell grabbed the glass of wine Logan poured the second he placed it on the bar, and downed it in one. 'Another, please,' she said, ignoring Silas's raised eyebrows.

This drink she sipped at, and nodded to an empty table. 'Shall we?'

Once they were seated, she said, 'Cross doesn't cover it. I'm furious.'

'What's happened?'

'Riley,' she scowled, and told him all about her disturbing conversation with her ex-husband.

'The git. He's got a nerve. He's probably hoping to muscle in and take over, thinking you're not savvy enough to get your own legal advice.'

'One thing's for certain,' she said, 'I'm never going to have Riley as my partner. If I have to sell the business and give him half, then so be it. But I'm not going to work with him. Bloody hell, I thought I was well shot of him apart from his occasional contact with the boys. Looks like I was wrong.'

'It might not be as bad as you think,' Silas said, and even though she knew he was just trying to be nice, she appreciated it.

'There was another reason I wanted to see you – I had an email back from the house clearance company. Thankfully, they keep quite detailed records and were able to track down where the painting came from. They remember this one especially because it came from the estate of a gentleman who died without leaving a will and without any living relatives. They were instructed by the Treasury Solicitor Department. From what I can gather, it's a great deal more complicated than that, but the essence is that the money raised from the sale of the old guy's house and its contents now belong to the Crown.'

Silas was quiet for a moment. 'What are you going to do?' he asked eventually. 'You bought it fair and square, and everything is legal – if you hand it back now, the only people to benefit will be the Crown. I'm not anti-royal, but I think they've probably got enough to live on, whereas you could do with the cash.'

'I agree.'

'You do?'

Nell smiled at his amazement.

'I thought you'd stick to your guns,' he admitted.

'If I could give it to a person, then I would,' she said. 'But it'll just disappear into the royal coffers, probably never to be seen again. So I've decided I will sell it after all, and give half the money to charity. The old gentleman died of cancer apparently, and although I don't know anything about him – not even his name – I hope he'd be happy with my choice. What do you think?'

Silas was strangely silent, and Nell shot him a sharp look. He was staring at his pint of ale and seemed deep in thought.

When he finally met her gaze, his eyes were full of pain, and Nell flinched.

'I think it's a wonderful thing to do.' His voice broke at the end of the sentence, and he cleared his throat. 'Sorry, must have got a frog in my throat.'

Nell continued to stare at him for a while longer. She had no cause to disbelieve him, but for some reason, she thought there was more to the story than Silas was letting on. Was it the fact that she was intending to keep half of the money, or that she was giving half of it away?

'I don't know if I'm going to offend you and I hope I'm not, but after the auction costs and I've given the charity their share, I think you ought to have half of what's left. We'll go fifty-fifty – and before you say anything, if it wasn't for you I'd never have known it was a genuine Oakman.'

Silas gawped at her. 'You're serious, aren't you?'

'Totally.' She grinned. 'I'd like you to do me a favour, though. Keep this to yourself for the time being, until the issue with Riley has been sorted out. In fact, I think you should buy the painting off me for the price I was displaying it at.'

'But why would you… Ah, Riley? But that would mean I'd be the legal owner. I could do what I wanted with it – including selling it. I'm flattered you trust me, but—'

'I'd trust you with my life,' Nell told him, truthfully.

'Exactly! If I end up having to have the business valued, they'll want to do a stock take and see the accounts. I don't want to risk anyone discovering the Oakman. I've got it listed as an oil painting of some Welsh hills with a sheepdog. I haven't mentioned the artist – mainly because I couldn't make out the signature.'

'It's a good job you couldn't.'

'And an even better job you could!'

'What if I just hang onto it for a while; take it to my place for safe keeping.'

Nell shook her head. 'I want to sell it to you legitimately before Riley gets the ball rolling, as he puts it.'

'OK, but I'm not happy about it, and I think you should leave any decision until after you've spoken to Francis. Let's see what he's got to say. And if I do buy it, then I insist you buy it back as soon as possible. Deal?'

'Deal! Fancy another drink?'

'Just the one. I've got some work to do this evening.'

'Oh?'

'We need to get the Oakman appraised, and sooner rather than later. Carlfort's will do it remotely if I email them the letter of authentication from Vaughan, and some photos, although the auction house will need to see it in person at some point before they list it for sale. Oh, and I don't want any of the money. It's yours.'

Nell merely smiled at him. She decided not to argue. Not right now. She had plenty of time to get him to change his mind.

She suspected it might be a challenge, but one she was found herself looking forward to very much indeed.

CHAPTER 22

SILAS

The offices of Evan, Slade and Donavon where Francis was a partner, was in Cheltenham, a town which held mixed emotions for Silas. Denise still lived there and it was where Molly was buried. These days he usually only visited three times a year: on Molly's birthday, on Christmas Day and on the anniversary of her death.

Yet here he was, on the A40 with Nell in the passenger seat, and not sure how he felt about it. He was usually so consumed with grief that he could barely see to drive.

Not today, though. Today he was quietly optimistic that Francis would be able to come up with an action plan which would mean Nell would be able to keep The Treasure Trove out of Riley's clutches.

Even though Silas had never met the man (he'd

seen him and heard him in Bookylicious) the things Nell had told him made him want to knock Riley's block off. Riley was a suitable name for the guy, because he'd certainly riled Silas. There was something about him that was sleazy and unsavoury, and Silas couldn't help wondering what Nell had seen in him.

He felt very sorry for her – fancy having a man treat you like that, and just when you think you're over him and have moved on with your life, he turns up and starts making waves.

Silas sneaked a quick look at her, and was relieved to see she didn't appear to be as nervous as when he'd first picked her up. She was dressed in a smart skirt with a flowery blouse, and was wearing heels, and looked every inch the businesswoman he knew her to be. Her face was a little pale, although she was sporting more make-up than he'd seen her wearing previously, and he thought how composed she was. She also looked extremely pretty, but he pushed that thought away. It was a path he didn't want to go down.

'How about an early dinner after your meeting?' Silas asked.

'That's a good idea. There must be a place or two in Cheltenham, that we could try. Do you know the town well?'

He'd been thinking of driving back to Ticklemore and stopping off in Ross-on-Wye for a bite to eat. 'Kind of, I used to live here.'

'Didn't you say your ex-wife still does?'

'Uh-huh.'

She must have heard something in his brief reply, because she said, 'I'm sorry – I could have come on my own.'

'It's fine.' And he was mildly taken aback to discover that it was. Having Nell by his side diluted some of the sorrow he usually felt on visiting the town that held so many memories for him.

'Why did you move to Ticklemore? Was it because of your divorce?' She pulled a face when he failed to reply straight away. 'Sorry, I'm being nosey. It's none of my business.'

'It's fine,' he repeated. 'Sometimes you just need a fresh start, you know? Cheltenham isn't that big a place, and bumping into Denise every five minutes wasn't doing either of us any good.'

'Did you have a studio there, too?'

'Yes. That's why I retained Francis to handle my side of the divorce. Denise is a teacher and has her own income but at the time…' He hesitated, not wanting to say too much. 'I wanted to make sure all of our assets were divided fairly.'

'I should have married *you*,' Nell joked, then was

immediately contrite. 'Sorry, that was insensitive of me.'

He smiled, to show her he hadn't taken any offence. 'I know of a little place not far from the theatre. They have an early bird menu to cater to the people coming out of the matinee performance. We can go there, if you like. Or we can stop off in Ross-on-Wye?' He was secretly hoping she'd say the latter.

'Shall we go to the one near the theatre? I'd like to see a bit of Cheltenham – I can't say I've ever been.'

'It's pretty and has some artisan shops, although most will be shut by the time your meeting with Francis ends. It also has lots of Georgian architecture and a racetrack.'

'Is there a boot sale, do you know?'

Silas chuckled. 'I can't say I do know. I'm not one for shopping.'

'You can find unusual things in a boot sale,' Nell said archly. 'Don't knock it.'

'Is that where you get most of the stuff that you sell in the Treasure Trove from, boot sales?'

'They are one string to my bow, along with second-hand shops and auction houses.'

'I could find out…' he said, hesitantly, hoping she wouldn't want him to accompany her.

'Let's wait and see if I'm going to have a shop to stock first,' she said. 'Is this it?'

Silas had driven into a private carpark alongside a building displaying the Georgian architecture he'd told her about. Once upon a time and many years ago, he thought it may have been a private house, with a butler and maids, and horse-drawn carriages. Now, though, it housed the offices of Evan, Slade and Donavon.

Nell gave her name to the receptionist and they took a seat in the waiting room, Silas silently noting that it hadn't changed much since the last time he'd waited in it. It was strange to be back here, almost surreal. He could still taste the tang of the undiluted misery he'd felt – his daughter in the ground, his marriage in tatters, his wife disconsolate. And all he'd been able to do was to be as fair as he could to Denise, and paint. Oh, and run away.

A door opened deep within the building and footsteps sounded on the parquet floor, then Francis appeared in the waiting area, his hand outstretched, a professional smile of welcome on his face.

He dropped both when he saw Silas.

'Silas... I didn't expect to see you. Do you have an appointment? Is it about Denise – if so, this isn't the time or place—'

'I'm here with Nell Chapman,' he said, confusion washing over him. Why would he be here about Denise... unless something had happened? But he couldn't imagine what.'

'Oh, I thought… I mean, Denise said she'd told you.'

'Told me what?'

'About us. Me and her.'

'Excuse me?'

Francis frowned. 'Denise and I are getting married.'

'You're the bloke she said has asked her to marry him?'

'Yes. Look, I thought you knew.'

'She didn't mention your name and I didn't think to ask.' Silas was, for want of a better word, gobsmacked. Who the hell could have seen that coming! Not him, that's for sure.

He was aware of Nell staring at the pair of them curiously, and he gestured to her. 'As I said, I'm with Nell Chapman, your next appointment.'

'Ah, yes, Mrs Chapman.'

'Ms – I don't want to associate myself with the Mr.' Nell stepped forwards and held out her hand.

Francis shook it. He sent Silas a curious glance, but Silas ignored it. 'Go on through,' he said to Nell, indicating she should walk ahead. 'I'm sorry you had to find out this way—' he began, sotto voce, but Silas shut him down.

'It doesn't matter. I'm just glad she's able to find

happiness again.'

'You haven't...? Is Ms Chapman...?'

'No and no. Through here, is it?'

'Yes, same office. Please, take a seat, both of you. Before we begin, I must say you're looking well, Silas; better than I've ever seen you look. How are you?'

'Fine. I'm fine.'

'Good, good. Denise will be pleased – she was worried about you for a while after—'

'Do you mind if we get on?' Silas interrupted hastily. 'Nell is worried enough already. She was hoping you could give her some advice.'

'Er, yes, of course. That's what I'm here for. Sorry, Ms Chapman. What can I do for you?'

Silas sat quietly, as Nell explained what had brought her to Francis's office, and he watched the play of emotions across her face, from anxiety and incredulity, to anger and hopelessness. Francis, for his part, said very little, only asking the occasional question for clarity.

Finally, she handed Francis the envelope containing the letter from Riley's solicitor, and she and Silas watched as Francis removed it, and read it. Twice.

Then he fingered the high-quality paper before turning the letter over to look at the back. Seeing nothing written on the reverse, he turned it back over and read it for the third time.

'What do you think, Mr Slade?' Nell asked.

'Call me Francis. It seems daft not to when Silas does.'

'I'm Nell,' Nell said.

'I suspect it's nothing to worry about. Can you leave this with me for the time being?' He waved the letter. 'I'll arrange for a photocopy to be taken, for your records. I'd like to keep the original, if I may?'

'Of course.' Nell got to her feet and thanked the solicitor for his time.

Silas, meanwhile, gave Francis a penetrating stare and hoped the man would get the hint not to mention anything about Molly. Or Denise. Or anything that wasn't to do with the subject in hand. Nell didn't need to hear about Molly. Not now. Not ever.

Silas didn't want her sympathy and he didn't need her pity.

What he wanted and what he needed was for things to carry on between them just the way they were.

CHAPTER 23

NELL

'Silas couldn't get out of there fast enough,' Nell said to Juliette the next morning, fingering the handle of her coffee mug thoughtfully. 'It must have been a shock for him to discover the man who his ex-wife was marrying was the solicitor who'd dealt with his divorce.'

'Isn't there a client privilege or something about that? Like when doctors aren't supposed to date patients?'

'Technically she wasn't his client,' Nell pointed out. 'Silas didn't look happy about it, and it was really awkward, especially when Francis thought Silas already knew about them. We were supposed to have had an early dinner at this restaurant Silas knows in Cheltenham, but we ended up going back to the car. We popped into a little place not far from Ross-on-

Wye, and had a meal in a gastro pub there.'

'And how did that go?'

'I'm not sure.' Nell stared absently into her mug. They were sitting in the kitchen in Juliette's house and she should have already opened the Treasure Trove, but she'd been desperate to unburden herself. 'Silas was clearly put out and uncomfortable, but I'm not sure whether that was because he'd only just found out about Denise and Francis, or whether it was because I was there to witness it.'

'You like him, don't you?'

Nell heaved a sigh. 'Yes, I suppose I do. But he's definitely not interested in me. He's still in love with Denise.'

'Are you sure about that?'

'As sure as I can be. You ought to have seen his face. The best way I can describe his expression was stricken. He went as white as a lace hankie.'

'I'm sorry, Nell. It can't be easy for you. He's the first bloke you've looked at twice since Riley left.'

'Just my luck.' She sighed again, the unexpected sting of tears making her blink.

'Oh, sweetie, come here.' Juliette wrapped her in a hug and Nell sniffled, trying not to lose control.

This was ridiculous. She'd known all along that Silas was only ever going to be a friend, so what was she getting so upset about?

'It's this thing with Riley,' she said to Juliette. 'It's really getting to me, and with the boys being away…'

'Of course, it is,' Juliette said sympathetically as she released her. 'You still haven't told me what your solicitors said about the situation with Riley.'

She hadn't, had she? She'd been more interested in telling Juliette about Silas. Why was that, she wondered. Her business and the potential loss of it should have been her leading story – to cadge a line from Juliette and the Tattler. She realised the news about the Oakman meant she had a financial cushion, and if Riley did do his worst and she had to give him half, she'd have the funds to start over. After all, she'd bought the premises outright with her share of the house, so he couldn't take that away from her.

'There's more,' Nell said, and went on to bring her friend up to date regarding events with Riley and the non-committal meeting with Francis.

'He said he'll be in touch in a few days,' Nell said. 'I've given him access to all the divorce stuff, and I dare say he'll do the legal thing of sending a letter refuting all claims to Riley's solicitor as his opening gambit.'

'He wouldn't be doing his job if he caved at the first letter,' Juliette said. 'Do you honestly think Riley is entitled to anything? Did Francis give a hint?'

'He might be entitled to a portion – after all, I did

use the sale of joint assets to kick-start the Treasure Trove. But then again, Riley didn't want anything from the house that he hadn't already taken. I've been going over and over this in my head, and I'm not getting anywhere. I suppose I'll just have to let the legal-beagles get on with it.'

'It's going to take time and money, despite Riley thinking you can sort it out between you,' Juliette observed. 'I hope you're not thinking of doing that, because you know he'll stitch you up, right?'

'No chance, and I'll tell him that when I see him later. I was hoping Francis would have given me some ammunition, but...' She pulled a face. 'As for the money, remember me telling you about the Oakman painting?'

'As if I could forget. It'll make a great story!'

'I've been doing some digging and discovered an old man owned it previously, but he died intestate and without any living blood relatives, so his estate has passed to the Crown.'

'You mean, the royal family?'

'In effect, yes. The house clearance company were paid an agreed amount for everything in the house, and then sold what they could. I own the painting fair and square.'

'You owned it fair and square before,' Juliette said.

'Yes, but I was planning on giving it back to the

original owner.'

'And now?'

'I'm going to sell it.'

'Good for you!'

'It's not as straight forward as that, though,' Nell said, and told her all about her plan to have Silas buy the painting from her, and his insistence that he sells it back.

'Do you trust him? I mean, once you sell it to Silas, you've not got a legal leg to stand on.'

'I do trust him. Totally. If he'd wanted to, he could have bought it off me in the first place and not said a thing about it. I wouldn't have known.'

Juliette swore. 'Darn it, is that the time? Sorry, Nell, but I need to get going.'

Nell drained her mug. 'Me too, I've got the shop to open and I'm late as it is.'

But late or not, she couldn't resist popping into Bookylicious for a Danish pastry to go. She'd skipped breakfast and now her tummy was protesting. Besides, she was supposed to be meeting Tanesha tomorrow and she didn't feel ready for it, so she needed to tell Hattie.

No matter how much pressure Hattie put on her, Nell simply wasn't in a position to take anyone on – not with all the legal stuff floating about. It simply wouldn't be fair on the girl.

Thinking it best to get it over and done with, Nell was relieved to see Hattie on duty. She was in the book part of the shop, restocking the shelves, and as soon as she'd paid for her pastry, Nell walked over to her.

'I'm sorry, Hattie, but I can't go ahead with this apprenticeship thing. It's an admirable idea, but I simply can't. Not for a while. Maybe not for a long while.' If ever, because assuming the valuation and fair distribution of the business was to go ahead, as Juliette pointed out it could take months. The boys might be more or less back by then, and she was hoping one or the other of them would help her run it.

Hattie studied her, her gaze sharp. 'Would this have anything to do with your ex-husband, by any chance?'

'Why? What have you heard?' Nell wondered who on earth the old lady could have been talking to. Neither Juliette nor Silas would say anything, and the twins were out of the country.

'No one. He's been sniffing around, that's all. I didn't expect to see him around these parts again. I remember him from when you used to live in Chrysler Lane – I didn't like him then and I don't like him now. You're well shot of him. Now that Silas Long…?' Hattie winked at her.

Nell ignored the obvious fishing for info – she was more concerned about Riley. 'When did you see him?'

'Last week was the first time; he had a cup of tea and a scone. Didn't leave a tip.'

'When were the other times?

'Now, let me see… Three days ago, or was it four, I saw him on the high street. And then again yesterday.'

'Where? What was he doing?'

'He was trying to see into your shop. Is there a problem? Can I help?'

'No, no problem.'

'Could have fooled me,' Hattie muttered as Nell stumbled out of Bookylicious and made her way swiftly to the Treasure Trove.

What had Riley been doing outside her shop? He must have known Wednesday was her half-day – it quite clearly said so on the sign on the door.

With her heart in her mouth, she glanced up and down the street before she slipped inside, but she couldn't see any sign of her ex. He was probably in work, she reasoned, so he was hardly likely to be lurking in Ticklemore this early in the morning. She wished she'd thought to ask Hattie what time she'd seen Riley sniffing around the Treasure Trove, but it was too late now.

There *was* something she could do, though, and

she'd better do it now – she had to get the Oakman off the premises urgently. Just in case.

CHAPTER 24

SILAS

'I don't mind storing it at the Gallery,' Silas said to her, less than half an hour later as he arrived to collect the painting. It was still wrapped up, and in the storage box he had placed it in to bring it home after Vaughan had examined it. Keeping it wrapped was the best things for it until it was safely in the hands of the auction house, where any damage would be their responsibility. 'I was going to suggest bringing it to mine anyway – I already took some photos, but Carlfort's are going to want close-ups and such, and the light is so much better in the studio than it is here. Are you sure Hattie saw Riley hanging around?'

'I'm sure she believes she did. He lived in Ticklemore long enough for him to be a familiar face, even if he didn't spend much time in the village itself. Have you thought any more about you buying it?'

'I have and I still think you should wait until Francis has given you his advice.'

'But you will store it at the Gallery?' she asked for a second time, and Silas could see how worried she was.

'I've said I would, and I will. It'll be safe in the studio. No one goes up there except me.'

She shuffled nearer to the window and peered out, most of her hidden by the sideboard which took up the majority of available space on the raised display.

'Anything?' he asked.

She shook her head. 'He'll be in work,' she said, 'but I can't help being twitchy.'

'I'd be twitchy, too, if I was in your shoes.' He had an urge to take her in his arms and tell her everything would be all right, but he didn't think she'd welcome the gesture.

'Show me where it is and I'll get out of your hair,' he said.

'It's in the office.' Nell didn't move from her look-out position, and he went to fetch it. The painting wasn't particularly large, about twenty by twenty-four inches, and even in the box he could carry it easily.

A phone rang just as he stepped onto the shop floor and he saw Nell frown at the number then put the mobile to her ear.

Silas mouthed goodbye to her as he walked past,

but felt her hand on his arm and he paused. When he saw her face, his eyes widened. Something was clearly very wrong. Oh God, he hoped it wasn't bad news about one of her boys—

'Wait a sec, Francis, Silas is here – I'm going to put you on speakerphone. I want him to hear this. Tell him what you just told me.'

Francis began talking, and as he did so, Silas's mouth dropped open.

'The letter is a fake,' the solicitor said. 'I had my suspicions yesterday, but I didn't want to say anything until I was sure. The wording of it, the type of paper used… it didn't add up. The firm of solicitors who supposedly sent the letter to you most definitely exists, but they have never heard of Riley Chapman and have never been instructed by him.'

'Dear God,' Silas whispered.

Nell's eyes were huge in her face and she'd gone incredibly pale, apart from a bright spot of colour on each cheek.

'He forged it?' she asked, her voice only marginally louder than his own, but he could nevertheless hear the anger simmering in her tone.

'Yes. You might want to take it to the police. This is clearly fraud, from what you told me yesterday about Mr Chapman wanting to settle the matter without involving solicitors.'

'The bloody cheek of it,' she said, her voice louder, the anger more apparent. 'But does he have a legitimate claim on my business?'

There was a pause and Silas heard the shuffle of paper, then Francis said, 'I've had a quick look at the terms of the divorce settlement and the division of assets, and I can confirm that he does not. He made no claim on the contents of the house, only on the property itself.'

Nell grimaced. 'Only because Vanessa didn't want any second-hand stuff that had once belonged to me – she wanted everything brand new. What about the value of the items he left behind? If Riley had known what they could be sold for, he would have wanted a cut – maybe all of it, because it was his money that had bought it originally.'

Francis said, 'Firstly it was down to him to check on the value of any jointly possessed items. Secondly, the items would have been deemed to have been owned jointly by both of you, not just by him, and thirdly, you gave up rights to his pension in lieu of the contents of the house.'

'I did? I don't remember doing that.'

'If I had been the solicitor who had handled your divorce, I would have argued against it. But it seems to have worked in your favour – Mr Chapman wouldn't be interested in your business if he didn't think it was profitable. Anyway, in my opinion he has no claim on you whatsoever, just as you have no further claim on him.'

'I don't owe him a penny?'

'You do not.'

'That's fantastic news.' Nell edged towards the nearest seat and dropped into it. She was trembling, which Silas guessed was from a mixture of temper and relief.

He carefully put the painting down on a sideboard and went to put the kettle on. He was tempted to see if she had any brandy or other spirit in the flat, but he didn't want to go upstairs without being invited, so a cup of tea would have to do.

The kettle had just come to the boil when Nell appeared in the doorway. She was still pale and she looked close to tears.

Without thinking, he crossed the space between them and gathered her to him.

Nell burst into tears, and Silas let her sob, holding her closer. He'd been half-expecting it – no matter how much Nell came across as strong and independent, over the past few days he'd come to see a different side of her. As she melted into his arms, he kissed her hair, murmuring the sort of nonsense words you might say to a small child or a frightened animal.

He didn't know how long he held her for, he just knew he was happy to do so. Seeing her so upset distressed him more than he thought possible, but at least the news had been good, even if her shitty ex-husband had put her through hell.

When she eventually gained some control and her crying had turned into hiccupping, jerky breaths, he released his hold a little in preparation to letting go of her completely. To his confusion, Nell tightened hers, and when he bent his head to look at her, she raised hers at that precise moment, and he was caught off guard to find his lips were inches from hers.

He hadn't meant to kiss her.

But he'd been unable to control the impulse as it surged over him.

God, she tasted good, her lips soft and warm, her curves moulding themselves to him as he crushed her to his chest, and he let out a groan, his body knowing what it was doing and what it wanted, whilst his mind was telling him this wasn't such a good idea.

Nell's soft sigh as he teased her tongue with his was nearly his undoing, and he had to force himself to drag his mouth away from hers before he tore her clothes off and did to her what he so desperately wanted to do.

The hurt in her eyes when he pulled away was almost more than he could bear, but he told himself it was for the best. He wasn't relationship material, and he hadn't been since his world had turned upside down. Nell deserved better than him – she deserved someone who could make her happy, someone whose mind wasn't haunted by a small girl with the most beautiful smile.

His own smile, when he managed to force his mouth into the right shape was probably more of a rictus he guessed, and he attempted to soften it by saying, 'Shall I make the tea?'

Nell caught her swollen bottom lip in the teeth and his eyes were immediately drawn to its bee-stung redness. What he wouldn't give to kiss her again…

But he couldn't. It wasn't fair on her.

Or him. He'd only be torturing himself.

'I'm sorry,' she said. 'I shouldn't have done that.'

'You've nothing to apologise for. It's me who should be saying sorry. I got carried away for a moment. It won't happen again – I promise.'

There was that flash of hurt again – or had he imagined it? Emotions were running so high right now, especially hers what with the news she'd just received, that he wasn't shocked they'd gone off the rails for a second or two.

There was an uncomfortable silence and he wondered whether he should go ahead and make some tea anyway, or whether he should leave.

He opted for leaving, and he moved past, careful not to brush up against her in case all his good intentions went out of the window and he was tempted to grab hold of her again.

She followed him onto the shop floor slowly, almost as though she was scared to be too close to him. She needn't worry – the mood was gone. If he tried hard enough he could convince himself nothing had happened in the first place.

'Do you still want me to keep this at the Gallery?' he asked, picking up the painting and wincing. He'd only gone and left it right by the front door; with the shop unattended and the pair of them snogging in the office anyone could have reached in and taken it. He'd only been minding it for a few minutes and he'd already put it in jeopardy. What the hell had he been thinking?

It seemed he hadn't been thinking at all – or not with his head, at least. Another part of his anatomy had taken charge for a while.

'If you still want to,' she replied, and he thought how gorgeous she looked with her large eyes, flushed cheeks, and tousled hair. Had he run his fingers through her locks?

He thought he might have.

'Of course I want to.'

'I meant after…' She gestured to the office.

'Let's forget it ever happened, shall we?' Even as he said it, he knew he wouldn't; it was too big an ask.

'Silas?' She was hesitant, reluctant, and he wondered what she was going to say, and whether he'd want to hear it.

'Riley is coming over later, to discuss the business. I haven't told him I was seeing a solicitor.'

'Are you going to tell him what Francis said?'

'Yes, but…'

'You're worried what his reaction will be?' Silas guessed.

She shrugged. 'A bit.'

'Do you want me with you?'

'Maybe. I don't know. He's never been aggressive but you seemed to bring out the testosterone in him last time.'

'Where are you meeting him?'

'He's coming here. '

'The shop or the flat?'

Nell shuddered. 'Not the flat. Having him in the shop is bad enough.'

'How about if I hover on the stairs. He won't be able to see me there, will he?'

'No.'

'That's settled then. What time do you want me?'

'We agreed six o'clock.'

I'll get here for five, in case he's early,' Silas

offered, and his heart clenched when he saw how grateful she was.

It wasn't the only reason his heart was doing odd things — the thought of seeing her again so soon, the knowledge that she wasn't pushing him away despite the kiss, had him more flustered than he could ever remember being.

CHAPTER 25

NELL

At the appointed hour, Nell let Silas in, looked up and down the street, then closed and locked the shop door behind him.

'We might as well have a drink while we wait,' she said nervously, showing him upstairs. 'Fancy a G and T?'

'Sure.'

As she poured the drinks – a weak one for her because she wanted to keep her wits about her – she was conscious of him glancing around her living room. It was a large space, running the full width of the building, a mirror footprint of the shop downstairs. The kitchen sat on top of the office and the little stockroom.

As Nell handed Silas his drink she was careful not to touch him. She was far too aware of him, and having him so near made her pulse race; his kiss had left her wanting more, but he'd rebuffed her, even though he'd seemed to have been enjoying it as much as she.

She couldn't blame him, though. He'd only been trying to comfort her; she was the one who'd instigated the kiss and she guessed he'd probably felt he couldn't push her away right then, not after she'd been so upset. Grateful that he'd tried to let her down gently, yet mortified he'd felt he had to do so in the first place, she'd been relieved when he'd left.

She'd watched him walk up the street, the painting under his arm, filled with sadness for what could never be. Nell hadn't meant to fall for him; romance had been the last thing on her mind, but it had crept up on her, stealthily taking her unawares, and it had all been so quick, too. One minute Silas was an acquaintance, a fellow business owner whom Hattie had brought together by her determination to get the Ticklemore Toy Shop off the ground, and now here she was lamenting that he wasn't interested in a relationship with her, when having a relationship with anyone had been the furthest thing from her mind. She'd have thought she had enough going on in her life at the moment, but her heart appeared to have had other ideas.

Still, Silas was proving to be a good friend, despite

him not thinking of her in that way, and she'd have to be content with that. It was either have him as a friend or lose him completely, and Nell knew which option she'd take.

Wanting to clear the air, she said, 'About earlier—'

But he hurriedly jumped in before she could finish. 'Forget it. I have.'

He smiled at her, and she took it to mean that he hadn't been offended by her launching herself at him, and neither was he going to let it get in the way of their friendship.

'Bloody good news about your ex,' he said, and she was thankful for the change of subject.

She'd been so het up and Silas had left so quickly earlier that they hadn't had an opportunity to properly discuss Francis's revelation, although it had been going around and around in her head – along with the kiss – for the rest of the day.

'I can't believe Riley would stoop so low,' she said sadly. 'The man I fell in love with and married would never have behaved like that. I can't think what's got into him.'

'People change.'

'You can say that again.' Her reply was heartfelt. She didn't recognise Riley. Mind you, she hadn't recognised him for a long time. He'd always had the tendency to be a bit brash and it had grown over the years, until making more money and boasting about it had become the dominant trait in his personality. She never would have pegged him as a liar and a cheat though… Oh, wait – he'd done the ultimate in lying and cheating when he'd slept with another woman. So maybe she shouldn't be so surprised. He was clearly capable of anything.

Loud banging on the shop door made her jump, and Nell gave Silas a horrified look. Riley was early, and she wasn't ready. Oh, Lord, what was she going to say to him? He wasn't going to take it well, even though he was in the wrong and had behaved despicably. Was *still* behaving despicably. How dare he barge back into her life, demanding half of something he had no right to!

More banging.

Riley had never been known for his patience and, feeling more angry than anxious now, Nell got to her feet.

'You'll be fine,' Silas said, stroking her briefly on the arm. 'And I've got your back.'

Nell gave him a grateful smile. 'I know you have. Thank you.'

Squaring her shoulders and lifting her chin, she strode downstairs to give her ex-husband what for.

'You're early,' she said, stepping aside to let Riley in.

'You know me, I like to get things done and dusted.'

No, she didn't know him. She hadn't known him for a long time, since well before he'd walked out on her.

'There's nothing to be done or dusted,' she said.

Riley came to a standstill. He'd been heading towards the rear of the shop, probably intending to conduct the meeting in her office or, God forbid, wanting to go upstairs to the flat. But her words made him pause, and he turned to look at her.

'I thought we had an agreement?' He gave her a narrow-eyed glower that Nell assumed was meant to be intimidating.

'I didn't agree to anything, except to talk,' Nell said.

His face hardened. 'Do you want this to get ugly? Is that what you want?'

'What I want is for you to listen to me, then piss off out of my life.' She took a gulp of air. 'I know the solicitor's letter is fake.'

'You're mad. I don't know who you've been talking to, but they've given you duff advice. Of course it's not a fake. What do you take me for?'

'Greedy? Stupid? Immoral? Would you like me to go on?'

'Hang on a minute—'

227

'No, you hang on and listen to me. Did you honestly think I would be so dumb as to not seek legal advice? You send me a letter from a "solicitor".' She air-quoted the last word, 'And it didn't occur to you that I wouldn't contact a solicitor of my own? Do you think I'm that gullible?'

The look in his eye told Nell that's exactly what he'd thought. In fact, he'd been counting on it.

'He advised me to go to the police,' she continued. 'And I will if you don't bugger off and leave me alone.'

Riley's eyes narrowed, and his lips had become a thin line. His jaw jutted out and he took a step closer to her.

Nell took a corresponding step back, her rear end coming up against a particularly good example of a mid-eighteenth-century card table, and she put a hand out to steady herself. He didn't look at all pleased he'd been caught out, and she was seriously glad Silas was only a scream away.

Not that she thought it would come to that. Riley had never been violent. He preferred the dual offensive of charm and subtle intimidation.

He wasn't being subtle now, though; he looked positively furious. 'You owe me,' he snarled, 'So don't think I'm going to let it go. It was my money you were spending when you bought all that stuff. If I'd have known—'

'Stop right there.' Nell held up a hand, her palm facing out like a policeman halting traffic. 'You didn't care. You didn't show the slightest bit of interest; as long as you had a posh house filled with nice things so you could show off to your so-called mates, you didn't care. And if Vanessa hadn't been so keen on having everything new, you could have had your pick of anything in the house. But you couldn't wait to move on, could you? I expect you were rubbing your hands together because you'd left me to sort everything out. So, you can't blame me for selling it. You didn't want it – what else was I supposed to do with it?'

'I didn't know what it was worth, did I?'

'And that's my fault, how? Look, I'm prepared to be fair. I'll give you half what I paid.' She heard a faint noise coming from the rear of the shop, and she hoped Riley hadn't heard it too.

'*Half what you paid?* You must think I'm a fool! I want half what you *sold* it for.'

'No.'

'What do you mean, no?'

Nell was beginning to lose patience. 'Exactly what I said. No.'

'You're not going to get away with this. Half of this tacky little second-hand shop is mine, and if I don't get it, I'll—'

'You'll what?' Silas sauntered across the shop floor, his hands in the pockets of his jeans, looking calm and slightly detached.

Riley scrutinised Nell, then Silas, and back again. He nodded to himself. 'I see how it is,' he sneered. 'You've got yourself a fancy man. Is he calling the shots now?'

'Don't be silly. I'm perfectly capable of making my own mind up. And if he was my fancy man, as you put it, how would that be any of your concern? You gave away any right to know about my life when you walked out of it. How *is* Vanessa, by the way?'

Riley sneered at Silas. 'You're welcome to her.'

This was the second time Nell had asked him about Vanessa, and for the second time he brushed her off. Which made her wonder whether the woman was draining him dry financially so Riley was having to resort to any means possible to get his hands on some funds. Well, he wasn't getting his hands on hers!

Silas grinned, coming forward to wind an arm around her waist and hug her close. He planted a kiss on her temple. 'Not that I need your permission, but thanks anyway. Your loss is my gain, buddy.'

'*Buddy?* Ooh...' Riley sneered. 'You like second-hand women, do you?'

Nell bristled. 'About as much as your Vanessa likes

second-hand men, I expect. And don't tell me she's not had her fair share of boyfriends before you.'

How the hell do you know that?'

'An educated guess.'

Silas gave Nell a squeeze, then released her. 'Shall I see you out?' he said to Riley.

Riley bared his teeth. He looked as though he was about to argue, but must have thought better of it. Turning sharply on his heel, he snarled over his shoulder, 'You haven't heard the last of this, Nell.'

'I think I have,' she said, adrenalin surging through her. She watched Riley stomp through the door and slam it behind him.

Heart thumping, her pulse roaring in her ears, she grinned at Silas. 'I think this calls for a celebratory drink,' she said. 'And mine's a large one!'

CHAPTER 26

SILAS

'Have you had dinner yet?' Nell asked, heading for the stairs and not waiting for Silas's answer. 'Silly me, it's only a quarter to six – of course you haven't. How about I cook something? I'm sure I can find a tasty morsel or two in the freezer.'

Bemused, Silas followed her upstairs.

'We did it!' she said as soon as they reached her living room.

'*You* did it,' he told her.

'It was both of us. If you hadn't spotted the Oakman, you'd never have known about my trouble with Riley, and I wouldn't have met with Francis.'

'The Oakman aside, I'm sure you would have spoken with another solicitor who'd have told you the same thing Francis did.'

'I can't believe he came back to me so quickly. I

232

assumed it would be days – weeks even. Was that your doing?'

'Not at all. I've had no contact with him since we left his office yesterday. He probably told Denise – she must have asked him to hurry it along.'

'Are you terribly upset?'

'What about?'

'That Denise is marrying Francis?'

Silas didn't want to talk about it; not because he *was* upset (far from it, he was pleased for her – Francis was a good bloke) but talking about Denise made him think about Molly. And he didn't want to bring Nell's mood down with his melancholy.

'Of course not.' He changed the subject. 'I took some clear shots of the painting today and sent them off to Carlfort's. They'll give you an appraisal and a guide price based on that, but you'll have to take the painting into them for them to firm up the appraisal before they will list it in an auction.'

'Oh.' Her back was to him, so he couldn't see her face, but she sounded subdued. 'Thanks.'

'Isn't that what you wanted?'

'Yes, of course it is.' She still didn't look at him. Instead, she was staring intently into the fridge.

'You don't have to make dinner for me,' he said. 'I'm quite happy with a takeaway. Or, if you're tired, we can do this another time?'

Nell's expression was bright and her voice was a little on the high side when she looked at him and said, 'I don't mind cooking, if you don't mind keeping me company. You don't have to, of course. I expect there's somewhere else you need to be.'

Was she hinting he should leave? Silas didn't know what to think; one minute she was offering to cook for him, the next she was more or less throwing him out.

'I don't have to be anywhere, but I can leave if you want.'

'I'd like you to stay. But only if *you* want to.'

Eh? This was getting complicated, and he was beginning not to know which way was up. 'What do you prefer? Chinese? Indian? Fish and chips?' he asked, thoroughly confused. At least choosing what to eat should be straightforward enough.

'I don't mind. You choose.'

Oh, heck... 'Indian,' he said decisively. 'Do you like your curry hot or mild?'

'Medium?'

'OK. Shall we order a dish each and we can share?'

'Sounds good. I'll order, while you make us a drink.'

'Tell me how much I owe you.'

'My treat,' she said. 'I'm a wealthy woman now; or I will be when the painting is sold.

'You're planning on giving half of it away, remember?'

'Three-quarters, actually. I'm giving half to charity and we'll split the other half between us.'

'I don't want it. The money is yours.'

'I want you to have it. Let's not argue about this now. We've got plenty of time before it's sold to squabble about it.'

Nell phoned the curry house, her eyes on Silas as he poured her another gin and tonic. He opted for a cold beer, feeling her gaze like a caress, and he had a momentary flash of how it could be between them if things were different. He walked over to the window and stared at the street below, putting as much physical distance between them as he could.

When she came off the phone and picked up her drink, she said, 'I've been considering donating it to a children's cancer charity – what do you think?'

'Excuse me?' Silas's stomach did a slow roll. Nell didn't know about Molly – she couldn't possibly. No one in Ticklemore did.

'A children's cancer charity,' she repeated, swirling the liquid around in her glass, oblivious to his discomfort. 'I told you the old gent died of cancer, and I know one in every two people are destined to get it, but it's so much worse when a child has it, don't you think? Or should I split it?' She sighed. 'I'd like to be able to help lots of charities, but you can only pick one or two, can't you, otherwise the money would be spread too thin to make much of a difference.'

'How much to I owe you for the takeaway?' Silas asked again, desperate to change the subject.

'I told you, this one's on me. You don't owe me anything. I think you'll find it's the other way around. And about the money... please take it. If you don't want it, you could always give your portion to charity, too. If it wasn't for the boys and wanting to give them a little nest egg for when they return from their pit-stop tour of the world, I might be tempted to do the same. And now that Riley is out of my hair and I don't have to worry about him swiping the Treasure Trove from under my nose, I think I will take on one of those apprentices.'

'Hattie will be pleased,' he said, faintly.

Nell wasn't usually so garrulous, but he guessed the relief of ridding herself of her ex-husband was singing through her veins like so much spent adrenalin and making her talkative. He noticed she'd nearly finished her drink and he poured her another gin, and made one for himself. The beer was pleasant, but he needed something stronger if he was to get through the next couple of hours.

He wanted to kiss her again but he was determined

not to. It wasn't fair on her if he gave in to the impulse; he didn't want to lead her on, and that was exactly what he would be doing if he did.

'Thank you,' she said softly.

'Please stop. You've thanked me enough already.'

'I don't think I'll ever thank you enough. If there's anything I can do for you? Anything at all?'

Oh, crumbs.

He cleared his throat and lifted his glass to his lips, his mouth dry. Her eyes were on his face and her gaze felt like a caress.

Silas took another large mouthful of gin and tonic, and the alcohol immediately coursed through his veins. He'd better not drink any more.

The silence was awkward and he was grateful when she put some music on, although the haunting lyrics of Fleetwood Mac made it feel worryingly more like a date than a quick bite to eat with a friend.

'You look tired,' he said, as she dropped onto the sofa. He'd taken one of the squishy chairs and he relaxed back into it, stretching out his legs.

'It's been a busy day.' She rested her glass on the arm of the sofa, her fingers holding the stem. 'I feel a bit numb, to be honest. I can't believe Riley would do something like that.' Her mood had become pensive now that the shock had worn off. 'I thought I knew him.' She blinked rapidly then polished off the rest of her drink. 'Another one?' She got up and poured another, handed him his glass then sat back down.

He shouldn't have another one, but he did, coughing when he tasted it. 'Did you forget the tonic?' Blimey, that was so strong it was practically neat gin.

'Sorry.' She made to get up again, but he waved her back down. She really did look exhausted. He'd eat the takeaway, then go. She could do with an early night and he could do with not being alone with her.

'I'll get it,' he said, as the buzzer sounded, and he went downstairs to fetch their meal.

By the time he was back in the living room she'd laid the table. He unpacked the contents of the bag, the aromatic smell filling his nose, and he realised he was hungry.

'This smells good,' he said, opening one of the curries.

Nell sidled past him to fetch their drinks and he caught the scent of her perfume. She smelt even better than the food and an altogether different kind of hunger reared its head.

He took the glass from her, his hand brushing hers, and to cover his sudden longing, he drained half of his drink, gasping as the gin hit the back of his throat. It had been a mistake to swap from the beer, and he decided it was best if he didn't have any more.

But the curry was spicier than he'd anticipated and when she handed him another bottle of beer, taking one for herself, he accepted it. It complemented the curry perfectly, and before he knew it he'd finished the bottle.

'Don't go yet,' she pleaded, after they'd finished eating and the debris had been cleared away. 'I know it's silly because the boys have been at uni for the biggest part of three years, but the flat feels awfully empty since they buggered off around the world.'

How could he leave now, after that? He imagined her alone, the events of the day running through her head, and the image of her sadness that day on the bridge slipped into his mind. His painting hadn't done her justice.

Feeling more at home in her company than was good for him, he fetched the remaining two beers from the fridge. He noticed she'd hardly touched her first one, and her glass of gin was more than half full. It seemed he was drinking enough for the two of them, and he hoped the food he'd just eaten would absorb some of the alcohol.

This time when he sat down, it was next to her on the sofa.

She was curled up on it, her feet underneath her. Her toes touched his thigh, and he noticed they were encased in pink socks.

She looked delectable.

If you don't love me now... The words of the song cascaded over him.

Stevie Nicks's whisky and caramel voice trembled in the air, and he shifted slightly, incredibly aware of the warmth of Nell's foot, of her perfume, of the sad look in her eyes.

The music faded, the next song beginning to play. *Sweet, wonderful you...*

She caught him looking at her as their eyes met. A small tentative smile from her, abrupt and sudden desire from him, which he hastily tried to disguise.

She unfurled her legs and picked up a cushion. He took a deep draught of his beer, the bottle almost empty. He daren't have another.

'Please...?'

'I'll stay for a while, if you want me to.'

'I'm sorry, I'm being all pathetic and needy.'

'You've had a shock.' He didn't mind needy; it made him feel wanted.

'But you've done enough.'

He'd like to do more. Oh, Lord, he'd like to do much, much more.

Then he was kissing her, his lips hard on hers as he crushed her to him, a groan sounding in his throat when her arms came around him. Her tongue teased his, and her hands gripped his back as she sank into the cushions.

He followed, her body underneath his, their legs entwined. Her soft pliable curves belied her strength as she held him tight, and he groaned again, desire surging through him. He was consumed by his need for her and—

A shriek of laughter from the street below brought him to his senses.

What the hell was he doing? He couldn't do this. He wasn't ready; he didn't think he ever would be.

He wanted Nell more than he'd wanted any woman, but he had to put a stop to this.

Silas sat up. 'Sorry, I can't... It's no use. *I'm* no use, to you or anyone. I can't move on. I just can't.'

He had to get out of there, away from Nell and the confusion and hurt in her eyes.

'I'm sorry,' he repeated, mumbling the apology through lips still tingling from the kiss. His heart was thudding and his breathing was ragged, and he wanted nothing more than to push her back down on the sofa and make glorious, wonderful love to her.

But what then? What would happen afterwards?

She'd quite rightly would want, and expect, more than a one-night stand, and he simply wasn't able to give her that.

'Sorry,' he muttered for the third and final time.

Then he fled.

CHAPTER 27

NELL

'I don't know what's up with Silas,' Nell said to Juliette the following day. The pair of them were sitting in the Tattler's office, situated above the butcher shop in the high street. Nell, desperately needing to speak to someone, had closed the Treasure Trove for an early lunch, had grabbed a couple of sandwiches from Bookylicious and had taken herself off to bend Juliette's ear.

Nell sighed. 'One minute he's kissing me, the next minute he's pushing me away. I think he's still in love with Denise. Do you remember me telling you about his reaction when he discovered she was marrying the solicitor who had handled his side of the divorce? Last night after he kissed me, he muttered something about not being of any use to anyone because he can't move on.'

'It's a shame,' Juliette said. 'You two look good together.'

'We get on well; I agree it's a shame. Although saying that, I'm not sure if I'm ready for another relationship just yet, not after Riley.' Nell shuddered. 'You should have seen the way Silas stood up to him,' she said. 'I was more or less holding my own, but I have to admit I was worried Riley was going to lose the plot. I can't say he'd ever been aggressive but there's always a first time, isn't there? And he was seriously cheesed off I caught him out in a lie.'

'It was more than catching him out in a lie,' Juliette commented. 'I'd call it attempted fraud.'

'Francis suggested I take it to the police but I don't think I'm going to. As long as Riley is out of my hair, that's all I'm worried about. I know I can never get rid of him completely because of the twins – he is their father, after all – but the less I have to do with him the better.'

'Let's hope he's learnt his lesson,' Juliette said, and Nell wholeheartedly agreed with her.

'Now that you don't have to worry about Riley finding out about the Oakman painting, do you think I can run that piece?' Juliette leant forward her eyes sparkling.

'You're keen, aren't you?' Nell chuckled.

'It's such a great story. I can do a feature now, and

then another one later when it's sold, and maybe even a third when you're handing the cheque over to the charity. It'll be fantastic publicity for you, look how the Toy Shop took off after I ran the story and one of the nationals took it up.'

'I don't see any reason why not,' Nell said. 'You'll have to arrange a time and date with Silas, because he's keeping the painting at the Gallery for the time being. I asked him to store it because I was worried about Riley seeing it.'

'Surely you can bring it back to the Treasure Trove, now?'

Nell knew that continuing to keep the painting at the Gallery was an excuse to see Silas again. As soon as she took possession of the painting and gave him his portion of the money (which she was still determined to do, despite his protests) they would probably go back to being little more than business acquaintances. And she didn't want that to happen.

Silas had crept under her skin and she didn't think she'd be able to wrestle him out again very quickly. She didn't actually want to. It might not be the most sensible thing to torture herself by spending time with a man who didn't reciprocate her growing feelings, but to cut him out of her life almost completely wouldn't be good, either. She enjoyed his company, enjoyed being with him. She also enjoyed him kissing her, but she pushed that thought away.

Juliette said, 'I want a photo of the pair of you with it – it'll be good for both of your businesses. Besides, if it wasn't for Silas, you would never have known that it really was an Oakman, so it's only fair he should get some of the credit.'

'I agree,' Nell said. 'Tell you what, I'll ask Silas and we can arrange a time. He might not want to have his photo taken, though,' she said an afterthought.

'Why ever not?'

Nell asked, 'Have you ever Googled him?'

'No, I haven't.' Juliette giggled. 'I think you have, though.'

'There's not a photo of him to be found. There's a photo of the outside of the Gallery, and as you'd expect there are loads of images of his paintings, but not one of him. Don't you think that's odd?'

'Not at all, quite a few people don't want to have their photos splashed all over the Internet. Come to think of it though, I've been on at him for ages to let me run a piece on him and his paintings, but he's not got back to me.'

'He's an extremely private man,' Nell said. 'But I don't think it's just that. I think there's much more to him than meets the eye. I just wish I knew what it was.'

'He could be a serial killer, or in the witness

protection programme.'

Nell shot Juliette a startled look, then she realised her friend was laughing at her. 'You're teasing me,' she said. 'But I still think he's hiding something.'

'If that's the case, are you sure you want to find out what it is?'

'Perhaps not. Anyway, he's probably not interested in me because he is still in love with Denise. He doesn't want to let me get too close, in case I get the wrong idea.'

Nell had enough of talking about Silas. She'd hoped that by unburdening herself to Juliette, she might have got things a little straighter in her head. But it hadn't worked. She was just as confused as when she'd gone to bed last night, slightly drunk, her lips throbbing, her heart skipping a beat as she remembered his hand on the back of her head digging into her hair as his mouth claimed hers.

'Now that all this business with Riley is out of the way, there's something else I can do,' Nell said. 'I'm going to take on an apprentice.'

'Good for you. It's about time you had a bit of help around the place. It was bad enough when I was on my own, but at least I didn't have to be in the office all day every day. Not like you have to be in the shop. I don't know how you manage it.'

'If I'm honest, neither do I, and with the twins

away, it's even harder. I used to rely on them being around during the holidays so they could man the shop while I went to purchase new stock.'

'Let me know when you take someone on, because that's another series of features I'm planning. It looks like she's got a few people lined up in Ticklemore to take on these youngsters. I'm going to start with Zoe because she's the benchmark. Look at how well she's done for herself since Alfred took her on. Not only is she learning a trade, but she's also learning a fair bit about running a business from Sara.'

'I know it's going to take me a while to train someone up, and it will probably take me even longer to trust them but I've got to start somewhere, haven't I? And so have they. Hattie said she had a girl called Tanesha who is interested, so I hope she's still available. I popped into Bookylicious earlier when I picked up the sandwiches, and I'd hoped to speak to Hattie about her, but she wasn't there. I'll try again on the way back.'

This time Hattie was in full view, clearing tables, so Nell made a beeline for her.

'What can I get you?' the older lady asked.

'I'm not staying,' Nell said. 'I just wanted to let you know I'm now in a position to take an apprentice, and if Tanesha is still available and still willing, I'll be happy to interview her.'

Hattie narrowed her eyes. 'What's changed your mind?'

Nell didn't want to air her laundry in public and she certainly didn't want to get into a discussion about Riley, so all she said was, 'Circumstances have changed.'

'Silas has seen your ex off, has he?'

Nell wrinkled her nose. 'What do you mean?'

'I've seen the way Silas looks at you.'

Nell gave an unladylike snort. 'I don't think so. Silas doesn't look at me at all.'

'I think you'll find he does.' Hattie put her hands on her hips and studied her. 'I just don't know what's wrong with you youngsters,' she said. 'First we had Juliette and Oliver playing silly buggers, and now you and Silas. Why don't the pair of you just admit you fancy each other and be done with it?'

'Hattie, Silas doesn't fancy me.'

The woman barked out a laugh. 'Ha! So you admit that *you* fancy *him*?'

'I do not!'

'Yes, you do, I can tell.'

Nell shook her head. She clearly wasn't going to win this argument. Hattie could be incredibly stubborn and tenacious when she wanted to be. Nell sent her an enigmatic smile, hoping she looked more like the Mona Lisa and less like she was constipated, as she left Bookylicious with Hattie staring after her.

Hoping to goodness Hattie wasn't going to stage one of her interventions, Nell phoned Silas and arranged for her and Juliette to call around tomorrow morning to take some photos of the painting. Then she spent the rest of the afternoon trying to forget about Silas and the way he made her feel, as she concentrated on rearranging a few things in the shop and doing a little bit of admin.

She was still hard at it, having closed the shop about an hour ago, when her phone rang.

'Ooh!' she squealed, seeing Adam's number flash up on her screen. 'Adam! Ethan! where are you?'

'An island called Otok Molat, just off Croatia. The beaches are fabulous and it's so unspoilt.'

'It sounds wonderful,' she cried, filled with sudden longing. Although it was mid-summer and glorious in Ticklemore, Croatia sounded mysterious and exotic.

Adam told her their news and they chatted for a bit, then he said something that made her sit up and take notice.

'Dad phoned again. What's all that about? We don't hear from him in ages, then he phones twice in a couple of weeks?'

'What did he want?'

'We're not sure. He seemed pretty cheesed off about something. He wasn't making a lot of sense, to be honest. He said you'd cheated him out of some money and that we're not to believe a word you say about it. What's going on, Mum?'

'Your father thinks he might be entitled to half of the Treasure Trove, but he isn't. It's all a misunderstanding and it's been sorted out now.'

'Are you sure?'

'Absolutely.' But even as she was saying it, she couldn't help but wonder if that man would ever be out of her life?

CHAPTER 28

SILAS

Silas rolled his eyes and heaved a sigh. That was the third time this morning the bell in the Gallery had tinkled to let him know he had a customer and he'd only been open an hour.

Reluctantly he swilled his brush off in the jar of water he kept on the easel and made his way downstairs, his mind filled with the scene he was creating, the roll of the hill, the majestic soar of the mountain, the silver clouded sky. Pen y Fan, the highest peak in South Wales might have been painted countless times by so many artists, but its beauty never failed to inspire him – and that it was a popular purchase was an added bonus.

He stopped dead when he saw who his customer was. 'Nell. And Juliette. Hi.'

'You forgot we were coming, didn't you?' Juliette

teased.

'No, I just didn't realise the time. Is it one o'clock already?'

'Yep.'

Silas hadn't forgotten. He'd been looking forward to it. Not the being interviewed by Juliette part – the seeing Nell again part. Although he'd spoken to her on the phone yesterday, her coming by the Gallery today kind of broke the ice after the other night.

He still couldn't believe he'd drunk so much.

What must she think of him?

He'd seen the hurt and confusion on her face when he'd muttered an excuse or two and a half-hearted apology for kissing her. But, damn it, the alcohol had suppressed his inhibitions and he'd almost thrown himself at her.

The worrying thing was that she hadn't minded. If anything, she'd seemed to be enjoying it as much as he, until he'd come to his senses and realised what he was doing.

But Denise did it, a little voice in his head taunted. She'd found love again, so why can't you?

It wasn't a case of finding love – he understood that. It was more a case of pulling the fragmented pieces of himself together so he could function in a relationship. He was self-aware enough to realise he was still broken and probably always would be. No amount of love could put him back together again.

Love? Nell?

He froze, as he realised the direction his thoughts had taken him, and the understanding they'd brought with them. He'd fallen in love with Nell and he hadn't even realised it until now.

Juliette said, 'Are you going to show me this painting, or are you going to stare into space for the rest of the day? It might be OK for you artistic types, but I've got things to do.'

Silas came out of his reverie to find Juliette staring at him, her hands on her hips. Nell, he noticed, was also looking at him, but her expression was one of concern as she studied him, and he wondered what she saw in his face.

Hastily composing himself, he plastered on a professional smile (the one he used when talking to customers) and gestured to the open-plan stairs. It had once been an upper sales floor, but Silas had seen the potential for a studio, so he'd had skylights put in when he'd bought the property.

'After you,' he said. 'Mind the sign.'

The riser of the fourth step sported a sign saying *Private*. It generally worked, although once or twice he'd caught someone heading upstairs, having not spotted it.

Juliette hesitated, one foot on the first step, her

head swivelling from side to side as she glanced around the Gallery. 'I haven't been in here for ages,' she said. 'Have you painted all these yourself?'

'Yes.'

'When do you find the time? Do you ever sleep?'

He laughed. 'Early mornings, late evenings, in between customers. I don't sit down here twiddling my thumbs waiting for the next person to walk through the door and hoping they'll buy a painting or two.'

'Do you do prints? These all look original.' Juliette peered at the nearest watercolour.

'They *are* originals, hence the price.'

'Have you thought about doing prints? You could sell tea towels, and coasters, or T-shirts.'

Nell stifled a giggle and Silas glowered at her. She could tell what he thought of that idea.

'Not really.' The thought of one of his paintings being used to dry dishes horrified him. Selling prints as actual pictures in frames was another matter, and one he'd considered but hadn't got around to doing anything about yet. He'd look into it further if there came a point when he didn't sell enough original stuff to keep the wolf from the door. And when he had the time.

'The Oakman is in my studio,' he continued. 'Upstairs. Shall we?'

Juliette shrugged. 'He's missing an opportunity here,' he heard her say to Nell but Nell didn't reply.

He noticed the look she gave him though, and he thought she appreciated his reluctance to turn his art into a gimmick. The closest he'd come to that had been creating the artwork to advertise the Toy Shop. He'd enjoyed it, surprisingly; it had been different.

Silas had already taken the Oakman out of the packaging and had placed it on an easel at just the right angle to catch the light flooding in from the large picture window. It was illuminated perfectly, giving it even more depth than it already possessed. You could almost believe the sheepdog depicted in the foreground was real and was waiting for just the right moment to leap into action and round up the errant sheep.

'It's smaller than I thought,' was Juliette's first words.

'They say that about the Mona Lisa,' was his dry reply.

'I'm not sure I see what all the fuss is about,' she added, stepping forwards to examine it closer. 'I can see why Nell bought it – it's nice enough – but it can't be worth more than a few hundred pounds, surely?'

'It can and it is. Peter Oakman was a well-known and much revered artist, but he usually depicted moody Scottish scenes, especially the islands. He rarely ventured further afield, and it's believed he only left his beloved Scotland twice. Once was when he went to London in the early 1890s, and the other was when his wife forced him to visit Wales shortly before his death. From what I can gather, this is only one of two paintings he did which wasn't of Scotland. His paintings sell very well anyway, but because this one is so rare, it's worth more.'

Nell's eyes were wide. 'You didn't tell me any of this,' she said. 'All you said was that it was genuine and worth a small fortune.'

'Sorry, I should have done.' He'd been more interested in her than in the painting, to his shame.

'No, I should have asked, but I was so wrapped up in finding the original owner… Maybe I should give it to a museum, or something?'

'But what about the charity you mentioned?' Juliette said.

'I suppose they'd benefit more,' Nell said, worrying at her lip with her teeth.

Juliette took charge. 'I'd best hurry up and take some photos. Silas, you come and stand this side, Nell that side.'

As he got into position, feeling distinctly uncomfortable at having his photo taken, Nell came up to him, her hand reaching towards his face, and he flinched.

'Sorry, I was just…. you've got paint…' Nell snatched her fingers away and stepped back.

Silas could have kicked himself. The last thing he wanted to do was to make her feel uncomfortable or unwanted. 'Paint?'

She was standing on the other side of the painting, her attention on the floor. 'Here. She touched her cheek and Silas scrubbed furiously at the corresponding spot on his own face.

'Is it gone?'

Nell shot him the swiftest of glances. 'Yes.'

'Good.'

'Please look a bit happier,' Juliette pleaded. 'The pair of you look like you've lost a pound and found a penny.'

Silas forced his lips into a grin and hoped he didn't look as manic or deranged as he suspected he might.

Juliette snapped away from differing angles, then she told them to stand back so she could get a couple of shots of the painting on its own.

The bell downstairs sounded, and Silas had never been more pleased in his life to have a reason to leave his studio. The atmosphere between him and Nell was so intense, you could cut it with a knife and serve it with a cup of tea.

He was so acutely aware of her it was excruciating, and he didn't know whether he wanted to scoop her up and kiss her until she cried for mercy, or run for the hills and not look back.

'Do you need me for anything more?' he asked, 'because I need to see to a customer.'

'I think we're more or less done. I'll just get a shot of Nell and we'll get out of your hair.'

Relief coursing through him, Silas descended the stairs, taking them two at a time, and almost launched himself off the bottom one and onto the shop floor, startling the postman, who had just left a letter on the desk and was heading towards the door.

'Sorry, I thought you were a customer,' Silas said.

'Is business so bad that you have to throw yourself at them?' the postie joked, giving him a salute as he left.

Alone in the shop, Silas seized the opportunity to calm himself, taking deep breaths and filling his nose with the scent of oil-based paints and the mineral spirits he used to clean the brushes. It was a scent that had pervaded the Gallery since he'd began the painting of Nell and it was one he found comforting.

Nell had unsettled him badly just by her nearness, and what on earth had he been thinking when he'd recoiled from her? She'd hardly been about to jump on him, and had only tried to be nice. He'd reacted as though she was a leper.

'Way to go, Silas,' he muttered sourly, leaning on

the desk and shaking his head. At this rate she wouldn't want to be in the same room as him, and although he wasn't prepared to act on his growing feelings for her, he didn't want to drive her away completely.

The thought of life without her in it was awful.

But, and he had to be realistic about this, could they continue to be friends? Those passionate kisses would almost certainly come between them. Not seeing her again, except through the window of the Treasure Trove, was unthinkable, however.

Oh dear, this was worse than he'd thought. He was smitten and he hadn't properly realised it until today.

Blowing his cheeks out, he headed back upstairs to see what Nell and Juliette were up to, but before he'd put his foot on the first step, the door opened again and in strolled Hattie.

'About your apprentice,' she began.

'Can we do this another time?' he asked. 'I'm busy.'

Hattie looked beyond him and grinned. 'I can see that.'

Nell was coming down the stairs. She looked... different. He couldn't put his finger on why, though.

'It's not what you think,' he said to Hattie.

'Oh, it most certainly is. About time,' Hattie said, then her face fell as she saw Juliette following Nell down the stairs.

'Told you,' Silas said out of the corner of his mouth.

'Pity,' she hissed back. 'Hello, Nell, I didn't expect to see you here? Or you, Juliette?'

Hattie was almost bouncing with curiosity but Silas didn't enlighten her. If Nell wanted to say anything about the Oakman, that was up to her.

Nell and Juliette shared a look.

'You can if you want to,' Juliette said. 'I'm running the story this week, and a bit of advance interest wouldn't go amiss.'

Nell said, 'Why don't we leave Silas in peace? I'm sure he's got lots to do, and I should get back to the Treasure Trove. Hattie, you can come with me if you like, and I'll tell you all about it. Juliette, do you have time for a coffee at mine before you shoot off?'

'Tell me all about what?' Hattie asked. She kept looking at Nell, then at him, and back again, and Silas prayed she wouldn't say anything out of turn to Nell.

'Let's go,' Nell said firmly, grasping the old lady by the elbow and steering her towards the door, Juliette hot on her heels.

As she passed him, Juliette gave Silas a knowing smile.

What was all that about, he wondered.

'You haven't heard the last of me, Silas Long,'

Hattie warned, as she left. 'I'll be back to have a chat about a lovely young lad who'll make a perfect apprentice for you. He helped his mum paint her living room last week.'

Silas groaned. She wasn't going to give up, was she? It might be better for him to throw in the towel and just accept that he was going to be saddled with an apprentice whether he wanted one or not.

As he made his way upstairs to his studio, his thoughts turned from Hattie and her plan, towards Nell and the decidedly strange expression on her face. And what was up with Juliette?

As he walked into his studio, his heart sank.

He knew exactly what was up with the journalist and the reason for the strange expression on Nell's face, because his eyes went straight to the two oil paintings sitting side by side on their respective easels.

The covers hiding both of them were slightly askew, and he knew immediately that Nell had seen the painting he'd done of her, and the one of Molly.

His first reaction was dismay.

His second was relief.

Nell had sneaked a peek into his soul and he hadn't been struck down. Maybe it was time to share one of the paintings with someone else. Someone whom he knew would value it and treasure it.

Denise.

He'd keep the other. It might be the only part of Nell that would ever be his.

CHAPTER 29

NELL

It was safe to say Nell was in shock. The last thing she'd expected to see when Juliette had naughtily lifted up a dust sheet covering a painting was an image of herself.

'Have you got any biscuits?' Hattie asked as the three of them trotted down the street towards the Treasure Trove.

'Um, I expect I can rustle some up.'

'Hobnobs are my favourite for dunking, but Rich Tea will do.

Nell blinked. This was surreal – talking about dunking biscuits when the only thing on her mind was that painting. Why did Silas have two paintings covered up? One of a child, and one of her. Why her? And who was the girl? She looked to be no more than about three or four years old.

Even with her limited experience of Silas's artistic style, Nell could tell he'd painted both of them, even if he had used a different medium – oil rather than watercolour – and the subject matter wasn't his usual landscape scenes.

The painting of her was melancholic and sad; moving, even. She remembered being on the bridge recently – it was the day the boys told her they were travelling the world for a year.

Both paintings were full of raw emotion and even from the brief glimpse she'd had of them, the one that evoked the greatest emotion in her hadn't been the one of herself, it had been the one of the little girl.

Nell opened the shop and left Juliette and Hattie to wander while she went to make the tea and hunt around for some biscuits, finding an unopened packet at the back of the cupboard.

She turned it over in her hands, thinking that if her boys were at home they'd demolish the lot in a few minutes. But they weren't – they were in Croatia, or goodness knows where, and she missed them so much she thought her heart might break. Covering her longing to smother their faces in kisses (they'd hate that) and hug them tight (more acceptable), she made three hot drinks and took them onto the shop floor.

Juliette was prowling around, picking things up

and examining them, stroking the top of a table, running her fingers through the tassels on an old lampshade. Hattie, on the other hand, had plonked herself down on an ornate cream-velvet chair, with gold-painted filigree, and was tapping her fingers impatiently on its padded arms.

'Meh, Jammy Dodgers. Not so keen. The jam sticks in my teeth. I've got all my own, you know.' Hattie snatched the packet out of Nell's hands and took several biscuits, despite her protestations that she wasn't too keen. 'Now, are you going to keep me dangling, or are you going to tell me what you've been up to?'

'Juliette, can you do the honours?' Nell said. 'You can tell a story so much better than I.'

Juliette smirked and Nell was sorely tempted to throw the remainder of the packet of Jammy Dodgers at her. Nell shook her head and gave her friend a warning look.

'It all started when Nell bought a painting from a house clearance place,' she began.

Nell tuned out. She was more interested in another painting – the one Silas had done of her. Why had he painted it?

That was the same question she asked Juliette as soon as Hattie left for her shift at Bookylicious.

'Because he likes you. A lot,' was Juliette's reply.

'He might just have thought I was an interesting subject. He's not exactly caught my best side, has he?'

'He's painted your behind.'

Nell blushed furiously, remembering a certain conversation she'd had with Silas regarding her bum. 'As I said, I don't think that's my best side. He could have painted my face.'

'Maybe he thinks your butt is sexy.'

'There's no way you could call that painting sexy,' Nell protested. 'I look like I've got the weight of the world on my shoulders.'

'Hilarity aside, and I'm sorry for teasing you…' Juliette didn't look sorry at all. 'Perhaps that's what made you a good subject for a painting. It's very pensive, sad almost.'

'I'm not surprised. That was the day Adam and Ethan told me they were off backpacking for a year. I was utterly miserable.'

'I could tell. He captured your mood perfectly. He's rather a good artist, isn't he? I thought his landscapes were stunning but his paintings of people are particularly good. Maybe he's planning on branching out?'

'I hope he's not branching with my picture. I could do without having it sitting in the Gallery's window for all to see.'

'He might put the other one in, the one with the

child. I wonder who she is? It must be someone he knows.'

'I've no idea. I don't think he's got any children. He's not mentioned any to me, and I've prattled on about the twins often enough that I'm sure he'd want to talk about his, if he had any.'

'A niece or a nephew, maybe? When he puts it on display, I'll ask him. I still think he painted you because he likes you.'

'Yeah, he likes to paint me looking miserable,' Nell said sourly. 'I've told you before, he doesn't like me, not in that way.' She sighed. 'Listen to the pair of us – we sound like school girls in the playground talking about which boys we think likes us.'

'You don't just *like* him though, do you? You feel much more for him than that. And I believe he feels more for you, too.'

'How do you know?' Nell's reply was terse.

'Because it was the same with me and Oliver.'

'No, it wasn't – it was completely different. Neither of you had anything holding you back, apart from your unfounded belief he was only with you because of the biography he was writing at the time and you thought he was trying to dig up the dirt on you and Otis Coles. He's not bad as Prime Minister, is he?' Otis Coles hadn't long been elected and he was doing a good job so far. She'd yet to read the

267

biography Oliver had written on him, although she'd purchased a copy and it was sitting on her bedside table.

'If you think I'm discussing politics with you, you can think again,' Juliette said.

'But you've got to admit, once all that nonsense with Otis Coles was sorted out and you realised Oliver was with you because he loved you, there was nothing preventing you and him from getting together.'

'As far as I can see, there's nothing preventing you and Silas from getting together, either. You love him. Go on, admit it. And I don't think he painted you just because you were peering over a bridge and looking like you wanted to throw yourself off it.'

'Can we not talk about this anymore? Don't you have some negatives to develop, or a typewriter to annoy?'

Juliette chortled. 'It's all digital now. Just because you live in the past, doesn't mean the rest of us do.' She paused. 'Stop trying to change the subject! He's kissed you twice, hasn't he? Of course, he fancies you. And all that help he's given you…'

'He's still in love with his wife – that's what's going on.'

'I don't believe it – there's something else afoot. What do you think it could be?'

'Juliette…' Nell's reply was firm. 'If there is, and Silas wants to tell me, he will. If not, then I'll respect his privacy.'

Nell meant what she'd said, she would respect his privacy, but that didn't prevent her from being curious, and she knew deep in her heart that whatever it was that Silas was hiding, it had something to do with the painting of the little girl. She could understand why he'd covered over the painting he'd done of herself – she couldn't imagine how embarrassed he'd be if she'd walked into his studio earlier and had seen it there – but why did he feel the need to cover up the lovely painting of a young girl?

And why did he feel the need to cover up the painting of her?

CHAPTER 30

SILAS

'Hattie.' Silas said the old lady's name with a sigh.

'I told you I'd be back.' She bustled into the Gallery where Silas was debating whether to wrap up the painting of Molly to send to Denise. He'd be sad to see it go – it was one of his best pieces, but he could always paint another. Molly's beautiful face was seared on his heart and his soul, and even though it wasn't visible in this painting because her head was bent over the present she was opening, he didn't need a physical reminder. And if he felt the need to paint her again, he would.

Hattie spotted it before he could take it off the counter and hide it on the floor behind the desk. 'What's that? I didn't think you did people. Do you do cats?'

'Eh?'

'My cat is getting on a bit and I'd like a picture of him, before he pops his clogs.'

'Take a photo.'

'It's not the same thing. Do you do commissions?'

'No.'

'Who's that, then?'

'Never you mind.' He hastily put it on the floor and propped it against the desk.

Hattie stared into the distance. 'Now, what did I come in here for? Oh, yes, I remember! Apprentices. You need one.'

'I don't. I haven't got time to train anyone, and neither do I have the inclination.' He wished she'd give it a rest; she was starting to get on his nerves.

'Balderdash. You don't need to train anyone to watch the shop floor for you. The number of times I've walked past and thought you were closed because I didn't see anyone in here – not even you!'

'I don't need to be sitting at my desk all day, every day – I can hear people come in and I can see them, too. He pointed to a camera at the back of the shop which was angled to view the whole room.

'It only takes a second for someone to run in and grab the money out of the till.'

'I don't have a till.'

'What do you have?'

'A card machine, and some notes in my pocket.'

'That's hardly professional, is it? Scrabbling around in your pockets for some loose change?'

'I don't need loose change. If you notice, every painting is priced at a nice round number, no ninety-nine pences to worry about. And I've always got enough notes in my wallet to give change to anyone who needs it. Besides, at these prices most people pay by card.'

'I suppose you keep the card machine in your pocket, too?'

Silas raised his eyebrows. 'Now you're being facetious.'

'It's better than being a moody sod.'

'You think I'm moody?'

'Don't you?'

'I prefer introspective.'

'Grumpy, I'd say.'

'Calling me names doesn't improve your chances of me taking on an apprentice,' Silas pointed out. 'Anyway, why are you so invested in this?'

Hattie leant her elbow on the desk. 'It's like this, see… Alfred would never have managed without Zoe and where would Zoe be without Alfred? Do you know how fast the old skills are dying out?'

'Painting pictures is hardly an old skill. They still teach art in schools, I believe. Universities, too.'

'Art business, history of art, graphic design –

they're all well and good in their place, but who teaches people to paint? Artists, not lecturers.'

Silas was about to argue with her, then thought better of it. If there was one thing he'd learnt about Hattie was that she always won. She always got her own way too, and he could feel himself wavering. Solitude was what he preferred, but having an assistant in the shop would allow him to have more time to do what he loved.

'He wouldn't be learning to paint, Hattie,' Silas said, his conscience pricking him. 'All he'd be learning to do is to watch the shop and shout upstairs for me if I'm needed.'

'Couldn't you give him something useful to do?'

'He can't paint – not down here – and having him upstairs with me would kind of defeat the object. Besides, I need my own space when I'm working.'

'He could pack things up for you. He could clean, he could… I don't know – do whatever you do when you're down here.'

'You're grasping at straws,' Silas teased, his tone gentle. She might be a force to be reckoned with, but Hattie's heart was in the right place. 'Besides, I don't think helping to paint your mum's living room is the sort of experience needed to paint pictures.'

'All I was saying is, that the kid isn't work shy. He'll have a go at anything. I know painting walls isn't the same as painting landscapes. I'm old, not stupid,' she huffed.

Dismayed that he'd caused her offence, Silas came out from behind his desk and put his arm around her, giving her a squeeze. 'You're far from stupid, and you're not that old either,' he added, gallantly.

'Oh, you! I'm eighty, you know. And I've got all my own teeth, as I was telling that young lady of yours.'

'Young la——? You mean Nell?'

'Unless you've been messing around with Juliette? And if you have, I'm sure Oliver would have something to say about it. He was as bad as you, you know – the pair of them danced around each other like a pair of flighty cats, scared of committing. She had a secret and so did he, and it took a bit of wrangling before they finally sorted themselves out. You and Nell need to do the same. Although I think her secret is well and truly out of the bag – Juliette told me all about the Oakman painting. Can I see it?'

Silas showed Hattie upstairs, and this time he vowed not to leave her alone.

'It's smaller than I thought,' Hattie said, frowning at the Oakman, her face crinkling into folds and wrinkles.

'That's what Juliette said.'

'I like it though. It's different to the ones you do,

but just as nice.'

'Thank you.' His work had never been compared to an Oakman before and he doubted it would be again. He'd take the compliment and be grateful.

Once she'd had her fill of looking at the painting, Hattie glanced around his studio. 'This is bigger than I thought,' she said, her eyes darting everywhere; they briefly came to rest on the safely-covered painting of Nell but just as quickly moved on again.

Silas tried not to let his relief show. 'It was originally two smaller rooms but I had it knocked through and put a couple of skylights in.'

'I think I'd like to paint up here,' she said.

'I didn't know you painted?'

'I don't.'

'Ah.' Silas smiled to himself. She was quite a character.

'You can see your shop,' she said, squinting at a computer screen sitting on an old table.

'Which is why I don't need an apprentice. I've got nothing to teach him, he won't be able to do a lot to help, and he'd be bored out of his mind.'

'His name is Max and he's sixteen and three-quarters. You'll like him.'

'I'm sure I would, if I met him.'

'I'll bring him in tomorrow, shall I? You can meet him then.'

'No, Hattie.'

'Please, just give the kid a chance. That's all he wants. He can put on his CV that he was employed by you, which will stand him in good stead when he applies for jobs. Just sticking work experience on your resume is a waste of time.'

'You care about this a lot, don't you?'

Hattie grunted. 'I wouldn't be here bothering you if I didn't. Life's too short to waste it on things that don't mean anything, and at my age, it's getting shorter too damned fast. Give the kid a chance, would you? You've had your chances, it's someone else's turn.'

Silas couldn't make head nor tail of her convoluted logic, but she was right about a paying job on a CV being better than work experience.

'If I say yes, how will it work?' he asked her and by the way she yelled 'Yes!' and fist-pumped the air, followed by a little jig, he guessed there was no "if" about it.

Silas was getting himself an assistant.

CHAPTER 31

NELL

Nell had fully expected Hattie to be part of the apprentice interview process but, just as she would have done if she was going for an interview for a proper job, Tanesha came alone.

The girl was slight, dark-haired and pretty. She was also nervous and trying not to show it, holding out a hand for Nell to shake as she introduced herself. Nell took it, seeing beyond the outward confidence. Despite Tanesha's direct gaze, her cheeks were flushed, her voice wobbled and she held herself rigidly. Nell immediately took pity on her, imagining this to be the girl's first interview for anything, and picturing one of her boys in her place.

It was early, only nine-thirty and the Treasure Trove didn't open for another half an hour, so Nell took her through to the office and filled the kettle.

'I don't know about you, but I'm gasping for a cup of tea. Would you like one? Or would you prefer coffee?'

Um… can I have a glass of water, please?'

Tanesha licked her lips and Nell poured her a glass and placed it on the desk. Tanesha lifted it with both hands and took a sip. She looked even more terrified, if that was possible.

'OK, tell me a bit about yourself,' Nell asked, and the girl launched into what sounded like a prepared speech. But at least she was looking more comfortable and Nell guessed she must have had some coaching.

As Tanesha spoke, Nell studied her. She was presentable and had dressed appropriately in black trousers and a white shirt, which Nell briefly wondered had once been part of her school uniform. She was fluent, spoke nicely, and Nell had a sudden vision of her in the shop, dealing with a customer.

When Tanesha paused for breath, Nell said, 'I don't need to hear any more. You've got the job.'

'*Really?*'

'Yes.' Nell smiled widely at her.

'That's brilliant! Thank you, Ms Chapman.'

'You'd better call me Nell. When are you able to start?'

'Now? Today? If I can, and you don't mind.'

Nell laughed at the girl's enthusiasm. 'You can, and I don't mind. But are you sure? It's a bit short notice for you.'

'Can I just call my Mum? She'll be well pleased.'

'Of course you can. Would you like that cup of tea now?'

'Yes please, Ms Cha— Nell.'

'Good. There are a couple of mugs in the cupboard.' Nell pointed. 'And you'll find tea bags, coffee and sugar in there, too. Milk is in the mini-fridge. Just milk and no sugar for me, please. And while you do that and phone your mum, I'm going to open up.'

Nell hoped she wasn't being too harsh in expecting the girl to make the tea, but she wanted to start her with the most basic of tasks and work up from there. It would be strange to have someone who wasn't one of the twins working alongside her, but Nell was sure she'd soon get used to it.

She hoped the boys wouldn't be put out, but then again they couldn't expect everything to remain the same forever. And she could certainly do with the help. It would be a relief to be able to catch up on paperwork during the day and know the shop was being supervised, instead of having to beaver away in the evenings.

Nell grimaced as an unwelcome thought leapt into

her head; what was she going to do with the additional free time? Ugh – the flat was empty enough as it was, and recently she'd felt lonely, especially since everyone else seemed to be so loved up. Even Hattie, at her advanced years, had found love, and Juliette was now with Oliver.

As if her thinking about love had conjured him up, Silas walked through the door.

'Hi,' he said, and Nell thought he seemed shy.

'Hi. I'm just about to have some tea. Would you like a cup?'

'Er, no thanks. I just popped in to say I've made an appointment to take the painting to London on Sunday. Carlfort's are expecting us at noon. Is that all right?'

His attention was captured by something behind her, and Nell glanced over her shoulder and grinned.

'Silas, meet Tanesha, my assistant. Today is her first day.' She took a mug from the girl's hand and said to her. 'This is Silas Long. He owns the Gallery up the road, and he's popped in to tell me that he's arranged for me to go to an auction house in London. I've got this painting I want to sell...'

Silas chuckled. 'If Tanesha is going to be working here, I think it's only fair to tell her the whole story. Nell bought a painting, and she wasn't sure who it was by. I saw it and spoke to a friend of mine who works in the Tate Gallery in London... By the way, Carlfort's have agreed with Vaughan's valuation in theory, but they won't definitely commit until they've had a chance to examine it themselves. Anyway, my friend told me it was painted by a man called Peter Oakman, who is a famous artist, and it's worth a fair bit. Right, I'd best be off. The Gallery won't open itself.'

'What you need is an assistant,' Nell teased as he turned to leave.

'Guess what? I've got one. I hope. There's a young man popping in to see me later today.'

'Couldn't resist Hattie, could you?'

'Nope,' Silas said cheerfully. 'I don't know why I even bothered trying. '

'I think it's worthwhile,' she said in a lowered voice as she accompanied him to the door. 'And now that I've got some money coming in from the sale of the painting, I'm planning on paying Tanesha more than the apprenticeship rate. It'll be a proper job, so she should be paid a proper wage.'

'If I remember rightly, isn't that what Hattie said about Zoe when she was taken on to help in the Toy Shop? It's a good idea – I'll do the same. I just hope I get on with the lad. I haven't had much to do with kids.' A flash of an emotion Nell thought might be pain appeared fleetingly on his face, but was gone before she could pin it down.

'Just treat him like you would me,' she suggested, and there was another surge of emotion in Silas's expression, but this time she thought she knew what it was – embarrassment? Or maybe dismay? 'So, noon on Sunday, eh? Good. I'll be there. So will you. If you still want to come with me, that is.' Nell knew she was babbling, but it was all she was capable of right now.

'If you still want me?'

'Oh, I do,' she breathed, then realised it sounded way more suggestive than she'd meant it to, and she felt her stomach drop. Why was it that whenever she was in Silas's company she began to sound like a 1970s comedy show – all waggling eyebrows and innuendo.

Dear me…

'I'll drive, shall I?' he offered. 'Pick you up at eight? That should give us plenty of time.'

'Great, see you then. Good luck with your apprentice.'

'Good luck with yours,' he said, smiling over her shoulder. 'I don't think you'll need it, though.'

He jerked his head and Nell turned around to see Tanesha carefully dusting.

Nell was delighted. The never-ending dusting was one of her pet hates and it should be done most days. No one wanted to buy anything from a dirty shop, and she did her best to make her stock and the shop look as appealing as possible.

She waved Silas off, then spent a minute drinking her tea and watching her new assistant as she gently picked items up, dusted underneath, then just as gently replaced them.

Nell had a feeling they were going to get along just fine.

'Is that painting you were on about in here?' Tanesha asked, scanning the walls. 'I only wondered because I'd be frightened to touch it.'

'Dusting is fine, as long as you don't use polish. You can use beeswax on some of the furniture but not all of it, and paintings should never ever have anything sprayed on them.'

'Phew. I'm glad you told me that – I was looking for the tin of polish but I couldn't find any.'

'That's because I don't have any.' Nell smiled to show she wasn't displeased by Tanesha's initiative. 'As for the painting, Silas is keeping it in the Gallery for me.' Nell didn't explain why. The poor child was here to work and to gain some valuable experience, and Nell didn't think she needed to hear about Nell's sordid ex-husband – although Tanesha would undoubtedly gain some life experience from the tale!

'Can I see it?'

'I don't see why not. How about tomorrow? I

close the shop for an hour for lunch, so I'll take you to see it then. Don't feel obliged though – your lunch hour is yours to do with as you please. Oh, and the Tattler will be running a piece on it, so it should be in the paper in a few days. I doubt there'll be much interest, though.'

Tanesha beamed. 'I think I'm going to like working here.'

Nell sincerely hoped so.

She hoped Silas would get on with his apprentice, too – then she was cross with herself for thinking about him. That man seemed to spend far too much time in her head than was good for her.

The problem was, he wasn't just in her head. He was in her heart too, and she had a horrid feeling he was there to stay.

CHAPTER 32

SILAS

For some reason, one he couldn't put his finger on, Max reminded Silas of himself when he'd been the same age. It might have had something to do with his gawkiness or his eagerness to dive straight in, but whatever it was, Silas took to the boy immediately.

'Hattie said you'd teach me to paint,' had been the first words out of Max's mouth that morning.

'Do you enjoy painting?' Silas asked.

It was the boy's first day. The pair of them had only met yesterday, Max had started working at the Gallery today, and he was already wanting to run before he could walk.

Max nodded. 'I guess. Don't think I'm any good at it though.' He strolled up to a painting of a wild and windswept coastal scene and peered at it. '*How much?*' The lad turned incredulous eyes to Silas. 'Did you paint this?'

Silas's reply was mild. 'I painted everything in here. Including the walls.'

'Er, they're white.'

'White is a colour, too. And it's the best one to showcase my art.'

'I like comics.'

'Like the Beano?' Silas was bemused. Max appeared to have the attention span of a goldfish.

'I don't know what that is.'

'It's a comic. I used to read it when I was a kid. I wonder if you can still get it?'

'I like manga.'

'To read or draw?' Silas knew manga was a type of graphic novel and the artwork was quite stylised.

'Both.'

'You'll have to show me.'

'OK.'

'But not today, eh?'

'That's good, because I don't draw on demand.'

'Neither do I,' Silas told him. Max stared at him curiously, so Silas added, 'I might run a business, but that doesn't mean I can churn paintings out by the dozen. It's got to get me here.' Silas thumped his chest.

'No offence, but they're a bit...' Max searched for the right word.

'Old-fashioned?' Silas supplied.

'Yeah.'

'I take it you're not a fan of watercolour landscapes?'

'Nah.'

'Is this just a job to you? You've not got a burning desire to be an artist?'

'Dunno.'

Silas could tell Max felt uncomfortable; the boy was trying to be honest with him, but he clearly didn't want to offend his new employer.

'Are you here because you feel you have to be?' Silas asked.

Max shrugged, and Silas wondered if there wasn't anything else out there which would suit the lad's needs better.

'I take it you don't want me to teach you to paint?' Silas persevered.

Another shrug. In a way, Silas was relieved. He wasn't a teacher. He did what he did, but he wasn't entirely sure how he did it. It was instinctive and he wasn't convinced he could pass that on to someone else. He could impart some technical details, but that was about it.

'How about I concentrate on the painting side of things, and you concentrate on the business side? Will that work for you?' he asked the boy.

'Sound.' Max looked slightly more cheerful.

'Right, let me show you around,' Silas said, and for the next hour or so he instructed him on various practices such as stock rotation (moving paintings around, so the Gallery always looked fresh), the importance of lighting, and how Silas marketed his work.

'It doesn't matter what you're trying to sell,' Silas said in conclusion. 'The principles are the same. Come on, I'll show you the studio. Down here is for selling, up there is for painting.'

To his surprise, Silas was quite enjoying himself despite Max's lukewarm attitude to his art. He didn't mind – appreciation of art was often subjective and depended very much on one's own personal taste. For Silas, a painting, sculpture, or any other piece of art, had to speak to him. He might appreciate the skill, or the technique, or the subject matter, and he might even appreciate its importance or value to the art world as a whole, but he didn't always like what he saw.

'Ideally, I'd like you down there, keeping an eye on the shop floor and doing the selling, leaving me free to concentrate on my painting,' Silas told him, as the lad prowled around the studio, taking in the array of pots and brushes, watercolour paper stretched on boards in preparation for being painted on, and paintings waiting to be framed.

'Did you do this one?' Max asked, pausing in front of the Oakman.

'Why do you ask?'

'I dunno. It looks different to the ones downstairs. Older.'

'Is that all?'

Max studied it. 'It's not a watercolour?'

'No, it's painted using oils.'

'We used acrylics in school most of the time, and sometimes watercolour paint, but we weren't allowed to use oils.'

'Probably because it takes too long to dry. I didn't paint with oils in school, either. Anything else?' Silas could have simply told the lad, but telling was nowhere near as effective as getting the boy to figure it out for himself.

'It's not your style?'

'The subject matter is similar,' Silas pointed out. 'The natural world.'

'Yes, but it doesn't look like one of yours,' Max insisted.

'That's because it isn't. It was painted at the end of the nineteenth century by a man called Peter Oakman, and it's rather valuable.'

'More than the ones downstairs?'

'Much, much more. Hundreds of thousands of

pounds more.'

'Sh— Wow!

Silas went on to tell him the story of the painting, adding, 'There will be an article about it in the paper soon.' When the Tattler runs it, Silas decided he'd send a copy of the newspaper to Denise – she'd be thrilled. They might have drifted apart since Molly died, but his ex-wife had always been his staunchest supporter, despite the resentment she'd felt at the hours he'd spent pursuing his art.

'It'll be going to auction soon,' he explained, 'where it will hopefully sell for a lot of money.'

Max gave it another long, close look. 'I never would have guessed.'

'Neither did Nell,' Silas joked, as Max moved away.

Before Silas could ask him not to, the boy tweaked aside the dust sheet covering the painting of Nell.

'You deffo painted this one,' Max said, without hesitation. 'I like it.' He sounded surprised. 'She looks sad.'

'She was.'

'Who is she?

'The woman I love.' Silas grimaced as the words slipped out of his mouth. Now that he'd said it out loud he was terrified to acknowledge the truth. He'd had his heart broken so badly it was still in shattered bits; he couldn't afford to have it broken any further.

'Who's this? Your kid?'

Silas briefly closed his eyes. 'Yes.' He forced the reply out through suddenly wooden lips and a clenched jaw.

'Cool.'

'She died.' Silas reeled back in shock. Sharing such an intimate detail hadn't been his intention.

'Aw, man. That's a bummer.'

You can say that again, Silas thought.

'I like this one, too.' Max was still staring at it. 'You painted them both with oils. Is the woman your wife?'

'No.'

'Is she the girl's mother?'

'No.'

'Why not in watercolour?'

Relieved that the boy wasn't offering pity or sympathy, Silas said. 'It seemed fitting.'

'Are you going to be doing more pictures of people? I think you should. No offence, but they're better than the scenery ones.'

'None taken,' Silas said dryly.

Max shot him a quick glance, and Silas smiled at him to show he genuinely wasn't offended. He, himself, had to admit these two oils were probably his best work to date. It was a pity he had no intention of selling either of them. He'd keep the one of Nell – no one else would want it – but he had yet to pack up the painting of Molly. Unable to let go of it just yet, he'd brought it back up to the studio. But now was as good a time as any.

'Grab that box there.' Silas pointed to a packing container. 'And that roll of glassine paper and the bubble wrap, and follow me. I'm going to show you how to prepare a painting for shipping.'

Reverently, Silas lifted Molly's painting off the easel and tucked it under his arm, then grabbed the dust sheet which had been used to cover it. He'd put it on the desk to cushion the canvas whilst it was being packaged.

'What did you call this?' Max asked, tearing a length of paper off the roll.

'Glassine paper. It's the best thing to wrap paintings in because it's water and grease resistant.' He watched Max carefully package it up, trying not to wince that someone other than himself was handling Molly's image.

'Do you want me to take it to the post office for you?' Max asked afterwards.

Silas lifted the box off the desk and propped it up against the wall. 'No, it's OK. I'll hand-deliver this one.'

It was about time he congratulated Denise in

person on her forthcoming nuptials. Besides, the painting was far too valuable to entrust to the post. He'd poured everything he had into this, and although he could paint another it wouldn't be the same. Similar perhaps, but not exactly like it because no two paintings were ever the same, which was one of the reasons artists had prints made of their work, and not solely to boost sales.

Ah, there was a thought... 'How are you with computers?'

Max gave him a withering look.

'Yes, of course, you probably played with an iPad before you took your first steps.' Silas remembered Molly being fascinated by the fast moving, colourful images on Denise's tablet. If she'd lived, his daughter would probably be running rings around him when it came to technology.

'Do you want a project?' he continued. 'I've been thinking of making prints out of my original artwork, but I don't know where to start. Can you find out everything I need to know, such as the process, who does it, what the prices are like, how long does it take, and so on, and report back to me? It'll help me out enormously.' And it would give the poor lad something to do. 'Before you do that though, I need you to pack the Oakman painting, and use double the amount of bubble wrap this time,' he said, only half-joking. 'Nell can't afford to have anything happen to it. As I said, we've got to take it to the auction house in London on Sunday.'

Silas popped upstairs to fetch it, being ultra-careful on the way back down. With Silas closely supervising – he could tell that Max was both chuffed to be given the responsibility of handling such a valuable painting and terrified – Max slowly and carefully prepared it for its journey to London. And whilst he did so, Silas's thoughts kept returning to Nell.

He was looking forward to getting her on her own, and not only because he loved being with her; he also needed to come up with an explanation of why he'd painted her which wouldn't reveal his feelings for her. Somehow he didn't think "I felt compelled to paint you" would be sufficient reason, despite it being the truth.

CHAPTER 33

NELL

Nell would have been perfectly happy to have taken Tanesha to view the Oakman yesterday, (she told herself it had nothing to do with wanting to see Silas again) but she'd thought it best to give the girl a chance to settle in a little at the Treasure Trove for a day first. Besides, she'd heard on the grapevine (aka, Hattie) that Silas had a new addition to the Gallery starting today, and she wanted to check the boy out – and tease Silas once more for caving in the face of Hattie's determination.

'Your lunch hour is yours to do with as you want,' she reminded Tanesha. 'Please don't feel obliged to come to the Gallery with me.'

In her head, Nell prayed Tanesha would want to view the painting today, otherwise she wouldn't have an excuse to pop in.

'I want to,' Tanesha said. 'My mum wants me to tell her all about it.' She suddenly looked contrite. 'It was OK to tell her about the painting, wasn't it?'

'Of course, it was. The whole village will know shortly, once it's splashed all over the Tattler.'

Nell felt quite apprehensive as she locked up for lunch. Although she was thrilled to have an excuse to see Silas again, the painting he did of her was playing on her mind. If he had been renowned for painting people, or even if he had the odd figure or two in his landscapes, she mightn't have thought so much of it. But he didn't, and what she was rapidly coming to think of as "her" painting wasn't a landscape with her in it – *she* was the subject matter.

Had he painted her because he had feelings for her, like Juliette said, or was there a far more plausible reason in that he was expanding his portfolio to include people, and he'd painted her solely because she'd been in the right place at the right time?

Nell opened the Gallery door and the buzzer sounded as soon as she stepped foot inside. There was no way anyone could creep up on Silas, but having her arrival announced quite so loudly was disconcerting, especially since he was behind his desk watching a teenage boy setting up a laptop. The boy in question was on his knees fiddling with a cable.

Both of them looked up when the door opened, and both of them wore the same delighted expression when they saw who'd come in.

Nell's heart skipped a beat when she realised Silas was pleased to see her.

I've brought Tanesha to see the Oakman,' Nell said. 'She wants to know what all the fuss is about. You must be Silas's apprentice,' she said to the lad. 'Hi, I'm Nell; I own the Treasure Trove down the road. And this is Tanesha, who is *my* apprentice. It seems everyone's got an apprentice these days.' She was rambling, but she couldn't seem to stop herself. No wonder the boy was giving her an odd look.

'You're the woman in the painting,' he said. 'The woman Silas lo—'

Silas jumped in. 'Nell, this is Max. Max say hello.' Silas was glaring at the boy.

'Er, yeah, sure. Hi, Nell, hi, Tanesha.' Max gave them a small wave, and a hesitant smile.

'Hiya, Max. I didn't know you'd started here.' Tanesha beamed at him.

'I take it you two know each other?' Silas asked.

Max grinned. 'We're in college together.'

The way the teenagers were eying each other up, Nell guessed they fancied each other, and she smiled. It was incredibly sweet.

'Sorry,' Silas said to her. 'I've already packed it up,

and I don't want to have to get it out again. Max, why don't you show Tanesha the photos I took of the Oakman? They're on the laptop.'

Max smiled shyly at Tanesha. 'Wanna come and see? It's a bit boring.'

'I bet it's not,' Tanesha said, following him as he took her over to the desk.

Nell noticed how the girl checked out Max and she nudged Silas and jerked her head to get his attention, and they shared a knowing look.

'How's he getting on?' she asked quietly.

'Difficult to tell yet as it's only his first day but he seems nice enough. How's yours?'

'She's a sweetie. Totally different to having the boys around the place. Girls are much more talkative.'

'I know.'

Something in his tone made her glance at him. He looked pained, as if he had toothache,

'Can I show Tanesha upstairs?' Max interrupted. 'The paintings down here are great, like, but the one you're working on is ace.'

'Go ahead.'

'What are you working on?' Nell wanted to know.

'Nothing special – the mountains above Hay-on-Wye – but I think Max is fascinated by the process rather than the finished article. You never know, I might make an artist out of him yet. I ought to let him

298

loose with a sheet of watercolour paper and some paint, and see what he can do.'

Nell hesitated, the silence stretching between them. 'I'm sorry if Juliette and I overstepped the mark, but we had a peep at what was under the dust sheets,' she admitted.

'Both of them?'

'Yes.' She might be genuinely contrite (after all it wasn't any of her business) but she was also consumed with curiosity.

'I see.'

'I didn't think painting people was your thing?'

'It isn't.'

'Yet you painted me?'

He stared over her shoulder and she hoped she hadn't offended him, but from the expression in his eyes, he appeared more concerned than offended.

'It's not going on show or anything. It was meant for my eyes only.' He looked a little guilty.

'I've never had my portrait painted before.'

'You don't mind?'

'No. The way you painted me is quite thought-provoking, I look sad, wistful I suppose.'

'It's not strictly a portrait,' he told her. 'A portrait concentrates on the face; yours can't really be seen. Would you *like* to have your portrait painted?'

Nell wasn't sure whether she would, and whether

Silas was offering to paint it for her or whether he was merely making conversation. 'I don't know…'

'Thank goodness for that! For a minute there, I thought I'd offered to paint you.'

Nell smiled. 'Would it be so bad?'

'Gosh! No! That's not what I meant. Oh, dear—'

'It's the bum thing all over again, isn't it?'

Silas winced. 'Please don't mention it. It wasn't my finest hour.'

Silence descended again for a few moments and Nell listened to the footsteps overhead as Max showed Tanesha around. 'Do you trust them up there on their own?' she asked.

'Surprisingly enough, I do. There isn't anything they could damage, and they seem like sensible kids.'

'Who is the girl in the painting?' Nell asked suddenly. She hadn't meant for the question to slip out, but now that it had…

She hadn't been prepared for the fleeting anguish on his face though, nor for the pain in his eyes; and when he opened his mouth Nell felt certain he was about to tell her something momentous, something that was the key to understanding him.

But just then Tanesha and Max clattered down the stairs, and the moment was gone.

'Another time,' was all he said, and she had to be content with that.

CHAPTER 34

NELL

Nell read the article in the Tattler for what must have been the fourth time that morning, and hoped Silas was pleased with it. She thought it was fab, and so did quite a few people who had already paid the Treasure Trove a visit today.

Ah, and here came Benny and Marge.

'Good morning,' Benny said. 'Good piece in the paper, isn't it?'

'Lovely photo of the pair of you,' Marge added, and Nell felt a slow blush spread across her cheeks.

She had been like this every time anyone mentioned her and Silas in the same sentence. Someone was bound to notice sooner or later, and Tanesha was already giving her strange looks.

'You make a lovely couple,' Marge continued, and

Tanesha sniggered.

Nell frowned at her. 'Haven't you got any work to do?' she said. 'How about you dust the window display?'

'I already have.'

'Polish the silver?'

'You told me not to – you said that patina is everything.'

'Go make us a brew, then,' Nell snapped.

Thankfully, even after just three days of working at the Treasure Trove, Tanesha understood Nell didn't mean to sound harsh. Nell also had the feeling Tanesha realised something else – that Nell had feelings for Silas. The girl hadn't mentioned anything, but it was the way she looked at her whenever his name came up. She wore an expression that was far too observant for her tender years. What did this teenager know about being in love, eh, Nell thought to herself – nothing, that's what.

If she was honest, Nell wasn't sure what she knew about being in love, either. What she felt for Silas was a far cry from what she'd felt for Riley, although to be fair, she could barely remember what it had felt like. She recalled how happy she'd been on their wedding day and how she'd been convinced it would last forever. It might have done if Riley hadn't slept with someone else. Those heady days of the first flush of love had long gone, but she'd assumed what remained had been deeper and more substantial.

Clearly not. On either side – otherwise he wouldn't have been able to do what he'd done, and she hadn't been heartbroken.

'Can we see it?' Benny and Marge were gazing at her avidly, in between shooting quick glances around the walls of the shop.

Nell told them what she'd told everyone else who'd asked. 'Sorry, it's been packed up ready to take to London for the auction.'

'That's a shame. We were looking forward to having a gander at it. Apart from houses, I don't think we've seen anything as expensive before,' Marge said.

'And you're not going to now, either,' Benny pointed out.

Tanesha returned with the mugs of tea just as Nell was showing the couple out. 'Fancy a flapjack? My mum makes them.'

'Ooh, go on then.' Nell took her mug and a flapjack and leant against the counter. 'I don't think I've ever been so busy,' she said, taking a bite. 'Mmm, this is lovely. Say thank you to your mum for me, won't you?'

'I will. She loves baking, so I expect I'll bring something in most days.'

'I knew I employed you for a reason,' Nell joked,

around a mouthful of sweet gooeyness. She cupped a hand underneath the treat, so as not to get any crumbs on the floor. 'I wish more people were here to buy and not just to look,' she said. 'Listen to me, I sound ungrateful, don't I? I'm not – I'm thrilled people want to pop in.'

'Why don't you put it on display until Sunday?' Tanesha asked, picking up her tea and taking a swallow.

Nell had considered it, but it was probably safer where it was. Having it on display when its worth was general knowledge might be asking for trouble.

'It's OK where it is,' she said. 'When I've finished my tea, I'm going to tackle my accounts, if you don't mind holding the fort? If anyone is a serious buyer, just shout and I'll be out straight away. I'll only be in my office.'

'Cool. Is there anything you'd like me to do, apart from keep an eye on the customers?'

'There's a box of oddments I picked up in a boot sale ages ago. I've been meaning to go through them, but I haven't had the time. You could sort them out if you like? Put any similar items together and check everything carefully for damage, but don't throw anything out, no matter what condition it's in, because even damaged things can be worth something; it depends on what it is, how old it is, how rare it is, what it's made of and who made it.'

'Blimey! There's a lot to learn, isn't there?'

Nell chuckled and went into the small stockroom to fetch the box. She thought it highly unlikely there'd be anything of any value in it, but one never knew – she hadn't realised the true value of the Oakman painting, had she?

She left Tanesha sifting through the contents of the box, secure in the knowledge that the girl could handle any Oakman queries and she was only a shout away for anything else, and Nell immersed herself in invoices, receipts, and her trusty spreadsheet, soon lost in the dubious delights of making sure her accounts were up-to-date.

She was abruptly brought out of the world of numbers and formulas by the sound of a familiar voice saying, 'No, don't interrupt her if she's busy. I'll swing by later.'

Goddammit, but she was certain that was Riley she'd just heard, and she shot out of her seat and rushed onto the shop floor just in time to see the door close and her ex-husband stride down the road.

'What did *he* want?' she demanded.

Another curious look from Tanesha. 'To see the painting. I told him the same as I told the others – the same as you've been telling them – that it's packed up ready to take to the auctioneer.'

'What exactly did he say?'

Tanesha tilted her head to the side. 'He asked where the painting was and if he could see it. I told him it was packed away, like I've said to the others. Then he said he hoped you'd got it insured, and I said I didn't know – is it?'

Nell nodded. 'It is. Go on.'

'He asked if you were keeping it upstairs in the flat, and I said Silas at the Gallery was storing it, and then he asked where you were, and I said you were in the office doing the accounts and who should I say wanted you, and he said he was your husband and he'd just got back from a business trip. And then he said not to interrupt you and he'll see you later.' Tanesha paused for breath. 'I didn't know you were married.'

'I'm not.'

'But he said—'

'He's my *ex*-husband, with the emphasis very much on the ex.'

'Oh.' Tanesha bit her lip. 'Have I said something wrong?'

Nell forced a smile. 'Of course not. I just didn't expect him to ask to see it, that's all.' Nell was kicking herself – she should have anticipated it. Although, to be fair, the Tattler only came out that morning and because the publication was local to Ticklemore and the surrounding areas, she hadn't expected Riley to find out about it so soon, if at all.

She wasn't overly concerned him knowing about the Oakman because, as Francis had told her, Riley had no claim on either her or her business, but she should have guessed once he did find out about it, he'd come sniffing around, hoping to get a share.

He didn't give up, did he? What was it going to take for him to get the message that he wasn't going to get his greedy mitts on the Treasure Trove or anything in it!

CHAPTER 35

SILAS

Silas stroked a finger down a length of packing tape on the box which contained the painting of Molly, and he smiled softly. Denise would love it, he was sure. He should have painted Molly ages ago, but he hadn't been ready. He was pleased with the one he'd done of her, all from memory. He'd painted his soul into it, mixing his love for his daughter, his grief that she had been taken too soon, and his sorrow for the life she hadn't lived and the life she should have had, into the very canvas.

It briefly crossed his mind to unpack it and take it back to the cottage, where he'd hang it on the wall. He had plenty of space – for an artist he displayed surprisingly little of his own work. But it was all packed up now. It would be silly to unpack it again.

Yes, but Denise would never know, he argued to himself. It wasn't as though she was expecting it. She had no idea he'd even painted it. So he could keep it, couldn't he?

For goodness' sake! If he felt that strongly about it, he should just keep it.

The problem was, he felt even more strongly that Denise should have it. And he told himself for the umpteenth time that he could always paint another.

But for some reason the urge to capture Molly on canvas had gone for now. He guessed it would probably return, and when it did he'd welcome it. Right now, though, it was time to let this painting go to its rightful owner – Molly's mother.

Picking it up, he took it outside and placed it reverently in the boot of his waiting car. He'd already put the back seats down (even though the painting wasn't very big) and he'd folded an old eiderdown which he'd found in the cottage not long after he'd bought the place, on the floor of the boot to act as a cushion. The painting rested on that.

Silas hesitated. Was he doing the right thing? After all, it was Friday evening and Denise may well be out. He hadn't even called to say he was on his way.

Oh, what the hell? Even if Denise wasn't in, she'd be back at some point. Besides, he still had a key. He'd never relinquished it.

Denise continued to live in the house they had all lived in as a family; when they had *been* a family. After they'd lost their daughter Silas hadn't been able to bear to remain there, but Denise hadn't been able to bear to leave.

Silas set the alarm and locked up the Gallery.

Maybe it would be better if Denise was out? He could let himself in, and leave the painting and his key. Denise would understand the symbolism; they would always have Molly's memory to bind them together, but he was acknowledging this new chapter in her life.

Was it time he wrote a new chapter of his own? Did he have the courage? More to the point, was he ready?

Silas patted his pockets. Drat – he'd forgotten his wallet.

With a deep sigh, he got out of the car and went through the whole process of unlocking the Gallery, disabling the alarm, finding his wallet, and securing the shop once more.

It was only after he'd listened to the reassuring long beep telling him the alarm was set, that he turned towards the car and noticed he hadn't closed the boot properly.

And it took him a second or two to understand what he was seeing.

The boot was empty.

The painting had gone.

With ice freezing his heart, Silas frantically lifted the eiderdown and peered underneath it, just in case.

It wasn't there. And neither was it in the footwell between the front and the rear seats, and the passenger seat was empty, too.

Molly's painting had vanished.

Silas peered up and down the street, hoping against hope he'd spot someone carrying a large, flat box, but the only people in sight were three teenage girls heading towards the Tavern, an elderly gent walking his dog, and Hattie.

Silas let out a noise that was half sob, half groan.

'No, no, no,' he muttered, running his hands through his hair, and scanning the street once more.

Whoever had taken it couldn't have gone far and he was tempted to leap into his car and chase after them. Unfortunately, he had a 50 per cent chance of heading off in the wrong direction.

Why would anyone want to steal a painting of Molly? It wasn't worth a lot, despite the composition being appealing. Hell, he hadn't even signed it.

'Is something wrong, my lovely?'

Silas was standing there with both hands interlaced on the top of his head frantically wondering what he should do, and he lowered his arms slowly to see

Hattie standing next to him.

'It's gone,' he muttered.

'What's gone?'

'The painting.'

'The painting? What do you mean, *it's gone*. Where has it gone?'

'Someone's stolen it.' His voice broke and he swallowed hard.

'Who? How? I mean, what—?'

'I don't know. It was in my car. I was taking it to Denise and—' He staggered back, the wall of the Gallery breaking his fall, the enormity of what had happened making him feel weak and unsteady.

Hattie said, 'You'd better sit down before you fall down.'

Silas's legs felt wobbly and, with Hattie's firm grasp on his upper arm, he slowly lowered himself until he was sitting on the pavement. He put his head in his hands.

'Who is Denise and why were you taking the painting to her?' Hattie asked.

'She's my ex-wife.'

'I still don't understand why you were taking the painting to her? Does Nell know? Have you called the police?'

Numbly he shook his head.

'Then I will.' Hattie took her phone out of her

pocket and poked at it with her index finger. 'Police, please. Yes, I'd like to report a theft.' She paused as the operator spoke.

Silas swallowed again, his mouth dry. He closed his eyes and felt like sobbing, knowing he should pull himself together, but unable to for the moment. It was only a painting, and a relatively worthless one at that. It wasn't as though anyone had died.

But to him, it felt like he was losing a part of his daughter, and he'd lost enough already.

'*I* think it's an emergency,' Hattie was saying. 'Have you seen this week's Ticklemore Tattler?' Hattie narrowed her eyes. 'You haven't? Well, you should, then you'd know what I was talking about.' She shifted the phone from one ear to the other. 'A painting. What? Just now. A few minutes ago. It's worth a fortune, so you'd better send someone pronto. Set up roadblocks or something.'

Silas was only listening with half an ear to Hattie's side of the disjointed conversation, when he abruptly realised something.

He tugged at the hem of her lightweight jacket. 'Hattie, it's not—'

'Shh! Can't you see I'm on the phone?'

'But it's not the Oakman. They didn't take the Oakman.'

'What?'

'Do you think it's the Oakman that's been stolen?' he persisted.

'You said it was! Where is it then?'

'It's in the Gallery, and I didn't say it was the Oakman.'

'Excuse me a second, love,' Hattie said into the phone. 'You might want to hang fire on the roadblocks. Silas,' she glared at him. 'You *did* say it was the Oakman.'

'I said…' He hesitated, trying to remember.

'You told me the painting had gone and someone had stolen it.'

'I wasn't referring to the Oakman. It's another painting.'

Hattie huffed. 'Scratch that,' she told the operator. 'It's not an emergency. But a theft has occurred, so you'd better send someone. This evening, preferably. Right. Yes. Of course. Thank you.' Hattie hung up. 'Come on, let's get you inside, and you can tell me what's got you so worked up.'

Silas clambered stiffly to his feet. With clumsy fingers, he unlocked the door yet again and stumbled inside to disable the alarm.

'OK, young man, you need to tell me what's going on.' Hattie's hands were on her hips and her mouth was set in a straight line.

Silas took a steadying breath and blew it out slowly

before he replied. 'I was on my way to give a painting to my ex-wife when someone stole it from the boot of my car.'

'Are you sure it's not the valuable one?'

'Definitely not. It's not worth much at all.'

'It is to you,' Hattie observed, shrewdly.

'Yes, it is.' He raised his eyes to the ceiling and blinked hard.

'Did it belong to you?'

He nodded.

'Did you paint it?'

Another nod.

'Silas, my lovely boy, you're going to have to help me out a bit here, because I can't for the life of me see what you're so upset about. If it isn't worth much, you haven't sold it, and you painted it originally, can't you paint another one? Or am I missing something?'

'Denise, my ex-wife, is getting married again.'

'Okaay... And you are upset, is that it?'

'Not at all. I'm pleased for her. And envious.'

'Because you want to get married?' Hattie had a gleam in her eye.

Silas walked heavily around the desk and fell into his chair. He waved an arm to indicate that Hattie should sit down.

Hattie sat. She shuffled around in the seat to make herself comfortable. 'Well? Do you?'

'I'm envious because she's moved on with her life,' he admitted.

'And you haven't?'

'No.'

'Do you still love her?'

'Not in that way.'

'What's the problem? And I still don't get why you're all het up about this painting.'

'It's of my daughter.'

'I didn't know you have a daughter.'

'I did, but I don't any more. She died when she was three.'

'Oh, my poor boy.' Hattie was on her feet in an instant and had thrown her arms around him and pulled him into her bosom before he had a chance to protest.

He thought about pulling away, but he hadn't been held like this in such a long time...

Hattie stroked his head, and he could feel the tears gathering in his eyes, the tiny prickling threatening an imminent release.

'There, there, let it all out,' Hattie crooned and suddenly Silas was unable to hold back any longer. He cried, deep heaving sobs; he cried until he could cry no more, and his breathing became jerky.

'Have a hankie,' Hattie said, as he sniffed loudly, and she pressed a white cotton square into his hand.

After blowing his nose noisily, Silas used the crook of his elbow to dry his face. 'Sorry, I don't know what came over me.'

'I do. Grief, that's what it was, and there's no need to be sorry. Shall I make us a nice cup of tea?'

'Yes, please.' He didn't want tea, but in making it Hattie would feel as though she was doing something useful. 'Through there.' He pointed to a door leading to a loo, a small kitchen, and another room which he could have used as an office, but which was mostly empty except for a mop and a bucket.

'I've been thinking,' Hattie said, when she returned after a few minutes, carrying two mugs. 'Oh, by the way, you don't have any biscuits.'

'No, I don't.'

'Everyone needs a biscuit in their cupboard. Tea is too wet without one.' She sighed, then slurped her drink noisily. 'What was I saying? Oh, yes, I've been thinking…do you believe you don't have any right to be happy again? Is that it?'

'Excuse me.' Silas left his tea untouched. What he really wanted was a large whisky.

'Because your daughter died, do you have the notion that you don't deserve to be happy ever again? It's quite common to feel that way. When my Ted died—'

'Sorry, but you can't compare your husband dying

to the death of my daughter. She was a child, for goodness' sake!'

'I'm not comparing,' Hattie replied calmly. 'Grief and mourning isn't a competition. We all deal with it in our own way. If you'd let me finish, I was going to say that I felt the same way after Ted died. That life wasn't worth living, and that I'd never be happy again. I felt guilty for surviving him, see? And I expect you do, too. I bet you also feel responsible. How did she die?'

'Cancer.'

'Ah, that explains why Nell is giving half the proceeds from the sale of the painting to those cancer charities. Breast and kiddies, it said in the paper.'

'Nell doesn't know about Molly. No one in Ticklemore does.' Apart from Max.

'Why ever not?'

Silas shrugged. 'Didn't want sympathy. Didn't want people talking about me behind my back. Didn't want to have to explain.'

'Didn't want to move on with your life?'

'That, too.' Silas was forced to admit the truth of it.

'It's OK to love again,' Hattie said. 'In fact, it's your duty. Don't let your poor Molly's death blight the years you have left. You can spend the rest of your life mourning her – and you will – but you don't have to spend the rest of your life *in* mourning. There's a difference. Life is too bloody short as it is. Don't get to my age and realise you've wasted most of it grieving over what you can't change. Especially now you have Nell.'

'I don't have Nell.'

'You do.' Hattie's reply was firm and unwavering. 'You've got to tell her, though, whichever way you decide to jump. She needs to know the reason why you're throwing her love back in her face.'

'Nell doesn't love me.'

'Good grief! If I've said it once, I've said it a hundred times – you youngsters need a kick up the backside when it comes to matters of the heart.'

'You had some trouble with that, too, if I remember rightly.'

'Alfred didn't know what was good for him.' She chuckled. 'He does now though. Sometimes people need a bit of convincing. Men especially.'

'Hattie, you can't say things like that. It's sexist.'

'I'm eighty years old. I've seen a damned sight more life than you have, so I can say what I like. So there.' She stuck her tongue out at him.

Silas shook his head at her in amazement. The woman was hopeless.

But she was also right. Hadn't he already admitted to himself that he had fallen in love with Nell? Maybe she felt the same way? Or, if she didn't, she might have feelings for him – ones which could be nurtured until they blossomed.

'You know what you've got to do, don't you?' Hattie asked, and when Silas stared at her in confusion, she rolled her eyes. 'Speak to Nell! Good God, do you need me to come with you and hold your hand?'

'I think I can manage this by myself.'

'Good. Make sure you do. Because if you don't, I'll have to get the pair of you in a room and knock your heads together.'

'I will, I promise, but first I need to phone Denise and tell her what's happened,' he said. He felt the need to explain to his ex-wife, and maybe even make his peace with her, before he spoke to Nell.

Hattie struggled to her feet and gave him a pat on the shoulder before she left.

Silas saw her out, then debated whether to head home and make the call from there. He had almost reached the door before he realised he was procrastinating.

He had to speak to her now, else he'd lose his nerve.

'Denise, it's me, Silas.'

'I know who you are.' Her voice was gentle. 'Is something wrong?'

'Yes and no.' He pulled a face. 'I painted Molly. I was on my way to give it to you this evening when it was stolen.'

'Oh, Silas, I'm so sorry. I wish I could have seen it.'

'You'd have loved it. Remember her third birthday? When she had that doll? She kept rocking it as though it were her baby.'

'How could I forget?'

'She was sitting on the floor and the sun was streaming in through the window.'

'It's about time you painted her. You should have done it years ago. Painting has always been cathartic for you. That you *didn't* paint her worried me.'

'I paint landscapes and seascapes,' he protested.

'You didn't always. You did a painting of Molly on the day she was born. I still have it.'

Silas remembered. Molly had been lying in her bassinette, wrapped up in a pink and white checked blanket. It had been the softest thing he'd ever felt, aside from his daughter's newborn cheek.

He hadn't painted her again. Caring for a new baby, as well as producing paintings to sell, had used up all his time and energy. And they'd taken hundreds of photos of their daughter, thousands. He hadn't felt the need to capture her in paint. He'd thought he'd have years ahead of him to do that.

How wrong could he have been?

And then she'd been diagnosed, and there had been the gruelling treatments and stays in hospital, the hope, the fear, and the final outcome.

He'd run out of time.

'It's been hard for you, hasn't it?' Denise said softly.

'For you, too. You were her mother.'

'I still am. But I grieved for her. You didn't. You boarded up your heart and trapped your feelings inside. Who has freed them?'

Silas breathed out gently. 'Her name is Nell. I painted her, too.'

'You must really love her – you never painted me.'

'That's because I had the real thing.'

'You don't have her?'

'I don't know.'

'You should find out.'

'Yeah… Listen, one day I'll paint you another picture of Molly. It might not be the same as the one that was stolen, though.'

'That's all right. But don't paint it just because you feel you have to. I don't need any images of our daughter to remember her by. Molly lives in my head and my heart. But I've learnt to live *with* my grief, not *despite* it. I embraced it, Silas, as proof that I loved Molly – I still do. There's room in our hearts to love more than one person at a time. Ask Molly to shift over a bit and give Nell some room. You need someone to love, someone who loves you back. I hate to think of you on your own for the rest of your life. You're a good man, a kind man, with so much love to give and so much life to live, so go out and start living it. Don't waste it. Molly's life might have been impossibly short, but she lived each and every moment of it. You should do the same.'

Denise's voice broke, and when she added, 'Go find someone special and love them with everything you are and everything you have,' Silas felt tears trickle down his cheeks.

'I already have…'

CHAPTER 36

NELL

Nell was intrigued; Silas had asked her to dinner – at his house, no less. He'd popped in early this morning just as she'd opened the shop, and she'd assumed he'd wanted to finalise the arrangements for their trip to London tomorrow. Instead, he'd invited her to his cottage for a meal this evening, adding that there was something he needed to tell her.

Nell had spent all day wondering what it could possibly be; which was grossly unfair of him, she thought. She would have accepted the invitation anyway, without him keeping her on tenterhooks. The only thing she was certain of was that it had nothing to do with the Oakman, because she'd asked him. But he'd refused to tell her anything further. Not able to decide whether it was a date or not, Nell aimed for the casual look, hoping he didn't think she'd made too much of an effort (she had – she'd agonised over what to wear in between wondering what he wanted to tell her), and had dressed in jeans, T-shirt, soft leather moccasins, and was carrying a suede jacket in case it got chilly later, and a bottle of wine.

Ticklemore wasn't large so she decided to walk. The evening was a pleasant one, the air retaining some warmth, the sun having not yet set.

Silas's cottage was situated on the outskirts of the village, at the end of a small row of similarly-sized houses, and she studied the outside of it briefly before she knocked the old-fashioned lion's-head knocker. The cottages she'd passed on her way to it had window boxes filled with colourful blooms or pots by their front doors. Silas's was markedly bare, as if it was trying not to be noticed.

It was quiet and unassuming, just like him.

She noticed Silas all right, when he opened the door, her breath catching in her throat at the sight of him. He looked delectable with his bare feet and dishevelled hair, but he also looked tired, and his eyes were wary. Her heart went out to him; whatever it was he wanted to say to her was preying on his mind.

'Come in,' he said, leaning towards her and kissing her lightly on the cheek.

She caught the scent of citrus and musk before he

stepped to the side, holding the door open for her. Nell handed him the bottle and waited for him to close the door behind her, taking the opportunity to look around. The hall was tiny, with one room leading off to the left and a flight of stairs. She shivered to think he slept at the top of them. Being here with him felt intimate; even more so when he moved closer, gesturing for her to go ahead.

The living room was larger than she'd anticipated from the outside, and held two small sofas, a bookcase, and a TV. For an artist, there was surprisingly little adorning the walls, just one painting above the open fireplace. At the rear of the room was a small table and four chairs. The table was laid for dinner.

'I've already opened a bottle of wine,' he said. 'Would you like a glass?'

'Yes, please.'

'Come through into the kitchen, and you can watch me cook. I'm not very good at it, but even if I do say so myself, I make a mean stir fry.'

She followed him into the room in question, her eyes darting everywhere, and she only realised she'd been checking for signs of female occupation when she failed to find any. No cushions, no candles, no ornaments; this was a bachelor pad.

It was neat and tidy though, and she saw the

ingredients for their meal were already sitting on the worktop next to the hob, on which was a wok and a saucepan. On the other side of the hob was a bottle of wine and two glasses.

Silas poured the drinks and handed one to her. 'Had a good day?' he asked, as he splashed some oil into the work and added rice to the saucepan, and turned on the heat.

'Busier than usual. Lots of people coming in wanting to see the Oakman. I'm not complaining, though. How about you?'

'It was interesting.' His eyes met hers, then he looked away. 'I had a visit from the police.'

Nell hadn't been expecting that and she was unsure whether it had any bearing on what he wanted to tell her. 'Is everything all right?' she asked, concerned.

'I think so. It wasn't, but I'm getting there.' He switched the heat off and turned to face her. 'I had a painting stolen yesterday evening.'

'Gosh, Silas, that's awful! What happened?'

'In a nutshell, I'd taken it out to the car but had to go back into the Gallery because I'd forgotten my wallet, and I stupidly left the car unlocked.'

'Oh, poor you. What did the police say? Do you think they'll catch who did it?'

'Unlikely, especially since it wasn't worth much.

They've given me a crime number, but I think that's as far as it goes.'

'I'm so sorry, but as you said, at least it wasn't valuable.'

He stared at the wall behind her and realisation dawned.

'It *was* valuable, wasn't it?' she said slowly. 'But not in monetary terms?'

'Yes, it was. It meant a lot to me.'

'Oh, Silas...'

'It was a painting of my daughter.'

Nell was taken aback. 'I didn't know you had children. You never said you had a daughter.'

She found it decidedly odd that he hadn't mentioned it until now, considering she'd freely chatted about Adam and Ethan, and he'd had plenty of opportunity to talk about his kids.

'I don't,' he said. 'Not any more. Molly died when she was three. Cancer.'

Nell slowly blinked as the enormity of what he was telling her sank in. 'Oh, God...I'm so, so sorry.'

'You see, I hadn't been able to paint her until recently. I couldn't. Something inside wouldn't let me. Not until I painted you.'

So that was who the other painting was of – his daughter. He'd covered both their paintings over, as though he hadn't been able to bear to see them.

Tears brimming and threatening to spill over, Nell put her glass down and went over to him. How the hell did anyone recover from something like that? She suspected he hadn't.

He let her put her arms around him, although he held himself rigid, and she could feel his grief reverberating through him like the barely-heard vibrations of a bell long after it had been struck.

If something happened to one of her boys, she didn't think she cope. How Silas managed to function normally was beyond her. She simply couldn't imagine what he was going through, but her instinct was to try to soothe his pain.

'I didn't realise,' she said, her face buried in the crook of his neck.

'Why should you? No one in Ticklemore knew.'

But Nell thought she should have realised something was very wrong in Silas's world. And deep down, she *had* sensed there was something, but she'd never have guessed it was the terrible loss of a child.

'Nell, I don't know how to move on,' he whispered. 'But I know I must. Can you help me?'

'Anything,' she vowed. 'I'll do anything.'

'Just hold me?'

That was easy; she could hold him from here to eternity if it would help. Her arms tightened around him and she let her tears fall. She felt him shudder, and he let out a long breath.

'There's something else you need to know,' he said, his voice hoarse.

Nell sniffled, the collar of his shirt damp against her cheek where she'd wept on it. She drew back and she saw his face. The anguish in his eyes almost broke her.

'I think I love you,' he said. 'No, don't say anything.' He put a finger to her lips. 'I don't expect you to feel the same way, though I hope maybe one day you can. I don't want to lose you.' He took his finger away from her mouth and gently thumbed away a tear.

'I love you, too,' Nell said quietly.

Silas stilled. 'Pardon?'

'I said, I love you, too.' Her voice was louder this time and more confident.

'You do? How? I mean, when—?'

'Shh....' She reached up, her lips finding his, and she gave herself to him, showing him through her kiss that she meant what she said.

Losing herself, her senses reeling, Nell's heart swelled with love. This sad, broken, wonderful man loved her. She would never be able to heal him completely, she knew, but she'd give him all the love she could and hope she could fill some of the emptiness she sensed inside him.

'Wait,' he murmured into her mouth, leaving her bereft as he pulled out of her embrace. Oh, God, she'd spoilt it. What was she thinking – practically jumping his bones when he'd only just confided in her that he'd lost his daughter?

'The rice is boiling.' Silas turned the ring off and moved the saucepan. 'Dinner can wait?'

This last was a question. He was asking for her commitment, he was asking if she was ready. He was telling her that he was, if she'd have him. And suddenly she knew this was what he'd wanted to tell her. Not that he had a daughter who had tragically died. Not that he was still suffering. He wanted her to know he loved her, and he wanted her.

'Dinner can wait,' she agreed. They'd have the rest of their lives to enjoy dinner together.

He took her hand and led her upstairs, Nell's heart thudding erratically in her chest, her mouth suddenly dry and a coiling excitement squirming in her tummy. It was a long time since she'd felt such desire, such unbridled lust, and she wasn't sure she remembered what to do with it.

Her body, thankfully, did, and as she surrendered to the deliciously wonderful things Silas was doing to her, all coherent thought flew out of her mind until the only thing that mattered was his fingers and lips, and the way he made her feel.

And after the first desperate flush of lust was assuaged and he held her in his arms, her head on his chest as she listened to the corresponding thump of his heart, she'd never felt so cherished and worshiped in her life.

Nell silently vowed to treasure him forever – what else was she supposed to do with the man who'd stolen her heart.

CHAPTER 37

NELL

Replete didn't begin to describe how Nell was feeling on Sunday morning, and she wasn't referring to the feeling of being full after a meal. Although she definitely *was* full – full of love and brimming with happiness.

She thought Silas was feeling joyful, too, as she could hear him in the kitchen humming along to some tune on the radio as he made them breakfast.

Last night (and this morning) had been special. They'd fitted together physically, mentally, and emotionally, as though they were two halves of the same coin. Even though Nell acknowledged there was still so much she didn't know about him, she felt in her heart and her soul that she knew Silas as well as any person could possibly know another. She knew he was kind, thoughtful, and considerate; she knew he loved deeply and thoroughly, and without reservation. She knew he was honourable and principled. She knew he was damaged by life and love, and that his wounds had finally healed enough for him to love again. What more did she need to know, although she was looking forward to finding out what his favourite food was, or what music he preferred (classical, if today's offering was any indication), or all of the other things that she had yet to discover, they didn't make the man.

'I've brought you breakfast in bed,' he said, appearing in the doorway with a laden tray in his hands.

'You shouldn't have.'

'I wanted to.'

'No really, you shouldn't have.'

'Why not?' He looked hurt and she giggled.

'Because now you're upstairs again, I'm tempted to have my wicked way with you.'

'The scrambled eggs will get cold.'

'Don't care.'

'What about the coffee?'

'Brew some more.'

Afterwards he didn't look in the least bit put out that he'd gone to the effort of making breakfast, only for it to go to waste. 'We'll grab something on the way,' he told her cheerfully when she emerged from the shower some time later, her hair wet and her skin glowing. Her heart was glowing too, she thought.

'What time do we need to leave?' she asked.

He narrowed his eyes at her. 'Don't even think it,' he warned. 'I'm not twenty, you know. I need a break.'

'You've had one.'

'Fifteen minutes isn't long enough.' He swatted her on the behind as he sidled past and she yelped. 'Anyway, I need a shower.'

'I could always join you?'

'Get dressed, woman,' he growled. 'If we don't get a move on we're going to be late. Do you need to pop home for anything?'

'If you've got a spare toothbrush, I'm good.'

'In the cabinet in the bathroom. Give me five minutes and I'll be ready – as long as you don't mind the unshaven look?'

'I don't mind at all.' Nell found his unshaven and tousled appearance incredibly sexy, and she had to concentrate on rubbing the water from her hair, otherwise she might have pounced on him again. The thought was delicious, but Silas was right, they did need to get going.

Once they'd collected the Oakman from the Gallery, they were on their way, with a stop off at a roadside café for a quick bite to eat en route.

Silas seemed thoughtful. 'When I told you a painting was stolen, did you think it might have been the Oakman?' he asked.

'It didn't occur to me. Why do you ask?'

'Hattie did.'

'When did you speak to Hattie?'

'She was there just after it happened. She was the one who called the police. I'll have to take her a bunch of flowers to thank her.'

See, Nell thought, that's what she meant by Silas being thoughtful and considerate, although from his expression she surmised there was more to the story than he was letting on.

Never mind, if he wanted to share it with her he would.

As they approached London, Nell could feel a slow build-up of excitement in her tummy. This was it; they were nearing the final stage of the process of putting the Oakman into an auction. She just hoped there wouldn't be any problems.

'It'll be OK, won't it?' she fretted. 'They won't say it's a fake, will they?'

'Definitely not! Vaughan is one of the top people in his field. If he says it's genuine, it's genuine. And I bet his estimation of the value won't be far out, either.'

'It's just that it would be awful if anything went wrong at this stage. I'd hate for the charities not to get their money, especially with the story being in the Tattler.'

'It'll be fine.'

Nell noticed his jaw had tightened and she thought she knew the reason. 'You don't mind me giving half of it to charity do you?'

'Nell, it's your painting, your money. You do with it as you see fit. But as you asked, I think it's a wonderful thing to do.'

'You seem uptight.'

'It brings back memories, that's all. Especially the children's one. We relied on them quite heavily towards the end.'

Nell winced. 'I'm sorry, I didn't think.'

'You didn't know, and even if you had done it shouldn't have made any difference. They need all the money they can get, not only for research but also for the wonderful care they provide. I don't think either Denise or I could have coped without them.'

'How does Denise feel about it?'

'The Oakman?' Silas laughed. 'Do you know, I haven't told her about it. I was going to take a copy of the Tattler and give it to her when I gave her the painting of Molly, but I didn't get to see her, and what with everything that happened I simply forgot.'

'It would be a nice idea to ask her along to the auction. What do you think?'

'You're incredible. Why didn't I think of that?' His face fell. 'Should I invite Francis?'

'You should,' Nell replied firmly, then she hesitated. 'Unless you'll find it too awkward?' What she wanted to say was that he might still love Denise and seeing her with the man she was going to marry might upset him.

Silas was one shrewd fella though, and he saw right through her. 'I love *you*, not Denise. Not in that way, although she'll always have a place in my heart and I'll always care for her. I was wondering whether Francis might find it awkward.'

'He might have done,' Nell agreed. 'But maybe not with me there.'

'You'd have been there anyway—? Ah, I see what you mean. You'll be there as my… Hmm, what should I call you? Lover is a bit suggestive – although you most certainly are – and partner sounds as though we're in business together. Girlfriend makes me sound like a teenager. You'd think there'd be a more grown-up word for what we have.'

'What *do* we have?' she asked, teasingly.

'Something very rare and very special.'

Nell had to agree with him.

CHAPTER 38

SILAS

Police officers, in Silas's limited experience, seemed to come in pairs, and today was no exception. They didn't look as though they were bearers of bad news, but Silas tensed anyway as they walked into the Gallery, their heads turning from side to side as they took everything in.

Max looked up from the computer where he tended to spend most of his time, and his eyes widened. He glanced at Silas, then back at the officers.

'Good morning, we're here to speak to Mr Silas Long. Would that be yourself, sir?'

'It would. I mean, I'm he. Him. I'm him. Is everything OK?'

They shared an amused look, and Silas guessed

they were used to odd reactions by members of the public. He hadn't done anything illegal in his life (unless he counted the graffiti incident when he was thirteen) but the sight of the officers immediately made him feel guilty, and he was convinced they could see guilt written all over his face.

'We're here about the theft you reported. The painting.'

'Have you found it?' Hope sprang to life in his chest.

'Yes, and we've made an arrest.'

'Where is it?'

'It's being held until the CPS – the Crown Prosecution Service – makes a decision on whether the case goes to court.'

'So I'm assuming I'll get it back eventually? Was it damaged?'

'No damage has been recorded.'

'Thank God for that. Where was it found?'

'An art dealer gave us a call. He became suspicious when he was offered a painting for sale and the man who was trying to sell it claimed it was painted by someone called…' The taller of the two consulted his notebook. 'Peter Oakman. Never heard of him.' He shrugged. 'The dealer said if it *had* been an Oakman, it would have been pretty valuable.'

My God, Silas thought, Hattie had been almost

right in that it should have been the Oakman that had been stolen – the person who nicked it had evidently thought he was stealing something valuable. But surely he'd seen a photo of the painting in the paper and realised it wasn't the same one?

'Are you allowed to tell me the name of the thief?' Silas asked.

'His name is Riley Chapman. Does that ring any bells?'

Silas felt a sudden heaviness in his chest. Oh dear, what the hell was he going to say to Nell? She didn't have time for the man and she already regarded him with contempt since his fraudulent letter, but he was her ex and she must have loved him once, and he was the father of her boys.

'Will he be charged?' Silas asked.

'He's already been charged with theft and attempted fraud.'

'Right.' He ran his hands through his hair.

'I take it you know Chapman?'

'He's the ex-husband of my, um, girlfriend I suppose you'd call her.'

Max sniggered and Silas cocked a warning eyebrow at him.

'I see. Why would he have thought it had been painted by this Oakman fella?'

'Because I did have an Oakman on the premises,'

Silas said formally. 'But it's now in an auction house in London.'

'Would Chapman have known the whereabouts of the painting?'

'He must have done. He certainly knew the painting existed, but I would have thought he'd have assumed it was at the Treasure Trove.'

Seeing the officers' confused expressions, Silas told them the story, ending with, 'Even if he hadn't read the story in the paper himself, I suppose he could have heard about it from almost anyone.'

When they finally left, Silas said to Max, 'Are you OK to hold the fort here for a while? I'd better go and see Nell before she hears the news from anyone else. I hate to leave you on your own but...'

'I'll be fine.'

'I'll have my phone with me. Call me if there's a problem. I'll only be down the road; I can be back in five minutes. Or three. More like three.'

'Just go. I'll be OK.' Max went back to studying the computer. 'Get in there!' he yelled abruptly, making Silas jump.

'What's wrong?' Oh, God, Silas wasn't sure he could take any more bad news this morning.

'We've had a price back from the printers I was telling you about. It's well less than I thought it was going to be.'

Silas sagged in relief. 'Tell me about it when I get back; I must speak to Nell. Oh, and Max?

Max looked up.

'Well done, yeah?'

The boy nodded, accepting Silas's praise.

Worry about leaving Max in the Gallery on his own was eclipsed by concern over how Nell would take the news about Riley, as Silas hurried to the Treasure Trove.

'Silas!' Nell cried, delighted to see him. 'I didn't expect to see you here this morning.' She hurried over and wrapped her arms around him, ignoring the curious looks from a couple who were studying an ornate umbrella stand.

Silas's heart sank even further. She wouldn't be so pleased when she heard what he was about to say.

'Where's Tanesha?' he asked, after they'd shared a brief kiss.

With a small frown at the serious look on his face, Nell said, 'It's her day off. Why?'

Drat, he was hoping the girl would be here to give Nell some support after he'd gone back to the Gallery.

'The police have been. They've found the painting of Molly.' He kept his voice low.

'That's brilliant news.' She studied him closely. 'Isn't it?'

'It was Riley who stole it.'

'Excuse me? I thought you said Riley? My God, you did say Riley! Why on earth——? *Oh.*'

'I'm sorry, Nell.'

'The bas—' She bit the word off mindful of the customers in the shop. 'He thought it was the Oakman, didn't he? He was in here the day the article in the Tattler came out. I didn't speak to him, Tanesha did. When he asked about it, she told him you had it in the Gallery and that it was packed up ready to be sent to auction.'

Nell's mouth was turned down and Silas was worried she was going to cry. 'What on earth did he think he was playing at?' she asked. 'He must have known he'd never get away with it. He's a financial consultant, for goodness sake, not a thief. Has he been arrested?'

Silas nodded.

'Hang on, I'd better get that.' Her phone was trilling loudly. 'Don't go yet, please?'

Silas waited while she answered, using the interruption to check his own phone in case he'd missed a call from Max. It was daft, he knew, because he'd have heard it ring, but—

'He said *what*?' Nell cried.

Silas looked up. Nell was pointing at her mobile which she was holding to her ear. 'Adam,' she mouthed at him, before returning to the conversation. 'I'm sorry, he shouldn't have. It's nothing to do with you.'

Silas moved to her side.

'No, I'll be fine. Honest. Where are you?' She pursed her lips and Silas didn't think he'd ever seen her angry before. 'Sounds nice. Be careful, and don't eat anything from a street vendor.' Her expression softened. 'Barbeques on the beach don't count, but make sure the food is cooked all the way through. Love you. Bye… bye.' She stared at her phone before slipping it into a drawer under the counter. 'That was Adam and Ethan. Riley phoned them.'

'Oh?'

'He wanted to give them his side of the story, first.' She put a hand to her mouth. 'He owes someone a lot of money. He didn't tell them who or how much, but they are chasing him for it.'

'That explains why he was so desperate to get his hands on the Treasure Trove.'

'I think desperate describes it perfectly. And stupid. I don't know what's got into him. He must have known he'd never get away with any of it.'

Riley might have done if Nell hadn't sought legal advice, Silas thought, as he remembered the bloke sitting in Bookylicious, making promises he'd been unable to keep. If only Silas had realised at the time who Riley was, then maybe Riley resorting to theft could have been averted.

'He asked the boys to pass on a message,' Nell said. 'He told them to tell me he's sorry.'

Silas thought the man was a coward, using his sons like that. He should at least have the courage to apologise to Nell to her face.

'And Vanessa has dumped him,' she added. 'I expect it's because the money has run out. I feel rather sorry for him.'

Silas, uncharitably, didn't think Riley deserved her pity. He didn't think he deserved Nell. She had been far too good for the man, if only Riley had realised it. Heck, she was far too good for *him*, but Silas had no intention of letting her go. Ever.

And when he drew her to him and held her close, he made a silent promise to love her and cherish her with every beat of his heart.

Nell deserved nothing less.

CHAPTER 39

NELL

The day of the auction had finally arrived and Nell used the catalogue to fan her warm face as she checked out the people in the room, wondering which one of them was going to buy her painting.

There weren't many present and concern washed over her, despite Silas telling her that there would undoubtedly be more bidders online and on the phone.

She'd been expecting lots of people sitting around or standing about, holding cards in their hands, eager to grab a bargain, like the auctions she sometimes frequented. But the reality of this particular auction was rather different to her previous experiences. Not that she bought from auctions very often, but she had been known to visit one or two in her time.

Carlfort's was grander, more upmarket, and she supposed it should be considering the quality and value of the items they handled. And that they were specialists in fine art.

Although Nell had treated herself to a new outfit for the occasion, she felt positively underdressed. Most of the clientele were in suits, and that included the women. Silas, too, had dug one out and dusted it off, and she thought he looked quite distinguished and incredibly handsome.

She smiled nervously at him and he slipped his hand into hers and gave it a squeeze.

Juliette stood on the other side of her, watching everything and taking notes, and Nell knew her friend was desperate to take a photo, but it was forbidden. Maybe if they asked nicely, the Oakman's new owner would allow the journalist to take a quick snap of him or her.

Oliver was here, too, and he and Juliette were making a bit of a holiday out of the occasion and were planning on spending the night in a hotel near the London Eye. Which was a pity, because Nell had been hoping everyone would join her and Silas for a celebratory drink in the Tavern as soon as they got back to Ticklemore.

Never mind, she was sure she and Silas could find another way to celebrate...

She thought she'd feel awkward meeting Denise for the first time, and maybe even feel a little threatened, but she didn't. Denise was lovely and had alleviated her worry, whispering in her ear as she gave her a hug, 'Look after him, won't you? He's a good man, one of the best.'

'I will,' she promised. 'I'm glad you and Francis could make it.'

'I wouldn't have missed it for the world,' Denise said, 'and I think it's a marvellous thing you're doing.' She turned to Silas and gave him a kiss. 'You're looking well, Silas.'

'So are you. How are the wedding plans coming along?'

'Don't ask! It's grown from close family only, to every man and his dog being invited. If Francis's mother had her way, the postman would be invited, too.'

'Er, Denise, I think he might already have been sent an invitation,' Francis said. 'He can sit next to the Amazon delivery driver. I swear my mother has ordered so many parcels lately that she's on first name terms with him.' He paused, then said, 'Denise and I were wondering – would you be one of the ushers, Silas?'

'I'd be honoured.'

Silas looked thrilled. Nell was going with him as his

plus-one and she found herself looking forward to it, despite realising that it would be bittersweet for both Silas and Denise.

Nell glanced behind to check on Tanesha and Max, who were remarkably quiet, considering they had whispered and giggled all the way down in the car, sharing earbuds and staring at each other's phones. Nell suspected they were an item, but she didn't like to say anything, fully aware of how easy it was to embarrass a teenager.

Filled with sudden longing for her own offspring, she wished Adam and Ethan could be here, but they were somewhere in Turkey, stuffing their faces with kofte and raki, and complaining about the heat. Adam would have enjoyed the auction, she knew; Ethan not so much. But at least Tanesha and Max were having a good time, and it was a new experience for both of them.

'Lot number 22,' the auctioneer announced, and Juliette nudged her.

'We're on,' Juliette hissed out of the side of her mouth as the auctioneer described the Oakman.

Nell sat up straight. Silas gave her hand another squeeze, and she sensed a ripple of interest in the room.

'Do we have £500,000? Three hundred, then? Two? £200,000 I'm bid. Two twenty, two-forty…' And they were off, the bidding rapid and climbing steadily.

Nell craned her neck to see if she could tell who it was, hoping to goodness the action wasn't mistaken for a bid.

The auctioneer kept tapping at a screen in front of him, and every now and again he'd say a figure and then say "on the phone", or "in the room" and she realised there was a considerable degree of interest in the painting from buyers who weren't here person.

'£650,000. Do I have seven? Seven I'm bid. £700,000 in the room. Do I have seven-fifty? Seven-fifty, anyone? I'm going to sell at £750,000.'

Nell held her breath.

'Seven-fifty on the phone. Eight hundred. Anyone for eight hundred? Eight hundred I have. Eight-fifty?' She was so excited she felt sick. To think the little painting was worth so much and she hadn't known

'I'm selling at £800,000...' He scanned the room and his attention came to rest on the two men and the woman who were manning the phone bids. All three shook their heads. The auctioneer banged his gavel. 'Sold for £800,000,' he announced.

Nell bit back a squeal of delight and managed to hold herself together until she was in the foyer. Unable to contain her excitement any longer she threw herself into Silas's arms. Juliette and Oliver piled on top, quickly followed by Tanesha and Max. Nell was dimly aware of Denise crying and Adam holding her, as they all jumped up and down, laughing and yelling.

'Shh!' They were glared at by one of the auction house staff, and, laughing so hard she had tears streaming down her face, Nell dragged Silas outside, closely followed by everyone else.

'£800,000!' Nell exclaimed for the sixth or seventh time. 'I can't believe it. I've got to tell the twins.' She took out her phone and sent them a message on their group chat, promising to speak to them later.

'I'm going back inside,' Juliette said. 'I want to see if I can get a few words from the new owner. A photo would be good, too.'

Denise hugged and kissed first Silas, then Nell. 'Thank you,' she said to Nell. 'It means a lot.' Denise and Silas shared a long look, before Silas nodded.

Molly's parents were able to give a little back to the charity which had helped them in their hour of need, and Nell was honoured to have been part of that.

'Take care, Silas,' Denise said. 'We'll always have Molly,' she added quietly, 'but we've now found each other again, as well as a new life and new love. I wish you all the happiness in the world.' She sent Nell a pointed look and Nell smiled tearfully back at her.

To Nell it felt like one chapter had ended and another had begun. The story still had Molly in it, but the book hadn't yet ended – there were so many more chapters to go, so many more words to be written.

But the most important word of all was woven into all of their lives – *love*.

Nell's heart was utterly full and her soul was complete as she thought of the love she shared with Silas. The rest of their lives was about to be lived, and she couldn't wait!

CHAPTER 40

SILAS

Silas was exhausted. Today had been emotional and exciting, and he was sorely tempted to suggest a quiet evening in, just the two of them, with a takeaway and the bottle of champagne he'd put in the fridge before they'd set out for the auction that morning. But Nell was still walking on air and he felt she needed a proper celebration in the pub.

He dropped Nell off so she could get changed into something a little more casual, and he went home to do the same. He never felt comfortable wearing a suit; they always reminded him of meetings with the bank manager. He was far happier in a pair of jeans and a T-shirt.

He strolled from his house into the high street to collect Nell. The collection took a little longer than either of them had anticipated because he couldn't resist kissing her, and then that led to other things, so it was a good half an hour before they were on their way.

'I'm starving,' Nell announced, as they stepped outside her flat.

The auction had taken place at around midday and after Nell had sorted out all the paperwork her end, they had all piled back into his car, for the return journey to Ticklemore. By "all" he meant himself, Nell, Max, and Tanesha, and they'd stopped off along the way for a spot of late lunch. He'd noticed that Nell had only picked at hers, and he guessed she had been far too excited to eat much of it. Now, however, her appetite had clearly come back.

'We can grab something in the Tavern if you like.' He checked his watch. 'It's not too late, they'll still be serving.'

Silas thought the pub seemed busier than usual; as they approached they could hear loud chatter and laughter drifting out on to the pavement. He didn't make a habit of going to the pub on a weekday evening, so he wasn't particularly well qualified to determine what was busy and what was not, but it did seem to be rather lively for Wednesday.

He saw just how lively it was when he pushed the door open and followed Nell inside, his jaw dropping open.

Nell turned to him and asked, 'Did you know about this?'

Silas shook his head. He gazed around the bar, quickly taking in the balloons and the banners which said "congratulations", the full tables, and the people who occupied them.

Everyone turned to look at them, and a sudden hush descended, then Hattie cried, 'Hip, hip, hooray!' and everyone else joined in, followed by a chorus of For She's a Jolly Good Fellow, which ended with somebody shouting, 'And so is Silas!'

Silas wanted to do an about turn and run away; he never did like the spotlight, preferring to hide behind his easels and paints, but he stood his ground; this was Nell's night and no one deserved it more.

'This is nothing to do with me,' he told Nell, who was beaming widely. 'I can give you three guesses as to who I think might be.'

'Hattie!' they said as one.

The old lady in question started clapping, and soon everyone was clapping, stamping their feet, and whistling. All the old gang were gathered, along with a couple of new faces. Alfred was there, with his daughter and David, Benny and Marge, Father Tod, Logan too, although he was dashing back and forth to the bar. Juliette and Oliver, who had clearly lied about their night away in London, were also present. They must have headed straight back and arrived before him and Nell. Zoe, Max and Tanesha, plus Alfred and Juliette's new apprentices occupied a table, Zoe looking smug because she was finally old enough to drink alcohol, the others having to make do with soft drinks.

'You sneaky thing,' Nell said to Juliette, hurrying over to give her a hug. And after that she was forced to hug the others, as they all wanted their turn. Silas noticed everyone had a champagne glass in front of them, and Logan and his mum were busy filling them. Juliette thrust a drink into Nell's hand, and another one into his.

Hattie stood up holding her glass aloft. 'Has everyone got a drink?' she asked, glancing around the room to check. 'Good, right then, let's have a toast – to Nell and Silas.'

'Nell and Silas!' The shout made the windows rattle.

'Gosh,' said Nell after the excitement had died down a little and everyone had taken a sip of their champagne. 'Anyone would think you are toasting a bride and groom, not the sale of a painting.'

Hattie smirked. 'Aren't we?'

Silas look puzzled. 'Aren't we what?'

'Toasting the bride and groom, as well as the

painting.' Hattie wrinkled her nose at him.

Nell's eyes met Silas's; she looked horrified.

His mood plummeted, and a feeling of dread radiated out from his heart. 'Would that be so bad?' he murmured in her ear, terrified of the answer, but needing to hear it all the same.

'No, I, it's just…unexpected.'

'It's unexpected for me, too.'

He turned his full attention on her, the rest of the room fading away, and said, 'I didn't expect to fall in love again. I didn't think I was capable of it. Yet here I am. Head over heels.' He gave her a wry grin. 'Just so I know where I stand, would it be so bad if we *were* bride and groom?'

A slow smile spread across Nell's delectable lips. 'No, it most definitely would not be bad. Silas Long, are you asking me to marry you?'

'I might be. Yes, I believe I am. I didn't think it was going to happen like this, though.'

'Neither did I,' Nell said, 'but the answer is yes, I'd love to marry you.'

A cheer erupted. Silas was only vaguely aware of it, because his attention was wholly and utterly on the woman who was in his arms and who was kissing him soundly.

She was the only thing that mattered. Her happiness was the only thing on his mind. He vowed he'd make Nell the happiest woman in the world, even if it took the rest of his life.

And he sincerely hoped it would!

THE END

Acknowledgements

Husband, of course, because he sees more of the top of my laptop than he does of my face most days (mind you, he might say that's a good thing!)

Catherine Mills, as always, for her unstinting enthusiasm for my stories and her willingness to gently put me right when I've drifted off course.

Mum for reading my stuff, Daughter for promising to (and for listening to me wittering about formatting when she has no idea what I'm rabbiting on about)

And my readers. Thank you for loving my books and making all the blood, sweat and tears – OK, coffee, sleepless nights and snivelling – worth it.

Liz x

ABOUT THE AUTHOR

Liz Davies writes feel-good, light-hearted stories with a hefty dose of romance, a smattering of humour, and a great deal of love.

She's married to her best friend, has one grown-up daughter, and when she isn't scribbling away in the notepad she carries with her everywhere (just in case inspiration strikes), you'll find her searching for that perfect pair of shoes. She loves to cook but isn't very good at it, and loves to eat - she's much better at that! Liz also enjoys walking (preferably on the flat), cycling (also on the flat), and lots of sitting around in the garden on warm, sunny days.

She currently lives with her family in Wales, but would ideally love to buy a camper van and travel the world in it.

Social Media Links:
Twitter https://twitter.com/lizdaviesauthor
Facebook: fb.me/LizDaviesAuthor1

Printed in Great Britain
by Amazon